"I hate this hat of yours, Amariah, hated it the moment I saw you in it."

She wrinkled her nose. "Because you hate it, Guilford, I shall henceforth hate it, too."

"Well, then, I'll banish the wretched thing and please us both." He flipped open the window and, before she could protest, sailed the hat out of the window and into the night.

"Guilford!" Amariah shrieked with surprise. "I cannot *believe* you did that! Oh, that poor, old, ugly hat!"

"Let it grace some poor, old, ugly scarecrow in a field of rye," he said grandly. "You, my fair Amariah, deserve something far more beautiful."

He slid closer along the swaying seat, leaning over her so that all she could see was his face in extraordinary detail: the dark lashes around his blue eyes, the way his black hair curled….

She blinked, and smiled. "You're going to kiss me, aren't you, Guilford?"

THE DUKE'S GAMBLE

Miranda Jarrett

MILLS & BOON™

Pure reading pleasure

First published in Great Britain 2007
Harlequin Mills & Boon Limited,
Eton House, 18-24 Paradise Road, Richmond, Surrey TW9 1SR

© Miranda Jarrett 2006

ISBN: 978 0 263 85203 5

Set in Times Roman 10½ on 12¾ pt.
04-1107-84619

Printed and bound in Spain
by Litografia Rosés S.A., Barcelona

THE DUKE'S GAMBLE

Miranda Jarrett considers herself sublimely fortunate to have a career that combines history and happy endings, even if it's one that's also made her family regular patrons of the local pizzeria. With over three million copies of her books in print, Miranda is the author of more than thirty historical romances, and her bestselling books are enjoyed by readers around the world. She has won numerous awards for her writing, including two Golden Leaf Awards and two *Romantic Times BOOKreviews* Reviewers' Choice Awards, and has three times been a RITA® Award finalist.

Miranda is a graduate of Brown University, with a degree in art history. She loves to hear from readers at PO Box 1102, Paoli, PA 19301-1145, USA, or MJarrett21@aol.com

Recent novels by this author:

PRINCESS OF FORTUNE
THE SILVER LORD
THE GOLDEN LORD
RAKE'S WAGER*
THE LADY'S HAZARD*

*A *Penny House* novel

Chapter One

Penny House
St. James Square, London
1805

In the experienced opinion of Eliot Fitzharding, His Grace the Duke of Guilford, there were few things better contrived to reduce a sensible woman to blithering idiocy than a wedding, and the nearer the relationship of the woman to the bride, the greater the intensity of that idiocy.

This is not to say that his grace did not enjoy watching the idiocy, much the way that other gentlemen enjoyed a good sparring match in the ring. As a confirmed and practicing bachelor, he was free to watch the spectacle surrounding a wedding as the purest of spectators: emotionally uninvolved, financially uncommitted, with no other goal than to amuse himself.

Which was why Guilford was sitting alone in the back parlor of Penny House this evening, enjoying an excellent brandy while he savored the exhausted quiet after the storm of the wedding earlier that day. He didn't mind in the least that he had the parlor to himself. Most nights, Penny House was like any other gaming club in London, vibrating with male bravado and high spirits, tempered by the despair of those who'd lost at the tables. Guilford had never seen Penny House as quiet as this, and he rather liked it. All the other guests had left long ago, and the servants seemed to have faded away for the night, too. The hothouse flowers were wilting in their vases, the fire nothing but gray ash and embers in the grate, and even the candles in the chandeliers had mostly guttered out, leaving the large, elegant room in murky shadow.

All were signs that would send most gentlemen to make their own farewells for the night and head for the door, as well. But Guilford never had been like most gentlemen, much to his late mother's constant disappointment, and instead of leaving, he stretched out his long legs before him and settled himself more comfortably in his armchair. Why should he leave when the best show of the night still lay ahead?

A yawning maidservant shuffled wearily into the room, and with the long-handled snuffer, began to douse the last of the lit candles in the chandelier until, finally, she noticed Guilford.

"Your grace!" she cried out, adding a little shriek for emphasis. "Oh, your grace, how you started me!"

"Forgive me, sweetheart," he said easily, his smile in the shadows enough to make the poor girl blush and fumble with the snuffer in her hands. Of course she'd recognized him; not only was he a peer, but he'd been a charter member of the club—as much from sheer curiosity as anything—and now served on its membership board. He'd also earned favored status because he cheerfully dropped the occasional large wager at the card tables, just to be agreeable.

"It's—it's me what should be asking forgiveness, your grace!" she stammered. "Truly, your grace!"

"Not at all." He raised his glass to the girl by way of apology. "Frightening you was never my intention."

Belatedly she remembered to curtsy. "Is there anything I might fetch for you, your grace? They're banking the kitchen fires for the night, but if there's something special you want, then I'm certain Mrs. Todd could—"

"But alas, not Miss Bethany." He sighed dramatically. Bethany Penny was one of the three sisters who owned Penny House, the one who'd overseen the kitchen, the one who could rival the king's own French cooks for her delicacy with spices, her wit with pastry. Of course, cookery fell within a woman's natural sphere, a concept her older sister had always failed to understand. "However shall I survive without Miss Bethany's roast goose and oysters?"

The maid looked at him uncertainly. "Miss Bethany will return to us, your grace. She's only gone away for a bit on her wedding trip with the major."

"Oh, the major, the major," Guilford said darkly, indulging in a bit of brandy-laced melancholy. No matter what Bethany Penny had promised, she'd be like any other new bride, besotted with her husband and her belly swelling with his brat as soon as it could be managed. Then she'd be ruined—*ruined!*—as a cook! "I scarce know the man, but he can't possibly appreciate the cook he's gotten in his wife."

"Beggin' pardon, your grace," the girl said, "but Major Lord Callaway is an excellent gentleman, and he loves Miss Bethany to distraction. You could see it in his eyes today when they wed."

"The sweetness of her turtle soup will far outlast mere love." Guilford sighed again. He appreciated the girl's loy-

alty to her mistress, even if it were mired in mawkish sentiment. "But thank you, no, sweetheart. I need nothing more,
and the kitchen may stay at peace. Go ahead now, finish your
tasks."

"Yes, your grace. As you please, your grace." She nodded
uncertainly, then bobbed another curtsy before she returned to
snuffing the candles. When she was done, she backed from the
room and gently closed the door, leaving him with only the
dying fire for light. Somewhere off in the large house, a clock
chimed twice, the sound echoing down the empty staircase.

Guilford smiled. The lights might be dimmed, but the stage
was most certainly set.

And right on her cue, the leading lady of Penny House
made her entrance.

The double doors swung open to reveal a woman silhouetted by the wash of light spilling from the room behind her.
Even from no more than this silhouette, Guilford would have
known it was her. Her height, the soft mass of hair piled high
on her head and crowned with a nodding white plume, her
very carriage as she stood there in the doorway: it could only
be Miss Amariah Penny, and no one else.

"Your grace." Her voice was charming yet firm, and still
very much in her role as the grand mistress of Penny House,
even at this hour and after such a day. "Might I ask if there is
something wrong? Something amiss?"

"Indeed you might ask, Miss Penny," he said, smiling
though he suspected she couldn't see him, "and I shall answer.
Nothing is wrong, or amiss, especially now that you're here
to look after me."

As always, she ignored the compliment. "Then might I inquire, your grace, as to why you are hiding in the dark and
alarming my staff?"

"I'm not hiding," he said, "I've merely been sitting here so long that the dark has swallowed me up."

She made a little *harrumph* of polite incredulity. "Then perhaps sitting here has made you unaware that everyone else has left this house for the evening, your grace. Shall I call for your carriage?"

His smile widened as he gently swirled the brandy in his glass. She was still wearing the same gauzy gown she'd worn earlier for the wedding, with the silver threads in the deep embroidered hem glinting faintly like stray sparks above her feet. He was certain she didn't realize that, with the light behind her, he also had a splendid view of her legs showing through her skirts.

"Everyone has left except for you, Miss Penny," he said, "and for me. How could I be rude, and leave you alone under such circumstances?"

"Because my staff is tired, your grace," she said, "and I wish to close the house for the night."

"Then close it, and send your staff to bed." He reached out and pulled another armchair closer to his. "Surely you must be weary, too. Come and sit, and keep company with me."

She sighed, betraying the weariness she shared with her staff, but was too stubborn to admit. "You know why I cannot do that, your grace. This is a gentlemen's private club for gaming, not a house for assignations."

"But tonight I'm not here as a member of the club," he reasoned. "I'm here as a guest at your sister's wedding."

She bowed her head, clearly perplexed, and didn't answer. He couldn't blame her, either, though she'd made this thorny little problem herself. Because the sisters lived on the top floor of Penny House, they'd already blurred the lines between their home and their trade. They weren't really much different from a butcher living over his shop, except that their shop was a grand house on St. James Street, and the customers were a highly select group of gentlemen drinking and gambling away vast sums of money for their reckless amusement.

But the ever-ambitious Amariah Penny had taken matters another step by inviting those members who served on the club's governing board to attend her sister's wedding as guests, including them amongst the family's oldest friends. Guilford was certain she'd done it only to strengthen the ties with those who helped her make Penny House the exclusive club that it was. That was how her unladylike mind seemed to work, always looking for an advantage to improve Penny House and increase profits, but now she'd have to face the consequences.

"You can admit you're tired, you know," he said, patting the chair beside him. "Any other woman would."

Her head jerked up, any weariness banished. "But I'm not like any other woman, your grace. Now I'll have your carriage brought—"

"Did you know there's a wager in the book at White's that predicts you'll be the only Penny sister not to marry?" he asked, dragging his question into an lazy drawl. "Not because you're lacking in beauty or grace—for you most certainly are not, Miss Penny—but because you're far too wedded to this club for any man to wish to play second."

"When my sister tossed her wedding bouquet today, your grace, it was my choice not to try to catch it."

"I noticed," he said wryly. "Everyone did. You kept as far away as possible from the other shrieking maidens vying for the prize on the staircase, your hands locked behind your back as if in iron manacles."

"And what is so very wrong with that, your grace?" she

demanded, her voice warming with a tedious missionary fervor. "Nearly all the profits my sisters and I earn from Penny House are given directly to charity. That was my late father's wish, and I mean to follow it always. Each time that you gentlemen amuse yourselves at our tables, you are helping feed and clothe and shelter the poor in ways you'd never do directly."

"No," Guilford said dryly, not in the least interested in the poor or how they dined. "I wouldn't."

"Well, then, there you are, your grace," she said, as if this were explanation enough, which it wasn't. True, she was a clergyman's daughter, but, in Guilford's opinion, her soul was as mercenary as they came. "Why should I wish to marry for the sake of one single man when I can do so much more good for so many others by being here?"

"Because you *are* a woman, my dear," Guilford answered, offering his own perfect explanation. "No matter how much you wish it, you can't do everything by yourself, and most especially you can't save the entire world. You can't even save the lower scraps of London. Of course, charity work is an admirable pastime for a lady, but a home, a husband and children must surely come first. It's in your blood, your very bones. Not even you can deny nature, Miss Penny."

"Is this part of the wagering at White's, too, your grace?" she asked suspiciously. "That I am somehow...*unnatural?*"

"Not exactly unnatural, no." With his eyes accustomed to the half-light, he'd no trouble seeing her, but he still couldn't tell if she were angry or amused—not that it would make any particular difference to him. "I do believe 'virago' was the term that was used."

She gasped, and to his satisfaction, he realized he'd finally struck home.

"They dared call me a virago?" she repeated with disbelief. "A *virago?*"

She charged into the room and straight to him, the heels of her slippers clicking across the polished floor. He could feel her anger like a force in the darkness, her blue eyes wide and her gaze intense, her mouth set in a line of furious determination. He'd known her for nearly a year now, ever since she'd appeared in London from nowhere to open Penny House, yet this was the first time he'd seen the ever-proper, ever-capable Miss Penny lose both her composure and her temper.

It was even better than he'd dreamed.

"A *virago,* your grace!" she said again, as if she couldn't say the hateful word enough times. "What—what *ninny* dared call me that?"

"How the devil should I tell?" Even though he'd given her leave to sit, she showed no intention of doing so, which made him suppose he must stand, too. With a sigh he rose, stretching his arms a bit as he now gazed down on her. "I don't know everything."

"Oh, yes, you do," she said quickly. "At least you'd know that."

"You're granting me an inordinate amount of knowledge, Miss Penny." Of course, he knew the name of the ninny who'd dubbed her a virago in the betting book at White's; he knew, because the ninny's name happened to be his own. "I'll admit to being vastly wise and clever, but I'm hardly omniscient."

She folded her arms over her chest and tipped her chin upward, so that she could still give the impression of glaring down her nose at him despite how he loomed over her. But he liked how she hadn't the rabbity look of most women with copper hair, her brows and lashes dark enough to frame her blue eyes. "No one has ever called you a virago, your grace."

"No one shall, either," he said. "Considering how a virago must be female by definition."

"A spinster, *and* a virago," she said with disgust. "I should take myself directly to the middle of Westminster Bridge, toss myself into the river and spare the world the burden of my dreadful shame."

He laughed softly, deep and low. "You're not old enough for such a grim remedy."

"No?" Her blue eyes glowed with fresh challenge as she took a step toward him—something that, under ordinary circumstances, he'd doubt she'd ever do. "I'm twenty-six, your grace."

"Congratulations." He'd already known she was past being a miss, and had grown into a much more interesting age for a woman. Dithering innocence had long ago lost its appeal to him, which was one of the reasons she fascinated him. "But I'll win that battle, Miss Penny. I'm twenty-nine."

"And what of it?" she scoffed, sweeping her hand through the air. "No one is telling you you've failed because you have chosen a life that includes neither a husband nor children."

"Actually I'm told that rather often," he said, remembering how shrill certain members of his family could become on his lack of an heir to his title. "Married life and children by the dozen are supposed to be good things for a peer, too."

"But for different reasons." She kept her head turned to one side, watching him warily from beneath her lashes. "I cannot fathom why you're confiding any of this to me, your grace."

"To show we have more in common than you might first think, my dear." Had she any notion of how wickedly seductive that notion was right now? Perhaps he'd misjudged her; perhaps she was more willing than anyone had realized. "We do, you know."

"Hardly, your grace." Her mouth curved in a small smile of undeserved triumph. "You were born heir to a title and a grand fortune, while I came into this world as the daughter of a country minister. This leaves precious little common ground between us."

"More than enough." He shrugged extravagantly, taking advantage of the moment and the cozy half-light to ease himself a shade closer to her. "*Vastly* more."

But instead of laughing as he'd expected, she folded her arms resolutely over her chest, a barrier between them. "I suspect you're not being entirely honest with me, your grace."

She was right, of course. He wasn't being entirely honest. That wager in the betting book at White's about wedding the formidably untouchable Miss Penny had been only the beginning. He'd made another, more private, wager with one of his friends, with odds—steep odds—for a much greater challenge: that no mortal man could successfully seduce her.

And Guilford—Guilford intended to win not only the wager, but to earn a welcome in the virago's bed for himself.

"I wouldn't say you've been entirely honest with me, either, Miss Penny," he said, lowering his voice to the rough whisper that reduced most ladies to quivering jelly. "Which is only one more way that we're alike, isn't it?"

She frowned. "Your grace, I do not see how—"

"Hush," he whispered. With well-practiced ease he reached for her hand where it clasped her other arm, slipping his fingers between her own to draw her hand free. "Consider the similarities, sweet, and not the differences."

"What I am considering, your grace, is exactly how much longer I must listen to this foolishness before I summon my house guards." Deftly she pulled her hand free, shaking her fingers as if they'd been singed by a fire. "I don't believe you've met them before. Large fellows, of few words, but significant height and muscle, and quite protective of my welfare. I'm sure they'd be honored by the privilege of escorting you from this house."

Undeterred, Guilford concentrated on flashing his most charming smile. "That's harsh talk between friends, Miss Penny."

She smiled in return, but with her it was all business and precious little charm. "Ah, but that is where you err, your grace. I am the mistress and proprietor of this house, while you are one of its honored members. Cordiality is not true friendship, nor shall it ever be otherwise between us."

He winced dramatically, placing his hand over his heart. "How can I accept such cruel finality?"

"You stand on Penny House's membership committee, your grace," she said, reminding him gently, as if he were in his dotage. "Perhaps you should recall the rules of behavior for all members that you helped draft and approve, rules that make expulsion mandatory for any gentleman who oversteps. How very much we'd hate to lose your company that way, your grace!"

Guilford shifted his hand from the place over his heart to the front of his shirt, as if he'd intended all the time to smooth the fine Holland linen. "Ahh, Miss Penny, Miss Penny," he said, coaxing. "You wouldn't do that to me, would you?"

In the grate behind them, the last charred log split and collapsed into the embers with a hiss of sparks and ash.

"If you knew me as well as you claim, your grace, you'd know that if you tried to compromise me or anyone else on my staff, or even Penny House itself, I'd do exactly—*exactly*—that." Amariah smiled serenely. "Now if you'll excuse me, your grace, I'll see that your carriage is brought around to the door."

Guilford watched her go, the plume nodding gracefully over her head with each brisk step. She might have won today, but this was only the opening skirmish. He'd be back. He wasn't going to let her get the better of him, not like this.

And no matter how she felt toward him now, he still meant to win that blasted wager.

Chapter Two

"Forgive me, Miss Penny, but are you certain you'll be well enough on your own here tonight?" Pratt, the manager of Penny House, lingered still in the doorway to her private rooms. Below his old-fashioned wig, his narrow face was lined with worry as he watched Amariah light the candlesticks on her desk. "I can ask one of the maids to come sit up with you if you wish."

As tired as she was, Amariah still smiled. "Thank you, Pratt, but I'll be fine here by myself."

He pursed his lips. "But, Miss Penny, if—"

"I told you, Pratt, I'll be fine." Amariah blew out the rush she'd used to light the candlesticks. "I need you far more as the club manager than as my personal broody hen."

"Very well, miss." Pratt sighed with resignation and bowed, a fine dust of white powder from his wig wafting forward. "Good night, miss."

"Good night to you, too, Pratt," she said softly. She really was fond of him, broody hen or not, and she certainly couldn't have made Penny House the success it was without his experience and constant guidance. "And thank you again for all your extra work today with Miss Bethany's wedding. Or rather, with Lady Callaway's wedding. Oh, how long it's going to take me to remember that!"

She laughed ruefully. It *would* be difficult for her to remember the change in her middle sister's name and in her rank, too, just as she still occasionally forgot to call her youngest sister Mrs. Blackley instead of simply Miss Cassia, and she'd been wed to Richard for months. But in Amariah's mind, they'd both always be just her two little sisters Bethany and Cassia, turning to her the way they had ever since their mother had died nearly twenty years before.

"You'll remember, miss," Pratt said, and bowed again. "Good night, miss."

He closed the door softly, and for the first time in this long, long day, Amariah was alone. Finally she let the weariness roll over her, and with an extravagant yawn she dropped into the chair behind the desk, pulling the coverlet she kept there up over her shoulders as a makeshift shawl. She kicked off her slippers and tugged the white plume from her hair and the hairpins with it, rubbing her fingers across her scalp as her now-loose hair slipped and fell down her back. She pulled the chair closer to the desk, poured herself a fresh cup of tea from the pot that Pratt had left her, and with a sigh she turned to the pile of unopened letters and cards and bills that needed replies. Though the club had been closed yesterday and today for Bethany's wedding, the work involved with running Penny House never seemed to pause.

Quickly she sorted through the stack of papers, dividing them into categories of importance. While handling her father's correspondence for the parish and the rectory was hardly on the same scale as Penny House, it had prepared her for trade and bookkeeping in ways that most young women of her station weren't. This was the special ability she'd brought to Penny House, balancing costs against expenses and remaining firm with tradesmen, just as Bethany's gift with cookery had made the club's suppers famous, and Cassia's knack for finding treasures in secondhand shops had turned the huge sow's ear that Penny House had been when they'd inherited it into the most fashionably appointed gaming house in London. The best part of all was knowing how much money they raised every night for charity, exactly as Father had intended. Running Penny House made Amariah feel like that ancient old rascal Robin Hood, taking from the rich to give to the poor.

Amariah smiled as she dipped her pen into the ink, remembering how the three sisters from the country had proved the doubters so completely wrong. But now marriage had reduced the three Pennys to one, and the never-ending work of running the club would be in her hands alone. There would be even more late nights and early mornings like this one for her, and resolutely she cracked the seal on the next letter, determined to make more headway before she went to bed.

But the harder she tried to concentrate on the sheet before her, the more the figures seemed to swim before her eyes, and the more, too, that her thoughts seemed determined to wander off onto the most unproductive path imaginable.

A path that led directly to the too-charming smile of His Grace the Duke of Guilford.

She put down her pen and groaned, rubbing her eyes with her hands. The duke was certainly not the first gentleman in the club to press his familiarity with her or her sisters, nor would he likely be the last, not with a membership made entirely of men from birth accustomed—and expecting—to have their own way.

Guilford, however, had taken her by surprise. Oh, he was worldly and witty enough for this kind of foolish, flirtatious game; there was no doubt of that. But until now he'd always been careful to keep most of his considerable charm reined in where she was concerned. He'd tease her, compliment her, tell her jests and banter with her, but that was all. No wonder he'd become one of her favorite gentlemen. He'd respected her and her role at Penny House. He'd understood why she must keep herself more pure and honorable than Caesar's wife for the sake of the club's viability, and why it would be so disastrous if she didn't. On one occasion, he'd even come to Cassia's defense when another guest had cornered her and made untoward overtures.

Now everything had changed. Of course, she'd try to give the duke the benefit of the doubt, and pretend the brandy had been speaking instead of him; but she could recognize a man half-gone with drink, and he hadn't been like that. He'd behaved as he did simply because he'd wanted to, because he'd thought he would succeed, and she'd never be able to feel at ease with him again.

With a grumble of frustration she shoved her chair back from the desk and padded across to the window in her stocking feet, drawing the coverlet around her arms like folded wings. She pushed aside the damask curtain and gazed out over the club's tiny enclosed backyard and across the slate roofs and chimneys of London. Though the stars still shone here and there in the sky, the horizon was beginning to pale with the coming dawn. All across the city, there would be hundreds of people whose workdays had already begun—bakers, milkmaids, fishmongers, stable boys, scullery maids—yet, as Amariah stared out over those rooftops, she felt as if she were the only one awake in the entire city.

You can't do everything by yourself, Miss Penny....

Why had he waited in the dark like that for her, turning the back parlor into his own seductively cozy lair? How had he known exactly the way to ruffle her usual composure, teasing her with that nonsense about being a virago? He'd smiled down at her, his single dimple punctuating his face and his dark hair falling carelessly over his forehead; his deep, lazy voice made for sharing secrets and wooing women into madness.

Was that why she'd almost weakened when he'd taken her hand, almost forgotten everything she worked so hard for every day and night, almost traded it all away for what the Duke of Guilford could offer by the half-light of a dying fire?

She rested her spread fingers on the windowpane, the glass cool beneath her palm, and bowed her head. She was so tired that even her bones seemed to ache. Surely that must be what was making her think like this, casting empty wishes to the morning star for a gentleman she'd never have: weariness, and nothing more.

No matter how much you wish it, you can't do everything by yourself....

"That's the one," said Guilford, tapping his knuckles on the jeweler's counter for emphasis. "That will do the trick."

"Ah, your grace, you do know what will please a lady." Mr. Robitaille nodded, and ran his hand lightly over the surface of the bracelet's rubies. As one of the most popular—and costly—jewelers here on Bond Street, old Robitaille himself knew a thing or two about pleasing a lady. The bracelet was a pretty trinket: rubies set like tiny red flowers, centered with pearls, and exactly what was needed to earn his place in the eyes of Miss Amariah Penny. In his experience, jewels never, ever failed.

"What pleases a lady is anything in this shop, Robitaille," he said cheerfully, "which you know as well as I do. But what lady doesn't like rubies, eh?"

Robitaille chuckled. "As you say, your grace, as you say. Shall I have it sent to Miss Danton, as usual?"

"I fear not." Guilford frowned, trying to look serious as he heaved a sigh as deep as the ocean. "It's a terrible tale, Robitaille. Charlotte Danton has thrown me over for the master of the Derby Hunt."

"No, your grace!" Shocked, the jeweler drew back, the bracelet clutched in his hand. "I cannot believe the lady would abandon you!"

"Oh, it's true," Guilford said with another sigh. The real truth was that he'd tired of Charlotte at precisely the same time that she'd wearied of him, but because she'd been the one who'd abandoned their sinking ship first, he considered himself free of any further obligations, either of the heart or the pocket. No wonder he'd jumped at that wager involving Amariah Penny as a new diversion.

"I am most sorry for your pain and your loss, your grace." Robitaille bowed his head in sympathy, as dutifully full of respect as any mourner hired for a burial. Almost as an afterthought, he looked down at the bracelet still in his hands. "Might I ask where the bracelet should be sent, your grace?"

"To Penny House, St. James." Guilford smiled, glad to be done with the sighing and moaning over Charlotte. "To Miss Amariah Penny."

"Miss Penny, your grace?" Robitaille's mouth formed a perfect oval of surprise. "Miss Amariah Penny of Penny House? Oh, your grace, you amaze me!"

His wonder was so complete that Guilford laughed. "Do

you think she's unworthy of me, Robitaille, or that I am unworthy of her?"

"Neither, your grace, of course not," the jeweler said
quickly, "but Miss Penny is…a different sort of lady, isn't
she?"

"She's some old parson's daughter, she has hair as red as
flame, and she's clever enough to earn her own keep," Guilford said, smiling as he recalled how upset she'd been with
him last night. "I suppose that does make her a change from
my usual fare."

The jeweler laid the bracelet back down upon the silk-
covered pillow on the counter, straightening the links with the
tip of one finger into a neat line.

"She won't take the bracelet, your grace," he said defini-
tively. "Not Miss Penny, nor her sisters, either. They won't accept gifts from this shop from any of my gentlemen. They
claim their position won't permit it."

"Hah, that's nonsense, Robitaille," scoffed Guilford. "I've
seen how she decks herself out every night at the club, sparkling like a queen. She didn't get diamonds and sapphires like
those from her papa in the vicarage."

Robitaille sniffed with disdain. "They're all paste, your
grace. I've seen her myself, from afar. Good paste, from Paris,
but paste nonetheless."

Guilford frowned a bit, unable to accept this. To him,
genuine or paste looked much the same, but he did believe
in the value of quality, and in paying for it, too. "Why the
devil would she wear paste, when she could have the real
thing?"

"Charity, your grace," said Robitaille with a fatalist's resignation. "She wants nothing for herself, nor did her sisters.
I cannot tell you how many pieces have been sent to the la-

dies of Penny House, your grace, and exactly the same number have been returned."

"But they haven't been sent by *me*," Guilford said, his confidence unshaken. "Miss Penny and I have always gotten on famously. You'll see. This bracelet won't come back."

But the jeweler's doleful face showed no such conviction. "As you say, your grace," he said with the most obsequious of bows. "Thank you for your custom, your grace. I'll have it taken to the lady directly."

"Good." And as Guilford turned away from the counter, he realized his pride had just made another, unspoken wager with Robitaille: that his bracelet would be the first accepted and displayed upon the lovely pale wrist of Amariah Penny.

It was the muted rattle of the dishes on the breakfast tray that first woke Amariah, followed by her maid Deborah's tentative whisper.

"Good morning, Miss Penny," Deborah said as she set the tray down on the table at the end of the bed. "Miss Penny? Are you awake, Miss Penny?"

Amariah rolled over in bed, shoving her hair from her eyes as she squinted at the face of the little brass clock on the table beside her head. She felt as if she'd only just fallen into bed, her head so thick and her eyes as scratchy as if she hadn't slept at all. Surely Deborah had come too soon; surely it couldn't be time to wake already.

"What time is it?" she asked, her voice scratchy and squeaky with sleep.

"Half past noon, miss," the maid answered apologetically. "I know you must still be dreadful weary after the wedding and all, but Mr. Pratt said you'd have his head if he let you sleep any later."

"Pratt's right." Groggy, Amariah kept her face still pressed into her pillow for another second more. It was time she woke; she usually rose at eleven, and now she'd lost that hour and a half of usefulness forever, never to be recaptured. "I *would* have his head."

Somehow she found the will to push herself upright just as Deborah drew back the curtains to the window, letting the bright noonday sun flood the room, and with a groan Amariah flopped back onto the pillow, her arm flung over her eyes.

"Forgive me, miss, but Mr. Pratt said it's the only way to—"

"I *know* what Mr. Pratt said," said Amariah, marshaling herself for another attempt, "though knowing he is right doesn't make it any more agreeable."

"Forgive me for being forward, miss, but everything will be more agreeable after a nice dish of tea." Deborah lifted the small silver pot and poured the steaming tea into one of the little porcelain cups, adding sugar and lemon. Then she tipped the fragrant liquid into the deep-bottomed dish and handed it to Amariah. "Your favorite pekoe, miss."

"Thank you, Deborah." Carefully Amariah took the saucer, her fingers balancing the worn, gold-rimmed edge. Painted with purple irises, the tea set was one of the few things the sisters had had from their mother, and for Amariah, using the delicate porcelain each morning was a small, comforting way to remind herself of her long-past childhood in Sussex.

Deborah shifted the tray to the bed, reaching behind Amariah to plump her pillows higher. "You see, miss, that Mrs. Todd cooked your eggs just the way that Miss Bethany—I mean, Lady Callaway—did for you, with them little grilled onions on the side."

"Shallots," Amariah said wistfully as she looked down at her plate. "They're a special breed of onions called shallots."

Deborah beamed. "See now, miss, isn't that just like Mrs. Todd, knowing the difference, *and* knowing you'd know, too?"

Amariah smiled in return, but without any joy. Mrs. Todd, Bethany's assistant in the kitchen and a master cook in her own right, had made an exact copy of one of her sister's best breakfasts, but it wasn't the same. It never could be, not without Cassia and Bethany to share it. Breakfast had always been the one meal the sisters had together, sitting in their night-clothes before the fire to laugh and gossip and plan their day before their work began in earnest.

Now Bethany and Cassia must be taking breakfast with their husbands, pouring their tea and buttering their toast, while she would be here at Penny House, with only—

"Miss Penny, miss?" The scullery maid standing before her was very young and very new, her hands twisting knots in her skirts and her face so pinched with anxiety that Amariah feared she might cry. "Miss?"

"What are you doing here, Sally?" Deborah scolded. "You've no business coming upstairs and bothering Miss Penny! Go, away with you, back where you belong!"

The girl's eyes instantly filled with terrified tears. "But Mr. Pratt said—"

"What did Mr. Pratt say, lass?" Amariah asked gently, preferring to earn her staff's loyalty through kindness, not threats. "Is something wrong?"

"No, Miss Penny. That is, it be this, Miss Penny." Sally made a stiff-legged curtsy before she darted forward, a folded letter in her hand. "I was sweepin' th' front steps, Miss Penny, an' found this there, up against th' door, an' Mr. Pratt said I must bring it to you at once."

"Thank you for your promptness. You did exactly the right

thing." Amariah took the letter from the girl, her heart making a small, irrational flutter of hope.

Why would Guilford leave her a letter by the door, instead of handing it to a servant? Why, really, would he write to her at all?

"You're new, aren't you?" she said. "What is your name?"

"Yes, miss," she said with another curtsy. "I'm Sally, miss."

"Then thank you, Sally," Amariah said, forcing herself to pause, and keep her curiosity about the letter at bay. "Continue to be so obedient, and you're sure to prosper here. You may go."

"Yes, Miss Penny." The girl fled with obvious relief, leaving Amariah alone with the letter in her hands. Though the stock was thick and creamy, the highest quality made for the wealthiest custom, there was no watermark or seal to reveal the sender. That alone was proof enough that it hadn't come from the duke, and enough to silence her foolish expectations; Guilford loved his title far too much ever to be anonymous by choice.

Still, the letter itself remained a puzzle. Only her name was printed across the front, in large, blockish letters written with an intentional crudeness to disguise the writer's true hand.

"That's a curious sort o' thing, isn't it, miss?" Deborah asked, purposefully lingering near the bed to watch. "Should I fetch one o' the footmen before you open it, miss, just to be safe?"

"Whatever for, Deborah?" Amariah scoffed. "In case some sort of villainy should puff fright from the paper? I'll grant that the writer must be a strange sort of coward to toil so hard at hiding his face and name, but I'm hardly afraid of his letter."

With a flourish, Amariah slipped her finger beneath the blob of candle wax that served as the letter's seal and cracked it open.

Mistress Penny,
Be Advised that you have a Great Cheat at your Hazard
Table & that I will Unmask him to Public Shame & Dis-
grace if you do not Do so First.
    A Friend of Truth & Honor

"I hope it's not bad news, Miss Penny," Deborah said as
she began laying out Amariah's clothes for the day.

"Not bad," Amariah said, briskly refolding the letter. The
message had been written in the elegant hand of a gentleman
and a coward, and she intended to discover his identity as soon
as possible. "Merely provoking. Please tell Mr. Pratt to send
for Mr. Walthrip directly, as well as all the footmen and guards
who have served in the hazard room within the last fortnight.
I should like to address them all as soon as they have arrived.
I will not have a gaming scandal at Penny House, especially
not based on the whispers of some knave too timid to show
his face."

Two hours later, Amariah stood at the head of the large oval
table, made of the most solid mahogany, normally used for
the playing of hazard. While the tall windows were thrown
open as they were each day to freshen the stale air left from
the night before, the room never could quite shake its noctur-
nal cast, like some dandy caught after dawn in the harsh glare
of morning. One by one, Amariah glanced at each of the faces
gathered around the green-covered table: some old and wiz-
ened, some fresh and young, some she'd inherited along with
the club itself, and all still dazed and rumpled from being
called into work so early.

"I'm sorry to have roused you from your beds," she began,
"but my reason is a serious one. I received a letter this morning accusing us of harboring a cheat at our hazard table."

"But Miss Penny, that is not possible!" Mr. Walthrip cried, his bony jaw jutting out with indignation over his tightly wrapped stock. He was the hazard table's director and had been for at least twenty-five years, and he took his job so solemnly that Amariah was not surprised he was the first to object. "There is a precision, a nicety, to hazard that does not favor cheating!"

"Are you saying it's impossible to cheat at hazard?" Amariah asked. "Or that it's impossible to cheat at hazard at Penny House?"

Walthrip sniffed. "There is not a single game devised by man that another man has not found a way to fox," he said, as stern as any judge. "But it would be difficult to cheat at hazard here at Penny House, miss, very difficult indeed."

"That is true, Miss Penny," Pratt said, nodding in agreement with the manager. "As you know, we have our dice made to our own specifications, as are our throwing-boxes, and no gentleman is ever permitted to introduce his own dice or box into the play."

"Yes, yes," Walthrip said, opening and closing his hands as if testing the dice even now. "The dice and the boxes are changed without warning throughout the night, especially if luck is favoring one gentleman more than others. We are open about everything, miss, as stated in the house laws. Nothing is ever done in secret or behind the hand."

Amariah leaned forward and ran her palm lightly across the green woolen cloth, marked with yellow lines, that covered the table. The room with the hazard table was the most popular in the club, and night after night, the game generated the most income. "Is there any way the table could be altered in some fashion to control the fall of the dice?"

"No, miss," said Talbot, the most senior of the footmen.

"Each afternoon the cloth is swept and secured fresh, and Mr. Walthrip tests it himself. There's no bumps or lumps to favor anyone."

"I would ask you to consider the very nature of the game, too, Miss Penny," Walthrip said, leaning forward. "While one man throws, there are any number of others who lay their wagers on his effort. They are watching him like so many cats around a mouse, and if he were to attempt anything out of the ordinary—anything at all, miss—why, they would tear him apart for his trouble."

"Then none of you have seen anything to catch your eye this last week or so?" Amariah asked. Once again she glanced around the room, and was gratified to see that none of the men looked uncomfortable with her question as they shook their heads in unison. "Nothing strange, or peculiar in any way?"

"Nothing," Walthrip said with relish, also pleased by the emphatic response of those around him. "It's the nicety of the game, miss, the veriest nicety."

Amariah listened, and nodded. Because she herself knew little of the games that supported the club, she had to depend on the experience and wisdom of those in her hire to advise her. Everything Walthrip and the others had said made perfect sense to her, for which she was glad and grateful, too. Still, she could not put aside her uneasiness. Scandal of the sort the letter-writer threatened could ruin Penny House, where the members counted on her discretion as they amused themselves. If that trust were gone, then they'd go elsewhere, just as they'd come to her earlier in the year.

Pratt coughed delicately. "Might I ask if you're at liberty to share the name of the accuser, Miss Penny?"

"I would if I knew it." Amariah tossed the letter onto the

green-covered table, and the men crowded closer to see it. "He signs only as a 'Friend of Truth and Honor,' though by doing so, he is neither."

"He's a gentleman," declared Pratt, whose instincts in discerning true gentlemen from false were impeccable. "The paper betrays him."

"I had thought that myself," said Amariah. "All we can do now is to wait, and watch to see if any of the guests seems particularly unhappy with us, and then—what is it, Boyd?"

The crowd around the table parted to let the footman come through to Amariah.

"This just came for you, Miss Penny," he said as he handed her a narrow package. "Mr. Pratt said to bring you any such at once."

One glance at the package told her this had nothing to do with hazard. With an impatient little sigh, she undid the wrappings and flipped open the leather-covered jeweler's box only long enough to pluck the note from inside. The card was thick, the coronet embossed so deeply that a blind man could have made it out. This was one correspondent who wasn't the least bit shy.

My dearest Lady,
Odds being what they are at Penny House, I knew I'd need to sweeten my stakes before I begged your forgiveness for last night's indiscretion.
    G.

Guilford. She sighed, more with dismay than anything else. Did he truly believe that she'd change her mind for the sake of a piece of gimcrack jewelry? Had he that little regard for who and what she was? How could he so completely disregard what she'd said to him last night?

Without even looking at the bracelet nestled in the dark red plush, she shoved the card back inside the box, closed the lid and returned it to the footman.

"Have Deborah take that to my rooms for now," she said. "Tell her that as soon as I'm done here, I'll write the usual note, and send it back."

She turned back to face the others. Nearly all the men were grinning, or rolling their eyes. Most of them had seen such gifts arrive before for her or her sisters, and just as promptly go back out the door again to their hapless senders. *They* understood. So why hadn't the mighty Duke of Guilford?

She leaned forward, her palms flat on the edge of the table and her voice full of determination.

"Consider yourselves all to be on your guard," she said. "You know what to do. Penny House cannot afford a breath of any scandal to tarnish its good name, and I know I can trust you to make sure that doesn't happen."

But could she dare say the same of Guilford?

Alec, Baron Westbrook, stood in the shadows of the wall across the street from Penny House and watched the members climb up the steps and into the club for a night of genteel gaming. Light from the scores of candles in the chandeliers streamed from every window, and even from here Westbrook could hear the happy rise and fall of all those well-bred male voices, happy to be eating rich food, drinking smuggled French wines, and winning and losing vast sums of money as if it were nothing but sand.

Westbrook stepped back farther from the street, pulling his hat down lower over his face. He knew all about Penny House.

He'd been one of the first flock of members approved by the committee when the club had first opened. He'd joined, of course, and come to see what all the fuss had been over the three red-haired sisters holding court as if the place was their palace. He'd come, because it was the thing to do, and he'd played, because he couldn't help himself, not where dice were concerned.

But after the first fortnight, he hadn't returned. He'd found the place too oppressive, too genteel, even stuffy, to suit his idea of amusement, as if the Penny women really were true ladies, ready to slap your wrist for any behavior they deemed untoward. Why, he might as well be at home with his widowed mother, being criticized for wasting his life and his fortune.

Most of all, he'd hated how the forced gentility of Penny House had altered the gaming tables. There was none of the wild excitement that Westbrook craved most from gaming, the raucous, drunken revelry and the underlying edge of danger that was so at odds with his ordinary life. He preferred to try his chances in the lowest gaming dens, ones full of thieves and scoundrels and sailors on leave, than to suffer the rarified pretensions of Penny House.

The only trouble with the dens was that they expected a man to pay his debts at once. They didn't make allowances for bad luck. They were chary with credit, even for a gentleman and a lord, and they hired bully boys with knives ready to extricate the losses from those who weren't quick about it.

Blast Father for leaving him a title, but no estate to support it! If only Father hadn't blown out his brains with a pistol and left his family penniless, then he wouldn't be forced to grovel to Mama's brother for every last farthing. Uncle Jesse was in trade, shipping and coal and tin and other vile, low activities, and though he would inherit it all once his uncle died, the old miser didn't understand that a lord needed funds to match his title. Instead he whined about losses and reverses, squeezing every penny and actually suggesting that Westbrook might look into trade himself.

Westbrook watched another chaise stop at the club, the light from the lanterns flanking the entrance catching the gold-trimmed coat of arms painted on the chaise's door. Westbrook didn't have a carriage of his own; he couldn't even afford to keep a chaise. Maybe one day, when his luck with the dice changed, or when Uncle Jesse finally went to the devil where he belonged.

When Penny House first opened, the sisters had been free with credit to the membership to encourage the play. But once the club had become so damned fashionable, they'd tightened up the lines again, and Westbrook couldn't be sure what kind of welcome he'd receive.

But that was going to change, wasn't it? Scandal would do that, and no scandal was bigger in a gaming house, high or low, than cheating. Cheats made everyone anxious, uneasy, ready to point a finger at everyone else. The fashionable world would shift to another club, the wealthiest gentlemen would go elsewhere for their entertainment. The sisters would welcome a gentleman like him in their doors, and they'd be happy to give him credit to keep him there.

He took one last look at the brightly lit club. Not yet, not tonight. But soon he'd be back inside, with credit to spare as he sat at the hazard table.

And this time, he meant to win.

Chapter Three

That night Amariah came early to the hazard room, standing to one side of Mr. Walthrip's seat at his tall director's desk where she could see the table and all the players gathered around it. There were also twice as many guards in the room tonight, tall and silent as they watched the players, not the play, and Amariah was glad of their presence. She'd never before entered this room at this hour of the evening, choosing instead to come only when it was near to closing and the crowds had thinned. From the club's opening night, Pratt had advised the three sisters that it was better for them to avoid the hazard table at its busiest. He'd warned them that the hazard room was not a fit place for ladies, even at Penny House, and how with such substantial sums being won and lost each time the dice tumbled from their box, the players often could not contain their emotions, or their tempers.

Finally seeing it for herself, Amariah had to agree with Pratt. Special brass lamps hung low over the table to illuminate the play, and by their light the players' faces showed all the basest human emotions, from greed to cunning to avarice to envy, to rage and despair, with howls and oaths and wild accusations to match. Only Walthrip, sitting high on his stool, remained impassive, his droning voice proclaiming the winners as his long-handled rake claimed the losers' little piles of mother-of-pearl markers.

Tonight fortune was playing no favorites, with the wins bouncing from one player to the next, yet still the crowd pressed like hungry jackals three and four deep around the green-topped table. It was a side of these gentlemen—for despite their behavior now, they *were* all gentlemen, most peers, among the highest lords of the land—that Amariah had never seen, and as she studied each face in turn, it seemed that any one of them could be capable of writing the anonymous letter, just as any of them might be tempted to cheat the odds in his favor. She'd always considered herself a good judge of a person's character, and now she watched closely, looking for any small sign or gesture that might be a clue. She was also there as much to be seen as to see, for the same reason she'd had Pratt double the guards: she wanted the letter writer to understand she'd taken his charge seriously.

Absently she smoothed her long kid gloves over her wrist as her glance passed over the men. Could it be Lord Repton's youngest son, newly sent down from school and working hard at establishing his reputation as a man of the town? Was it Sir Henry Allen, gaunt and high-strung, and rumored to have squandered his family's fortune on a racehorse who'd then gone lame? Or was it the Duke of Guilford…?

Guilford! With a jolt, her wandering gaze stopped, locked with his across the noisy, jostling crowd. He was dressed for evening in a beautifully tailored dark blue coat over a pale blue waistcoat embroidered with silver dragons that twinkled in the lamps' diffused light. While most gentlemen looked rumpled and worn by this hour of the night, he seemed miraculously fresh, his linen crisp and unwilted, his jaw gleaming with the sheen of a recently passed razor. He didn't crouch down over the table like the others, but stood apart, the same way she was doing. His arms were folded loosely over his chest, and his green eyes focused entirely—*entirely!*—on her.

Fuming in silence at his audacity, she snapped her fan open. Of course he'd sought her out, not just in Penny House, but in this room; there'd be no other reason for him to be here at the hazard table. She knew the habits and quirks of every one of the club's members, and Guilford never ventured into the hazard room, neither as a player nor as a spectator. For a man who prided himself on his charm and civility, the wild recklessness of hazard held no appeal, and it would take a sizable reason for him to appear here now.

A reason, say, like the bracelet she'd returned earlier this afternoon.

As if reading her thoughts, he smiled at her, a slow, lazy, brazenly seductive smile that seemed to float toward her over the frenzy of the game.

To her mortification she felt her cheeks grow hot. Gentlemen gawked and gazed at her all the time at Penny House—she was perfectly aware that being decorative was a large part of her role as hostess—but somehow, after last night, it seemed different with Guilford. It *felt* different, in a way that made absolutely no sense, as if they were sharing something very private, very intimate between them—something that, as far as she was concerned, did not exist and never would.

She made a determined small *harrumph,* and raised her chin. She couldn't believe he'd look at her in such a way in so public a place as this, with so many others as witnesses. Not, of course, that any of these gentlemen were ready to witness anything but the dice dancing across the green cloth. She and the duke might have been the only ones in the room for all the rest might notice. Guilford knew this, too, just as he'd known she'd be here, and his smile widened, enough to show his infamous single dimple.

Indignation rippled through her, and the fan fluttered more rapidly in her hand. Hadn't he understood the note she'd returned with the bracelet? She'd been polite, but firm, excruciatingly explicit in offering no hope. Had he even *read* it? She shook her head and frowned in the sternest glare she could muster, and pointedly began to look away.

But before she could, he nodded, tossing his dark, wavy hair back from his brow, and then, to her horror, he winked.

It was, she decided, time to retreat.

"I am returning to the front parlor," she said to the guard behind Mr. Walthrip. "Summon me at once if anything changes."

With her head high, she quickly slipped through the crowd to the doorway and into the hall, greeting, smiling, chatting, falling back into her customary routine as if nothing were amiss. Down the curving staircase, to her favorite post before the Italian marble fireplace in the front room. Here she was able to see every gentleman who came or went through the front door, and here she could stand and receive them like a queen, with the row of silver candlesticks on the mantelpiece behind her.

"Ah, good evening, my lord!" she called, raising her voice so the elderly marquis could hear her. "I trust a footman is bringing your regular glass of canary?"

"The lackey ran off quick as a hare the moment he saw me," the white-haired marquis said with a wheezing cackle, seizing Amariah's hand in his gnarled fingers. "You know how to make a man happy, my dear Miss Penny. If my wife had half your talents, why, I'd be home with her twice as often!"

"Double the halves, and halve the double! Oh, my lord, no wonder you're such a marvel at whist!" Amariah used the excuse of opening her fan to draw her hand free from his. It didn't matter that the marquis was old enough to be her grandfather; the same club rules applied. "What a head you have for ciphering!"

"Dear, dear Miss Penny, if only I could halve my years for your sake!" The marquis sighed sorrowfully as he took the glass of wine from the footman's tray. "Here now, Guilford, you're a young buck. You show Miss Penny the appreciation she deserves."

"Oh, I'll endeavor to oblige," Guilford said, bowing as the old marquis shuffled away with his wine in hand to join another friend.

"Good evening, your grace," Amariah said, determined to greet Guilford like any other member of the club. "How glad we are to have you join us. Might I offer you something to drink, or a light supper before you head for the tables?"

"What you might offer me, Miss Penny, is an explanation, for I'm sorely confused." He smiled, adding a neat, self-mocking little bow. "Did you intend to refuse my apology as well as the bracelet?"

"I refused the gift, your grace," Amariah said. They were standing side by side, which allowed her to nod and smile at the gentlemen passing through the hallway without having to face Guilford himself. "I gave you my reasons for so doing in my note."

He made a disparaging little grunt. "A note which might be printed out by the hundreds, as common as a broadsheet, for all that it showed the personal interest of the lady who purportedly wrote it."

"I *did* write it, your grace," she said warmly. "I always do."

"Following by rote the words as composed by your solicitor?"

"Following the words of my choosing!" she said as she nodded and smiled to a marquis and his brother-in-law as they passed by. "What about *my* words did you not understand, your grace? What did I not make clear?"

"If you didn't like the rubies, you should just say so," he said, more wounded than irate. "Robitaille's got a whole shop full of other baubles for you to choose from. You can go have your pick."

"Whether I like rubies or not has nothing to do with anything, your grace," she said. He was being purposefully obtuse, and her patience, already stretched thin, was fraying fast. "My sisters and I have never accepted any gifts from any gentlemen. It's not in the spirit of my father's wishes for us, or for Penny House."

"It's not in the spirit of being a lady to send back a ruby bracelet," he declared. "It's unnatural."

"For my sisters and me, your grace, it's the most natural thing in the world," she said. "If a gentlemen does wish to show his especial appreciation, then we suggest that a contribution be made instead to the Penny House charity fund."

Again he made that grumbly, growl of displeasure. "Where's the pleasure in making a contribution to charity, I ask you that?"

Her smile now included him as well as the others passing by. She'd long ago learned to tell when a man had realized he was losing, and she could hear that unhappy resignation now in Guilford's voice. But she wouldn't gloat. She'd likewise learned long ago that it was far better to let a defeated man salvage his pride however he could than to crow in victory. That was how duels began, and though she doubted that Guilford would call her out for pistols at dawn over a ruby bracelet, she could still afford to be a gracious winner.

"You will not take the bracelet, then?" he asked, one final attempt. "Nor anything else in its stead from old Robitaille's shop?"

"I'm sorry, your grace," she said generously. "But I shall be most happy to accept your contribution to our fund."

He sighed glumly. "You may not choose to believe me, Miss Penny, but you are the first lady I've ever known to send back a piece of jewelry."

"I'll believe you, your grace." She smiled, and finally turned back toward him. "Life is full of firsts. I suppose I should feel honored that one of yours involved me."

"I hope only the first of many," he said. "For both of us."

His glumness gone, his face seemed to light with enough fresh hope that she felt a little twinge of uneasiness. Whatever was he thinking? She hadn't promised him anything.

Had she?

At once she shoved aside the question as small-minded. It was only because she was still so weary from yesterday's wedding and the possibility of a cheating scandal that she'd let herself even consider such an unworthy possibility. Guilford had just conceded; she should be using this as an opportunity to benefit Penny House, not to suspect his motives.

"If you wish, your grace, I would be glad to show you exactly how the funds we raise are distributed and employed," she said. "It would be my pleasure."

He raised his brows with a great show of surprise. "You have forgiven me, then, even if you returned my peace offering?"

She wished she didn't have this nagging feeling that he was saying more than she realized. "Is there a reason why I shouldn't, your grace?"

He bowed his head, contorting his features to look as painfully contrite as any altar boy. "I've always heard it's divine to forgive, Miss Penny."

"It's more divine not to sin in the first place, your grace," she said, trying not to laugh. "Though I shall grant you a point for audacity, trotting out such a shopworn old homily for a clergyman's daughter."

He looked up at her without lifting his chin, his blue eyes full of mischief. "I always try my best, Miss Penny, especially for you."

"More properly, your grace, you are always *trying*," she said, unable to resist. They were falling back into their usual banter, the back-and-forth that she'd always enjoyed with Guilford. Maybe last night really had been no more than a regrettable lapse; maybe they really could put it past them. Because he'd always been one of her favorite members—and an important figure on the club's membership committee—she'd be willing to shorten her memory.

He laughed, his amusement genuine. "Let me truly repent, Miss Penny. Explain to me these charities, and I vow I'll listen to every word, and then make whatever contribution you deem fitting."

"The price of that bracelet would be more than enough, your grace," she said, feeling the glow of expansive goodwill. "But I'll do better than a dry explanation. Tomorrow is Sunday, and, of course, Penny House is closed. If you wish, I'll take you to one of our favorite charities, and show you myself what we have accomplished."

"What an outstanding idea, Miss Penny!" he exclaimed, ready to embrace this plan as his own. "I shall be here tomorrow morning with my carriage."

She paused for a second, then decided not to take the obvious jab back at him. Whether or not the duke chose to spend his Sunday mornings in churchgoing was his decision, not hers. She'd accept his money for her good works, true, but she knew better than to overstep and try to save his soul as she emptied his pocket.

"Later in the afternoon would be more convenient for me, your grace," she said lightly, without a breath of reproach. "And perhaps hiring a hackney might be less obtrusive."

"We'll compromise, and take my chaise," he said with a sweep of his hand. "That's plain enough."

Of course, it wouldn't be, not with a ducal crest bright with gold leaf painted on the door. Then again, Guilford wouldn't know how to be unobtrusive if his life depended upon it.

But she'd be willing to compromise, too. "Thank you, your grace," she said. "I'll be delighted to ride in your chaise."

"And in your company, Miss Penny, I shall be…" He paused, frowning a bit as if searching for the perfect word. "I shall be *ecstatic.*"

He bowed, then turned away and into the crowd of other members before she could answer. Apparently that was farewell enough for him tonight, or perhaps that was how he'd chosen to save a scrap more face. Amariah only smiled, and shook her head with bemusement as she began to greet the next gentleman. Good, bad or indifferent, there'd be no changing the Duke of Guilford, and resolutely Amariah put him from her thoughts until tomorrow.

Guilford pushed the curtains of his bedchamber aside to look out the window, and smiled broadly. Sunshine, blue skies, and plenty of both: the gods of good luck and winning wagers were surely smiling on him today. Despite the romantic plays and ballads proclaiming that dark mists and fogs were best for lovers, he'd always found a warm, sunny day put ladies more in the mood than a chilly, gray one. With a cheerfully tuneless whistle on his lips, he turned around and let his manservant Crenshaw tie his neckcloth into a knot as perfect as the rest of the day promised to be.

"A splendid day, isn't it, Crenshaw?" he declared, his voice a little strangled as he held his chin up and clear of the knot tying. "Would that every Sunday were so fine, eh?"

"As you wish, your grace," said Crenshaw, his standard answer to all of Guilford's questions for as long as either of them could recall. With puffs of wispy white hair capping perpetually gloomy resignation, Crenshaw was a servant of such indeterminate age that Guilford couldn't swear if the man were forty or eighty; all he knew for sure was that Crenshaw had been a part of the family since before Guilford had been born. Guilford had inherited him along with his title when his father had died, and he expected Crenshaw to be there waiting each morning with his warm shaving water and razor until either he or Crenshaw died first. And Crenshaw being Crenshaw, Guilford wouldn't bet against him to outlast the whole lot of Fitzhardings.

"It *is* what I wish," Guilford said. "Not that I have any more say in the weather than the next man. Is the chaise around front yet?"

"I expect it any moment, your grace." Crenshaw gave a last gentle pat to the center of the linen knot, like a nursemaid to a favorite charge. "Shall I expect you to return to dress for the evening, or will you be going directly to Miss Danton's house?"

"No, no, Crenshaw, I am done with Miss Danton, and she with me," Guilford said, without even a trace of rancor. "May she ride to the hounds happily into the sunset, and away from me. Today I'll have another fair lady gracing my side—Miss Amariah Penny."

"The lady from the gaming house, your grace?" Holding out Guilford's coat, Crenshaw's amazement briefly overcame his reticence. "One of those red-haired sisters, your grace?"

"The same, and the first and the finest of the three," Guilford said with relish as he slipped his arms into the coat's sleeves. He couldn't remember the last time he'd anticipated an engagement with any lady this much. "I shall return when I return, Crenshaw. I can't promise more than that. There's the chaise now."

He grabbed his gloves and hat, and bounded down the staircase. He had always liked Amariah Penny, liked her from the first night he'd met her. He'd first visited Penny House for the novelty of a club run by ladies, but Amariah was the reason he'd returned. It wasn't just her flame-colored hair and well-curved figure—his London was full of far more beautiful women—but her cleverness. She was quick and witty in the same ways he was himself, and because she always had the right word at the ready, she was vastly entertaining. You'd never catch her relying on a languid simper to cover her ignorance. She smiled wickedly, then came at you with all guns blazing, and Guilford had never met another woman like her.

Yet before this week, he hadn't thought of her as anything beyond her place at Penny House. He wasn't certain why; perhaps he just hadn't wanted to tamper with a perfectly good arrangement between them. The wager had changed that. It was almost as if he'd been granted permission to consider her in bed instead of just the front room of Penny House, and now he could scarce think of anything else. He wanted to see the whole expanse of her creamy pale skin, and learn every exact place she had freckles. He wanted to explore the body her drifting, constant blue gowns hinted at, and discover the lush breasts and hips he suspected were there. He wanted her to laugh that wonderfully husky laugh just for him, and he wanted to hear her moan with the pleasure he'd give her.

Most of all, he wanted to learn if she could amuse him in bed as much as she did each night in the parlor at Penny House. No wonder he couldn't think beyond such an enchanting possibility.

What was she doing now, at this very moment? Was she making herself ready for him, just as he had for her? He pictured her sitting before her looking glass while her maid dressed her hair. With the delicious torment of female indecision, she'd be choosing her gown, her stockings, her hat, all with him in mind, and he couldn't help but smile.

The chaise was waiting at the curb, its dark sapphire paint scrubbed and shining. Gold leaf picked out his crest on the door, and more gold lined each spoke of the wheels, like spinning rays from the sun. As he'd ordered, the windows were open and the leather shades rolled up and fastened, leaving the interior open to the breezes and light. He didn't want Amariah feeling trapped, or too confined; he wanted her comfortable and relaxed against those soft leather squabs, and wholly susceptible to his charm.

He climbed into the carriage and settled back with a happy sigh as the footman latched the door after him. This wouldn't be like the night at Penny House. This would be his domain, not hers; he wasn't about to grant her that advantage again. With the same tuneless whistle, he picked a white flower from the little vase bolted to the wall of the carriage and tucked it into his top buttonhole. He'd never known any woman this long before he'd seduced her—that is, excluding the cooks and relations and young daughters of old friends who were by nature unseducible—and he found the novelty of their situation at once intriguing and exciting.

The chaise had barely eased into the street when a rider on horseback came up beside them, the man reaching out to knock his fist imperiously on the side of the chaise.

Guilford pulled off his hat and thrust his head through the open window, the breeze plucking at his hair. "What, Stanton, will you raise the dead?"

"The dead are pretty well raised by this hour, Guilford," drawled Lord Henry Stanton, "else all the knocking in the world won't raise 'em further."

"Very well, then, you're raising the hair on all the living." Guilford sighed impatiently. True, he'd been friends with Stanton since school, good friends and companions in considerable mischief over the years, but seeing him here, now, took a little of the luster from Guilford's afternoon. Even a minute stolen from the time he wished to spend with Amariah was too much. "What are you doing here now, anyway?"

Stanton ignored him, his heavy-lidded eyes making a swift survey. "A carriage instead of your usual nag, and a posy on your chest?" he observed. "The lady will be pleased you made the effort for her."

"The lady will be better pleased if I arrive on time." Guilford knocked on the chaise's roof to signal the driver to begin, but Stanton only followed, matching his horse's gait to that of the horse in the traces.

"True enough, Guilford," he said. "Rumor has it that Miss Penny is the very devil for promptness."

That made Guilford smile in spite of himself, imagining how indignant Amariah would be to hear her much-practiced goodness linked to the prince of all badness. "You shouldn't call her the devil anything, considering her father."

"No?" asked Stanton, a leading question if ever there was one.

"No," Guilford said dryly. "Not that I ever said I was even seeing Miss Penny today."

"You didn't have to say a word." Stanton winked, and tapped a sly finger to the brim of his hat. "If you didn't want the whole town to know, then you shouldn't make your assignations in the middle of the crush at Penny House. Westbrook told me."

Now Guilford's sigh came out as more of a groan. "What I choose to do and where I do it are not any of your affair, Stanton."

"Where the luscious Miss Penny's concerned, Guilford, I'm afraid they are." He leered through the window. "As I recall, there's a substantial wager between us resting on the well-rounded backside of the lady."

"I haven't forgotten, Stanton," Guilford said, "and I still mean to win. I've planned every detail. After a drive through the park, a supper in a private room at Carlisle's, a few bottles of the best of that cellar's wines, I could be claiming your stake before dawn."

"Carlisle's, you say." Stanton raised a skeptical brow at the mention of the fashionable tavern. "And here I'd heard your itinerary was a tour of almshouses and beggar's haunts."

Blast Westbrook for having such excellent ears. "Oh, the day's only begun," Guilford said with as nonchalant an air as he could muster. "Good deeds will only put her into a more agreeable humor."

"Oh, indeed," Stanton said, and grinned to show exactly how little credence he gave to Guilford's theory. "But tell me, Guilford. Do you really believe the steps of some wretched almshouse would be the proper place to tumble her?"

"Stanton, Stanton." Guilford clucked his tongue in mock

dismay. "Am I truly that low in your estimation? Ah, to show so little regard for Miss Penny's sensibilities!"

Stanton drew back, feigning great shock in return. "Are you defending the lady's honor before you've even warmed her bed?"

"What if I am?" Guilford shrugged elaborately. "You know my ways, Stanton. I'd much rather play the gallant than the rake. Better to leave a woman sighing your name than cursing it."

He'd always liked women, and they had liked him in return, a satisfying exchange for all parties. He was also quite sure he'd never been in love, at least not the way the poets described, but the liking had been quite fine for him.

And he did like Amariah Penny and her creamy pale skin.

"She won't be as easy as your usual conquests," Stanton insisted. "She's her own woman. She owns that whole infernal Penny House. She doesn't need you, or anything you can give her."

"That's only because she doesn't yet know what I can give her." Of course, that didn't include ruby bracelets, but he'd conveniently forget that slight for now. "She'll learn soon enough."

"You're smiling like a madman," Stanton said glumly. "Next you'll be telling me you're too damned gallant to stomach the wager."

"You only wish it were so, Stanton." Even if he weren't so intrigued by the stakes, he still wouldn't back down. It was the principle of the thing, not the money. Any man who set aside a bet like this one would become the laughingstock of White's, and his friends would never let him forget it. "If you wish to call it off, that's one thing, but I'm not about to do it. How daft do you think I am?"

"You tell me." Stanton sighed with unhappy resignation. "Let the wager stand, then, and the terms with it. You have a fortnight to bed Miss Penny, and to collect reasonable proof that the deed's been done."

"Oh, you'll know," Guilford said, looking down to adjust the flower in his buttonhole. "As you observed yourself, all London hears everything that happens at Penny House."

"And I'll be listening, my friend." Stanton gathered the reins of his horse more tightly in his hand. "I'll be listening for every word."

Amariah crouched beside the bench, her hand holding tight to the girl's sweating fingers. "Not much longer, lass, not much more."

The girl cried out again, her face contorted with pain. She'd already been in hard labor, her waters broken, when she'd thumped on the kitchen door, and there'd been no time to take her to a midwife. Amariah had had her brought inside, here into her sister Bethany's little office down the hall by the pantry, and while the bench might not be the most ideal place to give birth, it would be far better and more private than the street or beneath a bridge.

"The midwife should be here any minute, Miss Penny," said the cook, Letty Todd, as she rejoined Amariah. "Though from the looks of things, any minute may be a minute too long."

"We'll manage, Letty." Amariah felt the force of the young woman's pains as she tightened her grasp. She couldn't be more than fifteen or sixteen, scarcely more than a child herself, and her worn, tattered dress and the thinness of her wrists and cheeks bore mute testimony to how cheerless her life must be. Though Amariah didn't know the girl's name or situation, she did recognize her as one of the crowd of poor folk that came to the back door each day for what might be their only meal of the day. A scullery maid ruined by the master's son, a sailor's widow, a milkmaid deceived by her sweetheart: Amariah didn't care what misfortune had brought the girl to this sad state, nor had she asked. All that mattered was that Penny House offer this young woman the haven she'd so desperately sought, and that she and her baby be treated with kindness and compassion.

"Ooh, it's coming, miss, it's coming!" cried the girl frantically. "The baby, miss, the baby! Oh, God preserve me!"

Amariah had attended enough births in her father's old parish to know that the girl was in fact close to delivering. But her experience had been as an observer, not as a midwife, and as she shifted between the girl's bent, trembling knees, she prayed for the skill and knowledge that she knew she didn't have.

"Listen to me, dear," she said. "At the next pain, I want you to take the biggest breath you can and push."

"I—I can't!" the girl wailed. "Oh, help me!"

"You can," Amariah said firmly. "Take a deep breath, and then try to—"

"Forgive me, I came as fast as I could!" Quickly the midwife tossed her shawl over the chair and draped one of the clean cloths over her forearms. She was brusque and efficient, and ready to take charge. "Don't fear, duck, we'll see you through. If you'll just hold her knee for her here, miss."

Gratefully Amariah obeyed, and at once was caught up in the drama of the birth. As she'd thought, the baby crowned and slipped into the midwife's waiting hands within minutes of her appearance. A boy, loud and lusty, and as the kitchen staff cheered his arrival, the new mother wept with mingled joy, exhaustion and despair as the midwife put her new son, wrapped in a clean dishcloth, to her breast for the first time.

"I'd nowheres t'go, Miss Penny," she whispered through her tears. "But you an' t'other Miss be so kind t'us in th' yard each day, I thought I could…I could—"

"You did exactly the right thing coming here," Amariah said softly, brushing her fingertips over the baby's downy head. "We'll find a safe home for you and your son once you've recovered. Now rest, and enjoy him."

"Sammy," said the girl. "His name be Sammy. Sammy Patton."

"Sammy, then." Amariah smiled. "Welcome to this life, Sammy. And may God bless you both."

She helped the midwife bundle the soiled linens, closing the door gently to let the new mother sleep. Yet even as she washed her hands and arms, the image of the new baby lingered, his tiny wrinkled fists ready to take on a hard life, his pink mouth as wide and demanding as a little bird's, ready to announce his hunger and indignation to the world.

"Miss Penny?" Pratt stood before her, even more anxious than usual. "Miss Penny, his grace is here for you."

"His grace?" Amariah stared at him, her thoughts still on the new baby.

"His Grace the Duke of Guilford, miss." Pratt nodded, as if confirming this for himself as well as for her. "I have put his grace in the front parlor."

"Guilford!" Oh, merciful heavens, how had she forgotten so completely about him? Swiftly she tore off her blood-stained apron and ran toward the stairs, smoothing her hair as best she could, then flung open the twin doors to the parlor.

"Good day, your grace," she said with a sweeping curtsy. "Forgive me for keeping you waiting, but I had an unexpected emergency that needed my attention below stairs."

She smiled warmly, but Guilford only stared, his expression oddly frozen.

"Good day to you, too, Miss Penny," he said at last. "It would appear that I've caught you at an, ah, inopportune time. Shall I wait for you to recollect yourself?"

"I won't make you wait at all, your grace," she said, puzzled. "I'll just send for my bonnet, and I'll be ready."

He shook his head, for once seemingly at a loss for what to say. "I shall be glad to wait, you know. Perfectly glad."

"But there's no reason for it, your grace," she began, then caught him looking down at her dress. It wasn't the usual kind of admiring gentleman's look, but a silently appalled and beseeching look, and quickly she turned toward the glass over the fireplace to judge for herself.

She was still wearing the plain gray wool gown she'd chosen for morning prayer, now rumpled and wrinkled and stained where her apron hadn't covered her enough. She wore no jewelry, and her hair, though mussed, was still drawn back tight in a knot at the back of her head.

It wasn't much different than how she usually looked for day, but Guilford wouldn't know that. Whenever he saw her, she was always dressed in one of her blue Penny House gowns, fashionably cut low and revealing, with white plumes pinned into her curled hair and paste jewels sparkling around her throat. How she looked for the evenings was as much a part of the club as the Italian paintings on the wall or the green cloth covering the hazard table upstairs, and no more a part of her, either.

She glanced back at him with that pathetically woeful expression on his face. Of course, he was wearing his same habitual coat, so dark a blue as to be nearly black, a green-flowered silk waistcoat draped with a heavy gold watch chain and cream-colored trousers, all chosen to please himself and without a thought for where they were going. Had he truly expected her to match him, and dress in the gaudy blue silk and paste necklace for calling on almshouses?

"I'm perfectly content to wait," he said again, adding a coaxing smile. "Take as long as you wish. I understand how ladies can be, you know."

"Oh, I'm sure you do, your grace," she said, smiling in return. She understood him, too, and likely a good deal better than he either realized or wished. "I suppose I am a bit untidy. I'll take those few minutes to refresh myself, and be back before you miss me. Shall I send for Pratt to bring you refreshment?"

"That excellent fellow has already tended to me." He gathered the glass from the table beside him, raising it toward her like a toast. "Hurry back, sweetheart. And mind that I'm most partial to the color blue on a lady like you."

"I'll take that into consideration, your grace," she said as she backed from the room.

But now it was outrage that sent her marching up the stairs to her private rooms to change, her heels clicking fiercely on the treads of the steps. For an intelligent man, the duke was behaving like a first-rate dunce. This was the other night after the wedding all over again. Did Guilford really believe her memory was this short? She'd asked him to join her today for educational purposes, not to amuse him, and she knew she'd made her intentions perfectly clear.

Quickly she shed the soiled gown, washed, and brushed her hair, then stood before the other gowns that hung in the cupboard. She didn't possess the vast wardrobe that Guilford seemed to believe. Beyond the dramatic gowns for evening that she and her sisters wore for their roles at Penny House, there wasn't much that would meet the stylish standards of a duke. The only one that might do was a soft blue wool day gown with a ruffled hem, complete with a matching redingote with more ruffles across the bust, and a velvet bonnet in a deeper blue—an ensemble designed by her fashionable sister Cassia, and the one Amariah wore when she and her sisters went driving in the park together. She touched her fingers to one of the ruffles and smiled, imagining how pleased Guilford would be to see she'd obeyed his request.

Then she resolutely turned to the gown beside it. A serviceable dove gray with dull pewter buttons, high necked and as plain as a foggy day: a dress somber enough for a poor neighborhood. Amariah's smile widened with fresh determination as she reached for the gown and drew it over her head.

Guilford wouldn't be partial to this color, or the sturdy plainness of her gown, either. She didn't care, or rather she did for the opposite reasons. At least *she* knew how to dress unobtrusively and suitably when the situation called for it.

And as for her so-called reputation as a virago: ah, for a virago the gray gown would be entirely appropriate!

Chapter Four

"Here I am, your grace," Amariah said, tugging on her glove as she stood in the doorway to the hall. "You've been most kind to wait for me, and now, you see, I'm ready whenever you please."

Guilford turned, the easy, welcoming smile already on his face for her, and stopped short.

What in blazes was she wearing *now?* A nun's habit? A winding cloth? Sackcloth and ashes?

"You are ready?" he echoed. As rumpled and unappealing as her dress had been earlier, he would have taken it over this without a second's hesitation. The gray shapeless gown and jacket were bad enough, burying all semblance of her delightfully curving body in coarse gray wool, but she'd scraped her hair back from her forehead so tightly that she'd lost every last coppery curl, and then tied a dreadful flat chip hat over a white linen cap. She looked like the sorriest serving girl fresh from the country, or worse, perhaps from some sooty mill town.

What had happened to the delicious Amariah Penny? And how could he possibly take her into Carlisle's dressed like this?

"Have you changed your mind, your grace?" she asked

sweetly. "You know I won't think an iota less of you if you've decided you'd rather retreat than accompany me."

One more look at that awful gray gown, and he very nearly did. Yet there was something in her eye—an extra sparkle of triumph—that stopped him. He couldn't forget that Amariah Penny was no ordinary female, and she wouldn't rely on ordinary female wiles, either. If she thought she'd shed him simply because she'd made herself as ugly as possible, why, then he was ready to prove her wrong.

"Nothing could make me abandon you, Miss Penny," he said with as gallant a bow as he could muster—which, coming from him, was impressively gallant indeed. "*Abandonment* is not a word I acknowledge when it comes to a lady."

"Of course not, your grace," she said as he joined her in the hall. A footman was holding the front door open for them, and she sailed on through. "I must thank you again for offering your chaise today, your grace. It will make everything so much easier and more pleasant."

"The pleasure is mine, Miss Penny," he said, then stopped short with surprise for the second time that morning.

There stood his chaise where he'd left it, standing before the carriage block, the blue paint shining in the sun. But now Amariah's man Pratt was there at the curb, too, directing three Penny House servants who were loading wicker hampers, covered with checked cloths, into the chaise.

His chaise.

She glanced over her shoulder at him, adjusting the flat brim of her hideous hat, and he caught that extra sparkle of a dare in her eye again. "I trust you are in a charitable humor today, your grace."

"Charitable?" he said indignantly. "You've turned my chaise into a dray wagon! What in blazes is in those baskets, anyway?"

"Food," she said as if it were perfectly obvious. "The places we are to visit are always in need of food for hungry folk, your grace, and I try to provide what I can. Come, there's still plenty of room for us inside."

"Well, *that's* a blessing," he said glumly as he followed her down the steps. How could he begin to seduce her when they'd be packed cheek to jowl with her wretched baskets like a farmer and his wife on market day? If he saw any of his friends with her like this, he'd never hear the end of it.

"Indeed it *is* a blessing for those we benefit, your grace," she said, clearly refusing to hear the sarcasm in his voice. "We all do what we can, don't we?"

He didn't answer. He'd wager a handful of guineas that if it had been after dark and she'd been standing with him inside the club, wearing one of those handsome blue gowns, then she would not only have understood his other meaning, she would have laughed aloud.

"Here you are, your grace, seat yourself," she continued as she climbed into the crowded chaise, "and I'll tuck myself into this little place. I'll grant you it's snug, but we shall manage."

"*Snug,* hell," he muttered crossly as he squeezed his long legs into the small space she'd allotted to him. "Snug is what we'd be if you were beside me, not with this infernal basket wedged between us."

She smiled, tipping her head to one side. Sunlight filtered through the woven brim of her hat, dappling her face with tiny pinpricks of light. "The basket won't be here for so very long, your grace, and I promise you it will do such a world of good that you'll feel infinitely better about yourself, much better than from the simple sensation of my skirts brushing against your leg."

He smiled in return, thinking of what might have been if she weren't being so damned perverse.

"It wouldn't have been the brush of your skirts, Miss Penny," he said, "but the pleasant warmth of your thigh pressed against mine. Nothing simple about *that,* I can assure you."

"How wonderful it must be for you to have such confidence in your opinions, your grace!" she exclaimed wryly. "To be able to give your *assurance* as easy as that—why, I almost envy you!"

"Except that envy is one of the seven deadly sins, and you, as a parson's daughter, would never, ever dream of sinning."

"One must have goals, your grace," she said serenely. "Likely yours has been to experience every one of those seven sins for yourself."

"Not at all," he declared. "I'm not even sure I could name the seven, let alone describe them on a comfortable, given-name basis."

Her smile widened as she held up her hands, ticking off each sin on a finger. "Envy, pride, covetousness, lust, anger, gluttony and sloth. Those are the seven deadly ones."

He frowned. He wished he hadn't asked; he didn't like realizing that, at one time or another, he had in fact been guilty of most of the seven. Come to think of it, he was practicing at least two of them at this very moment, sitting with her in his luxurious chaise with the crest on the door.

"There are more than seven sins?" he asked warily.

"Oh, yes," she said, too cheerfully for comfort. "There are the sins that cry out to heaven for vengeance, as well as the sins of the angels. I don't have fingers enough for them all."

"At least there's no sin in that," he said with a heartiness that he didn't quite feel. He was on shaky ground here, and they both knew it. "I suppose I should know better than to banter about sins with the vicar's daughter."

"At least bickering isn't a mortal sin, your grace," she said. "Not even on the Sabbath."

"I suppose not." He turned toward her, or at least as far as he could in the crowded seat. "Look here, why don't we speak of something more agreeable than all this hellfire and damnation?"

Amused, she leaned back against the seat, an almost languid pose that was much at odds with her prim dress.

"Sins alone don't earn damnation, your grace," she said. "It's only if you don't show repentance that you'll run into trouble when you die. But if you'd rather not speak of the state of your soul, I've no objection to finding a new subject."

"Very well," he said, more relieved than he'd want to admit. "What shall it be? The weather? The crowds in the street around us? Where we shall dine this evening? What member is cheating the club at hazard?"

Surprise flickered across her face, only for an instant—she was very good at hiding her emotions—but enough for him to know what he'd overheard between two servants last night was true.

"Wherever did you learn such a thing, your grace?" she asked with forced lightness. "A cheat at the Penny House table?"

He smiled, the advantage back in his court. "You're not denying it."

"Because it's too preposterous to deny," she declared. "Our membership consists of only the first gentlemen in the land. How could I suspect one of them of cheating?"

"Because gentlemen hate to lose, perhaps more than other men," he said. "Because gentlemen can be desperate, too.

Because if you are as pathetically trusting as you wish me to believe, then I must report you to the membership committee at once, before you let some villain steal away everything from under your nose."

Bright pink flooded her cheeks—an angry, indignant pink, not a blush at all. "That will not happen, your grace. You have my word."

He smiled indulgently. "You can't simply wish away a scandal, my dear."

"I'm not," she said tartly, "and I've taken action to stop it. You should know me well enough by now, your grace, to realize that I am not too proud to ask for assistance if I need it."

"And you in turn should know me well enough to come to me if the troubles rise around your ankles." He reached his hand out across the back of the seat so it almost—almost— brushed hers. "It's far better to reach out for a lifeline than to let yourself drown."

She shifted away from his hand. "How fascinating that you regard yourself in that way, your grace."

"Oh, I regard myself in a great many ways, Miss Penny," he said, "and you should feel free to do the same."

"You can play at being my Father Confessor all you want, but I still won't invent a scandal simply for the sake of telling it to you."

"Even if it's no invention?" he asked softly. "Even if it's true?"

"No," she said, raising her chin a fraction in a way he recognized as a challenge. "Especially because it's not."

He sighed, willing to concede for now. She'd confide in him eventually, anyway. Ladies always confided in him, and they'd have the entire rest of the day together. "You're a stubborn creature, Miss Penny."

"You're back to that virago nonsense again, aren't you?" She narrowed her eyes a fraction. "Why is it that when a man holds firm, he is steadfast, but when a woman does it, she's stubborn?"

He laughed. Oh, she was *good,* virago or not, and his admiration for her rose another notch. "I'll stand corrected. You, Miss Penny are steadfast, not stubborn."

"I suppose I should thank you for that," she said. "Or didn't you intend it as a compliment?"

"I did," he said. "And well deserved it is, too. I can offer more if you'd like."

"I'm sure you could." Her mouth curved wryly to one side. "But I've a better suggestion for conversation, your grace. Let us speak of you."

"Of me?" He hadn't expected that. "An agreeable enough subject, so long as we keep from my sins. Perhaps I'll begin by telling you how much I enjoy your company."

She leaned forward, toward him, her elbows on her knees and her hands clasped.

"Bother that," she said. "I already know you enjoy my company, else you wouldn't have asked for more of it this afternoon. I want to learn something new about you. Tell me of your childhood—your first pony's name, your favorite tree to climb, the vegetable you found most loathsome to eat in your nursery suppers. What manner of boy were you, anyway?"

"My manner was ill-mannered, truth be told," he said, laughing. "I was the only boy after four girls, the heir to my father's title that everyone had long abandoned hope of ever living to see. I arrived seven years after my youngest sister, a complete surprise that set every church bell in the county to pealing. I was so petted and coddled that it's a wonder I wasn't completely spoiled for anything useful."

She grinned wickedly. "Some might disagree with you, your grace."

He returned her grin, relishing its warmth. Women didn't generally ask him about his childhood, and it rather pleased him that she had. "Perhaps I am spoiled. But I had a deuced fine time as a boy, I can tell you that. I spent most of the year in the country, at Guilford Abbey, getting into whatever mischief I could."

"That's in Essex, isn't it?"

"Devon," he said, the pride clear in his voice as he let himself sink into a hazy, happy recollection of the past. "'Devon is Heaven,' my father used to say, and there was no finer place for any boy. I had a new pony every summer to match my height as I grew, a whole pack of dogs that trooped along with me and a boat to sail in the duck pond. I went hunting and fishing with my uncles and my sisters' husbands, played out the American war in the orchards with my cousins and ate my fill of sweet biscuits and jam with the servants at the big table in the kitchen."

"So even the servants spoiled you," she said softly, watching him from beneath the brim of that dreadful hat.

"Oh, they were the worst of the lot," he said. "Cook always had a soft spot for me, and she was always baking me special little pies, carving my initials in the top of the crust."

That made her smile. "So you wanted for absolutely nothing."

"Not a blessed thing," he agreed. "I was the happiest little rogue alive."

"I hope you won't forget that, your grace," she said, glancing out the window as the chaise slowed. "Ah, we've arrived."

Curious, he turned toward the window, as well; he'd been so caught up in his reminiscing that he'd no notion of how far they'd traveled. He looked, and saw, and his expression at once grew somber.

Could there have been a more different scene from the green Devon hills he'd been describing? They'd long ago left the neat, fashionable prosperity of St. James Square for a neighborhood in London that he knew he'd never visited before.

Here the houses were so old they seemed ready to topple into the street, ancient timbers and beams that somehow must have survived the Great Fire over a hundred years before. Broken windows were stuffed with handfuls of dirty straw, or simply left open and gaping, like a broken tooth in a drunkard's smile. No reputable trades kept businesses here, but every other building seemed to house an alehouse or gin shop. Even on a Sunday, last night's customers still sprawled on the steps, while a few desultory women with bodices open and cheeks painted with tawdry red circles tried to lure their first customers of the day.

Because the afternoon was warm, and the same sun that shone on the rich folk in their open carriages in Green Park also fell here, the street was also filled with dirty, barefoot children, cripples on makeshift crutches, babies wailing with hunger in their too-young mothers' arms, mongrel dogs scrapping over an old mutton bone, and costermongers hawking fruit and vegetables too rotten for the better streets. The street itself was unpaved, with a deep kennel in the center filled with standing, putrid water, thick with dead rats and human filth.

His coachman would have seventeen fits when he saw that muck on the gold-trimmed wheels of the chaise.

Amariah was unlatching the door herself, not waiting for the footman. "Mind yourself, your grace. They'll all ask you for something. But if you give one a coin, then fifty more will suddenly appear with their hands out, too, so I've found it's best not to begin. They'll only squander it on gin, anyway, which is why I prefer to give them food instead."

Just as she warned, beggars of every age were already crowding around the door with their filthy hands outstretched like so many claws, pressing so closely that they rocked the chaise on its springs and made the horses whinny nervously.

"Hold now, Miss Penny, you can't go out there with them!" he said, grabbing her arm to keep her back. "It's not safe!"

She looked back at him over her shoulder, incredulous and a little disdainful at the same time, as she shook her arm free of his hand.

"Of course I can, your grace," she said, looping one of the baskets into the crook of her arm, "and I do, every Sunday."

"But consider what you're doing, Miss Penny, the risk you are taking—"

"Being poor and hungry does not turn a person into a dangerous beast, your grace," she said firmly. "But if you are too frightened for your own safety, then you may feel free to remain here."

Before he could catch her again, she'd pushed the door open and hopped outside, holding the basket before her like a wicker shield as she made her way through the beggars. Now he realized they'd stopped before a woebegone little church, bits of stonework broken away like a stale pie crust and the once-red paint worn from the tall arched doors. The church's pastor stood before one of these doors, smiling and holding it open for Amariah and her baskets.

"Your grace?" One of his footmen belatedly appeared at the door, his expression as confused as Guilford's own must be. "If you please, your grace, what—"

"Damnation, take those infernal baskets down for Miss Penny!" He couldn't let Amariah go alone, not into this mess, and with a deep breath he pushed past the footman into the crowd after her. The stench was appalling, and it took all his willpower not to cover his nose with his handkerchief. Who would have guessed other humans could smell as vile as the refuse beneath their feet?

"A penny, guv'nor, only a penny!"

"Please, sir, please, for me poor mum!"

"Sure, sure, a fine gentleman like yourself can spare a coin for a sufferer!"

Resolutely Guilford pushed forward, focusing on Amariah and not those jostling around him. With a horrible thought, he pressed his hand over his waistcoat, relieved to feel the comforting weight of his gold watch and chain still there. The timepiece had been in his family for generations, and he'd hate to have it nicked by one of these sorry rascals.

"Please, m'lord, please—"

"Not today, I'm afraid," he mumbled. He told himself he was only following Amariah's suggestion, but he still felt like some wretched miser with his pockets stitched shut. "I've no loose coins with me."

Finally he reached the church, bounding up the worn stone steps and away from the beggars. His heart was pounding, and he could feel the unpleasant prickle of sweat beneath his shirt collar.

At least Amariah was beaming at him for his trouble, no inconsiderable consolation.

"Your grace, I should like to present Reverend Robert Potter," she said in exactly the same easy, gracious tone she used when introducing foreign princes and other grandees at Penny House. "Reverend Potter is the vicar here at St. Crispin's parish, and he sees that the food we bring from Penny House is given away to those who need it most. Reverend Potter, His Grace the Duke of Guilford. Lord Guilford is most interested in our charities, Reverend, and is accompanying me today to observe for himself."

His hands clasped over the front of his plain black cassock, Potter nodded and smiled warmly. He was tall and thin, almost gaunt, but the kindness in his weathered blue eyes softened his entire face.

"I cannot tell you how honored I am to meet you, your grace, and to have you here at St. Crispin's," he said. "Would that more great lords were like you and Miss Penny, and took such a worthy interest in the sufferings of the unfortunate."

Guilford cleared his throat and nodded in return, feeling like some sort of false play-actor standing on these steps. "Miss Penny can take all the credit," he said. "She's the one who brought me here."

"She also seems to have brought more than the usual amount of food, your grace." Potter watched with obvious approval as the footmen brought in the rest of the baskets from the chaise. "But how rare to have it delivered to us in a ducal carriage!"

Amariah looped her hand into his arm. "Come inside, your grace, and see everything that we brought."

He let her lead him inside the church, cool and damp after the sun, and into a small hall to one side of the church itself. The bare walls were whitewashed, the worn planked floor swept clean, and three rows of long board tables ran the length of the room. As soon as the footmen set the baskets on the tables, two plainly dressed women and a boy in an uncocked black hat began unpacking them and arranging the food inside into wooden trenchers. There were no benches at the tables; after seeing the crowd outside, Guilford guessed they wouldn't exactly sit and linger over their meal, anyway.

"As much as we brought, it won't begin to be enough,"

Amariah said as she, too, began to transfer apples from a basket to a trencher. "There are so many in London who are hungry, and they are quick to tell one another when they discover a place where charity food is to be had. As poor as this neighborhood is, I'd guess that more than half of those folk waiting outside are from other places, folk who've come here in hopes of being able to take away the hunger for even this day."

One of the women carefully unwrapped a large roast goose with only a few slices missing from one side, a goose that Guilford recognized as having graced one of the sideboards at Penny House last night.

"That was left from us, Miss Penny, wasn't it?" he asked, watching as the woman began slicing the meat free from the carcass. Their efficiency was making him feel uncomfortably idle.

"If from 'us' you mean from Penny House, then yes," Amariah said, pausing to toss one of the apples lightly in her hand, like a red polished ball. "The members expect everything to be fresh for them each night, seasoned and served to exquisite perfection, and then, like naughty children, they scarce nibble at it before they turn to a new indulgence."

"They're entitled to their whims," Guilford said, feeling he should defend his fellow members. "Especially considering what the membership is."

"Well, yes," she said, and smiled. "But I see nothing wrong in bringing what they choose to reject to others who are not quite so—so *discerning*."

For the first time, he thought of how much must be wasted in a single night, of the plates of barely touched food that were whisked back downstairs, and thought, too, of how corpulent a good many of his friends and associates were, their well-fed bellies straining against their embroidered silk waistcoats. The prince himself had launched the fashion for excess; Guilford had heard it whispered that the waistband of His Highness's breeches measured over fifty inches around.

"But those apples aren't left from the club's dining room tables," he said. "You must've bought them just for today."

"Ah, you are so vastly clever, your grace!" she said, and tossed the apple in her hand at him.

"You'd judge me clever, Miss Penny?" He caught the fruit easily in one hand, and flipped it back to her to cup in both hands. "At least I'm clever enough to know what became of old Adam after he took an apple from a lady."

"Oh, but your grace, this fruit has no such conditions," she said, laughing. "The apples, and the milk, bread, cider and cheeses all are bought with the profits from the gaming tables. We support these gatherings at St. Crispin's, more at St. Andrew's, and of course my sister Bethany's own little 'flock' that gathers each day behind Penny House itself, and yet it's only the barest beginnings. Are you lingering about with a purpose in mind, Billy Fox?"

"Aye, mum." The boy who'd been helping grinned at her, tipping his head back to gaze boldly at her from beneath the crumpled brim of his scarecrow's hat. "That's how I rule me life. Purposeful, mum. Purposeful."

"Purposefully impudent, I'd say," Amariah said, but she laughed and tossed him the apple. At once the boy bit into it with hungry enthusiasm, heedless of the bits of apple and peel that now dotted his grin.

Guilford guessed he must be nine or ten—because he was so thin and wiry, it was difficult to tell—and while his clothes were as dirty and tattered as the others outside, at least he'd washed his hands before he began helping with the food. He had a choirboy's blue eyes and golden curls combined with a born rascal's cockiness, and Guilford liked him at once.

"I eat purposeful, too, mum," Billy said between bites. "Nothing impudent 'bout that."

"If the lady says you're impudent, lad, then you are," Guilford said, laughing, too. Strange that he'd just been speaking of his boyhood with Amariah, for this little rogue could have been cut from the same bolt of cloth as he'd once been himself. "You must trust me. I know from my own sorry experience. It's not wise to cross Miss Penny."

"Go on, guv'nor." The boy looked at him sideways, his profile silhouetted against the angled brim of his black hat. "Miss Penny's an angel o' kindness an' forgiveness, even t'me."

"Then you must not test your luck," Guilford said darkly, glancing knowingly—no, *purposefully*—at Amariah. "Far better to keep her sweet tempered, and be safe. Here now, doff your hat and beg her forgiveness."

Before the boy could react, Guilford reached out to sweep the hat from his head for him.

Beside him, Amariah gasped. "Don't, your grace, please, *please!*"

But her warning came too late. With Billy's hat in his hand, Guilford froze, painfully, horribly aware of how much he'd just erred.

The boy didn't flinch, or duck away. He held his ground, staring back at Guilford as boldly as Guilford was staring at him, unable to make himself look away from what the hat's wide brim had hidden. Where there should have been another bright blue eye, instead was only a grotesque, tortured mass of scars, the skin drawn tight over the empty socket like melted wax.

The boy thrust out his upturned palm toward Guilford. "That be 'alf a crown, guv'nor. I don't let no one gawk at me for free, an' for swells like you, the fare be 'alf a crown."

"He's not a swell, Billy," Amariah said quickly, the warning in her voice clear. "He's His Grace the Duke of Guilford."

"What of it?" Billy shook back his blond curls, as if determined to hide nothing from Guilford. "If a cat may look at a king, why, then a duke may look at a Fox. Don't that be so, Duke?"

"You call him 'your grace', Billy," Amariah said as she took Billy's hat from Guilford's hand and set it back on the boy's head, slanting it at the same shielding angle as it had been before. "And if you don't start minding what comes from your mouth, you'll find yourself transported to the colonies for being disrespectful to your betters."

"Maybe he be the disrespectful one, staring like he'd never seen nothing so ugly in his life," Billy said, but now his belligerence seemed wearier, almost faded. He adjusted the brim of his hat, tugging it carefully lower over his scars. "I'm ugly as th' devil, Miss Penny, an' not even you can say otherwise."

"I never said you were ugly, lad," Guilford protested. "Not at all."

"You didn't have t'say it out loud," Billy said, his voice full of bitterness. "I seen it in your eyes. *Both* o' your eyes."

Filled with remorse, Guilford took a step toward the boy, his hand outstretched in reconciliation. "I didn't mean that, Billy, not when—"

"Bugger off, Duke," muttered the boy, backing away. "Just…just bugger off."

Before Guilford could speak again, Billy turned and ran, racing off through the back of the hall just as Reverend Potter began leading the first of the beggars from the street into the hall.

"Why did you do that to him?" Amariah demanded as they stepped back from the table and the jostling, hungry beggars. "He didn't deserve that from you!"

"How the devil was I to know about his face?" Guilford looked beyond the ever-increasing crowd, vainly searching across them for another glimpse of the boy. "You could have warned me."

"Oh, yes, how kind *that* would have been!" She lifted one of the empty baskets clear of the table. "'This orphan-boy is called Billy Fox, and beneath that hat his face is horribly scarred from having fallen into an open cook fire as a baby.' And did you truly believe he'd listen to that nonsense about not being ugly?"

"It wasn't nonsense," he said, remembering how in his thoughts he'd likened the boy to an angel before he'd seen the scar. "I meant it."

"Yes, and he'd believe it from you, as handsome and perfect a man as ever was born." She shoved the empty basket into his hands. "I'm going to hunt for him, before we lose him forever."

"No, I'll go." He handed the basket back to her. "If I did the damage, then it's up to me to try to mend it."

He dodged through the others, following the path the boy had taken, down a hall and into an empty kitchen. The kitchen door was still ajar, and Guilford's hopes sank. He walked outside, standing on the back step with his hands at his waist. Clearly Billy had fled into the twisted warren of the neighborhood's streets and alleys, where Guilford would never be able to follow, or find him. Not that Guilford blamed him; if he'd been in the boy's situation, he would have done exactly the same.

But Guilford hadn't counted on the powerful allure of his fine horses.

As he left the kitchen yard, he turned down the narrow passageway back to the street, and the front of the church. His chaise was drawn beside the curb where he'd left it, his driver and footmen keeping a wary guard against anyone coming too close.

That included Billy, who was standing as near as he could without being shooed away. His hands deep in the pockets of his oversize coat, he was studying the matched pair of bays as if he could stare all night and never see his fill. Guilford recognized the rapt intensity in Billy's face, even here in a part of London where the few horses were broken-down nags pulling carts— he'd seen it scores of times before in the men who lived and breathed for horseflesh and the track—and it gave him an idea.

As quietly as he could, he came up beside the boy and stood there in silence for a moment or two, so as not to startle him.

"You like horses, Billy, don't you?" he asked at last.

"Oh, aye," Billy said, still intent on the horses. "Are them yours, Duke?"

"They're mine, yes," Guilford said. "Their names are Hop and Buck. They have the same sire and dam, which is why they're matched so well. Buck's the older, and never lets Hop forget it. You can rub their noses if you like."

Billy caught his breath, twisting to look up at Guilford. "Can I? You won't care?"

"Not if you move slowly so they won't turn skittish. Come, I'll make a proper introduction."

He led the boy over to the horses, ignoring the wave of silent disapproval from his driver.

"This is Buck," he said as the boy began to stroke the horse's broad nose, "and this is Hop. Buck and Hop, this young man is Billy Fox."

The boy chuckled with delight, his face alight. "He's a fine, fine horse, sure enough," he said, "and so's his mate. I seen plenty of horses up at Newmarket, racing horses, but none so fine as these. Don't that be so, Buck?"

"They know when they're appreciated." Guilford smiled, sharing the boy's happiness. "Have you ever asked for a place in one of the stables? Seems to me they're always looking for boys to train up into grooms, especially ones that are as good as you are with the horses."

The boy flushed, his hand still on the horse's nose. "I asked once, an' they ran me out. They said I'd fright th' horses."

"Buck and Hop don't seem frightened at all," Guilford said, "and they're as good a judge of men as any horses I know. How would you like to try to justify their good opinion, and take a place in my stable?"

The boy turned quickly toward him, not sure whether to trust Guilford or not. "For wages?"

"I'll have to see what my stable master pays to boys your age," Guilford said. "You'll have to answer to him, and if he has any complaints, out you go. But of course, you'll have a cot in the stable, and take your meals with the rest of the staff."

The boy was holding his breath. "You'd take me on proper, Duke?" he whispered. "You're not makin' sport o' me?"

"Not at all." Guilford fished in the pocket of his waistcoat for one of his cards, handing it to the boy. "You come to my house tomorrow morning, and ask for Mr. Lawson. I'll make sure he's expecting you."

The boy stared down at the stiff white card in his hand, and too late Guilford realized he most likely couldn't read the black engraved letters. "That's Guilford House, number fourteen, Grosvenor Square, though the engraver's made a good deal more fuss from the words than was necessary."

The boy shook his head, still staring at the card in his hand, too overwhelmed to speak and clearly close to tears.

Guilford patted him on his bony, narrow shoulder. "I'll see

you tomorrow, then, Billy," he said gently, sparing the boy the thanks he couldn't say. "Buck and Hop will be looking for you."

He turned toward the church steps, and saw Amariah at the top, where she must have heard his entire conversation with the boy. Her face was hidden in the shadow of her hat's brim, and she was standing so still that he was sure he'd somehow blundered with her again.

"It's not that much," he said by way of explanation, or perhaps apology, whichever was necessary. "But I told you I'd try to mend things, didn't I?"

She raised her chin, and now he could see she was weeping, openly, shamelessly.

"Not that much," she repeated. "*Not that much!* Oh, Guilford! Can't you tell that what you just did was worth a thousand ruby bracelets?"

Chapter Five

◦◦◦◦◦◦

Amariah tipped the glass to drink the last of the Madeira. Through the crystal, she could just make out the duke's face across from her at the table: wavy and distorted by the glass and the wine, but his smile still unmistakable and his charm very nearly irresistible, especially after what he'd done this afternoon, and especially, especially when he laughed.

Oh, my, perhaps she *had* had too much to drink.

"This has been a most lovely evening, Guilford," she said, setting the empty glass down with a little *ping,* "but I really must be returning to Penny House."

"No, you don't," he said, his voice slurring just enough to turn into a drawl. "That is, you don't have to go back there yet."

"But I do." She sighed mightily, pushing her chair back from the table. It wasn't easy: there seemed to be far more incentives to stay than to leave. The old inn near the river was nearly empty on a Sunday night, and they had this small private dining room to themselves. The table was close to the open fire to keep away the evening chill, the cook had kept the dishes coming one after another, and the keep had insisted on refilling her glass again and again; the temptation to linger was strong indeed.

And that wasn't even including the handsome, smiling gentleman across from her.

She took her napkin from her lap, refolded it with great deliberation and set it at her place on the table. "I have to go home, Guilford. Home. To Penny House. I have a great deal of work waiting for me there to prepare for tomorrow."

"Hang the work." He waved for the servant, who hurried forward to refill both their glasses. "You work too hard, Amariah."

She set her palm over her empty glass before the servant could reach it. "And you don't work at all, Guilford."

"Touché." He stared down at their two glasses, his full and hers empty. "Still, pet, I must insist you consider following my lead. Less work, and more amusement shall make for a much more agreeable life."

"Agreeable, ha." She pushed herself to her feet, keeping a firm grip on the back of the chair so as to give her legs a moment to steady themselves. "Far better to lead a useful life than an amusing one."

"I say you can do both." He rose, too, and downed his glass for the last time. "But if you insist, my dearest Miss Penny, then home I shall take you. I won't have anyone saying I'm not a gallant."

"No one does," she said. "Not about you. Not *ever.* See, you're being gallant right now, holding your arm out to me like that."

He reached for her hand and tucked it gently into his, drawing her closer. She was glad he did, too, because she wasn't at all certain she would have been able to make such a momentous decision on her own, let alone act upon it.

"Thank you, Guilford," she said, nearly weeping with gratitude. He was *such* a kind man, a good, sweet, kind man, even if he was a duke. "Thank you, oh, for everything."

"Thank me again when I've gotten you home," he said, steering her from the little dining room toward the front door of the inn. "And mind you, if you begin to feel ill, give me a bit of warning. I'd rather you weren't sick in the chaise."

That struck Amariah as inordinately funny, so funny that she could not stop laughing even after he'd helped her into the chaise and they'd begun the long drive home.

"There now, Amariah," Guilford said, laughing with her. "I told you your life could afford to be more amusing, and you have wisely taken my advice."

Her laughter faded as she gazed at him, not bothering to keep the admiration from her eyes. "I still cannot believe what you did this afternoon."

"What, with the boy?" He shrugged, more embarrassed than anything, which only endeared him to her more. "I told you I'd try to make it up to him, and I did."

"But you heard what he said. He's treated like a curiosity at a fair. Once people see his scar, they want nothing to do with him."

"That's hardly his fault," he said. "I'd like to believe we're past the evil eye and other such nonsense."

"So would I, but the rest of the world doesn't agree." She sighed softly, thinking of how much she'd enjoyed his company. "You're a much nicer gentleman than you wish the rest of London to know, aren't you?"

He winked. "I am what I am, sweetheart, no more and no less."

"Much more, I'd say." She grinned, sliding down lower against the squabs. "I don't know how you imagine I'd be ill, Guilford, when I have never, ever felt better in my life."

Leery, he was watching her more closely, doubtless looking for signs of impending distress. "Let's hope you continue to feel that way, sweetheart."

"Oh, I will, Guilford." The stiff brim of her hat was pushing so awkwardly against the back of the seat that she pulled the hat off, dropping it on the seat between them. "I may call you Guilford, mightn't I? I know your friends all call you that at the club, and it's much easier than 'your grace.'"

"You call me Guilford, and I'll call you Amariah, just as we agreed to do, oh, at least three hours ago." He picked up her hat, scowling down at it. "I hate this hat of yours, Amariah, hated it the moment I saw you in it."

She wrinkled her nose. "Because you hate it, Guilford, I shall henceforth hate it, too."

"Well, then, I'll banish the wretched thing, and please us both."

He flipped open the window, and before she could protest, he sailed the hat out the window and into the night.

"Guilford!" Amariah shrieked with surprise, pressing her hands to her cheeks as she slid a little farther down the slippery leather cushion. "I cannot *believe* you did that! Oh, that poor, old, ugly hat!"

"Let it grace some poor, old, ugly scarecrow in a field of rye," he said grandly. "You, my fair Amariah, deserve something far more beautiful."

He slid closer along the swaying seat, leaning over her so that all she could see was his face in extraordinary detail: the dark lashes around his blue eyes, the gray shadow of his beard along his jaw, the way his black hair curled in little tufts before his ears.

She blinked, and smiled. "You're going to kiss me, aren't you?"

He smiled back, and she noticed for the first time the little chip in one of his eyeteeth. "I'm sorely tempted, yes."

"So am I, Guilford," she whispered, reaching up to loop her arms around his neck. "So am I."

It didn't surprise her at all that he kissed her then, or that she kissed him in return, either. What did surprise her was how kissing Guilford could be so enormously different from kissing any other man. To be sure, her experience was not so large as to give her much ground for comparison: a half dozen gentlemen at most, hurried kisses stolen outside the ballroom at the Havertown Assembly when she'd been no more than Reverend Penny's eldest girl.

But Guilford—Guilford knew *how* to kiss, and there was nothing either stolen or hurried about the way he did it. His kissed her with tenderness, with leisurely assurance, and with passion, too, his mouth teasing across hers, building the sensations until her lips parted in a breathy gasp, welcoming his deeper possession. Now she needed her arms around his shoulders to anchor herself, her fingers moving restlessly over the broad muscles of his shoulders. She'd never imagined the feel of a man's tongue against her own, or how the feel of him lying across her this way could rouse such heady excitement throughout her whole body.

And then, like that, it was over, and he was sitting up straight in the far corner of the seat, his arms folded over his chest in thorough retreat.

"If I were as nice as you claim," he said wearily, "then I wouldn't have done that."

She twisted around on the seat and pushed herself upright. "Yes, you would have," she said, "because I would have, too."

He sighed, pointedly looking away from her and out the window. "No, because you wouldn't even have thought of kissing me if I hadn't put the notion into your head first."

"Don't be such a conceited ass," she snapped. She sat in the other corner of the seat, as far away from him as possible. "I know you're the great, grand Duke of Guilford, but you could not have made me kiss you if I didn't wish it first."

He turned back toward her. "Is that a dare, Miss Penny?"

"I'm not daring you to do anything," she said crossly. The pleasant haze of the wine had nearly disappeared, leaving her only with a dull ache beneath her eyes and the unpleasant sense that she'd just done something she was going to regret for a good long time. "I'm simply stating an honest fact. How much farther to Penny House?"

He glanced back out the window. "Oh, I'd say we have only about five more minutes or so of hell left to share."

"That is not amusing," she said, each word clipped. "Accurate, perhaps, but not amusing."

He lowered his chin, glowering. "Spoken like a true virago."

"Indeed," she said tartly. As much as she hated that hideous word—she knew she wasn't a virago—*she* wasn't going to give him the satisfaction of arguing over it again. "*The Hapless Gallant and the Virago,* a folly in three acts, to be performed to great acclaim this night at the Haymarket Theater."

He shoved his hair back from his forehead. Now she noticed how rumpled his shirt and coat had become, how in general he was looking considerably more resistible than he had earlier. "What in blazes is that supposed to mean?"

"That you are not the only one possessing a wit, Guilford," she said, "just as you are not the only one capable of initiating a kiss, even if that kiss in hindsight was barbarously misplaced."

"You hardly objected!"

"Nor did you," she said, looking out the window herself, "which is precisely my point. Here's my alley now. Driver, stop here, if you please. Thank you for dinner, Guilford, and for your generosity toward Billy Fox, but I'll reserve my judgment regarding the pleasure of your company."

She opened the door and jumped out, not waiting for the footman to flip down the step.

"Damnation, Amariah, come back here!" Guilford called. "Come back directly!"

But she didn't turn around, her hatless head high as she marched down the narrow alley to the Penny House yard and kitchen door, and he didn't follow her, either. If she'd ever needed more proof of the error of consorting with club members outside of Penny House, then this day was it.

To her surprise, the kitchen was dark, and though she peered through the windows and rapped lightly on the door, no one came. True, the club had not been open and it was the staff's customary day off, but had she really been out so late that everyone had gone to bed? She reached in her reticule for the key to the lock—she always carried the keys to both doors of the club, in case of a fire or other mishap while she was out—opened the door, and entered the shadowy kitchen.

As she made her way toward the back stairs, her slippers crunched on something hard. A crust of bread, she guessed, something that should have been swept away earlier, and she crouched down. But instead of crumbs, she found the muted glitter of broken glass, and a little farther across the floor, beneath the table, lay a half brick with a paper tied around it. She glanced back over her shoulder, and now saw the broken window pane, low in the frame. She grabbed the brick from under the table and rose, then hurried to light a candlestick to give herself more light. She untied the paper, smoothed it out in her fingers, and tipped it toward the light to read the message written so neatly, and bordered with a pattern of stars.

My Dear Mistress Penny,

Why do You ignore my Warning?

You still Harbor a CHEAT & if You do not Turn Him Out I will see His Shame & Yours in the Press.

Do Not Doubt me, You will see I Mean my Word & You WILL be made to Pay.

Yr. S'rv't,

A Friend of Truth & Justice

Ah, she thought grimly, the perfect end to a perfectly wretched day. What more could happen to her? Swiftly she read it again, making sure she hadn't missed some unintentional clue tucked inside. It was from the same sender as before, the elegant penmanship unmistakable. She'd already done all that could be done at the hazard table, and taken every step to stop any cheating, she told herself again.

But this time the writer addressed her more familiarly, as his "Dear Mistress Penny," and this time, too, he'd threatened not just Penny House, but her. It didn't matter that the penmanship belonged to a gentleman; the act most certainly didn't. This package had been hurled violently through the window, and no matter how much she told herself to be brave, she couldn't keep back the sick dread that now raced through her. The longer she stared down at the page, the more she realized her fingers were shaking and her heart was racing from fear of what might have happened.

What if she'd blundered into the dark yard while this man had still been there? What if he'd decided to "make her pay" when she'd been alone, concentrating on unlocking the kitchen door? Why had she let her pride and irritation with Guilford overrule her common sense, walking down a shadowy alley alone in the middle of the night instead of letting

him take her to the front door, where a footman would be sta-
tioned and waiting to see her safely inside?

What if, what if, what if?

She heard the tap at the door behind her, quick and insistent. Swiftly she stuffed the note inside her sleeve, grabbed the
jagged chunk of brick from the table to defend herself and
turned back to the door. She could just make out the shadowy
shape of a tall man outside the window, and with her other hand
she held the candlestick close to the the glass to show his face.

"Guilford!" She unlocked the door and threw it open. "Oh,
thank God, it's only you!"

"Only me?" Quickly he looked from the brick in her hand
to the broken glass. "How it does gladden my heart to hear such
sentiment! Did you forget your key, sweetheart, or has breaking and entering become part of your stock-in-trade, too?"

"Listen to me." With the brick still cradled in her hand, she
took a deep breath to calm herself. She hadn't realized how
frightened she'd been, and relief was now making her almost
light-headed. "It's not what you think. Someone else broke
the window with the brick. The glass was already shattered
when I came inside. Look, this note came with it."

At once his face grew serious as she handed him the note.
"He could have been waiting for you, Amariah," he said
sharply as he read it. "You could have been hurt, even killed."

"But I wasn't, Guilford," she said, persuading herself as
much as him as she took a deep breath. "He was gone when
I came inside. The door was still locked. Whoever he is, he's
a coward. I'm fine. Truly. No harm was done."

By the wavering candlelight, Guilford's expression was uncharacteristically serious. "You must call for the watch immediately, and report this to the constable in the morning."

"No constable, no watch," she said firmly. "Penny House

cannot afford the scandal, Guilford, and that's all that would come of involving the constable. Especially since I half suspect that it's one of our own members writing this drivel. What would we do if the constable announced such a culprit to the world? Surely you, of any of the club's members, would understand the risk in that. And I told you before, no harm was done beyond the broken window."

"Not tonight," he said ominously. "Not this time."

"Not this time, or ever," she said as firmly as she could. "I'm not a child. I can look after myself."

"Not a child, but not a fool, either," he said, shaking his head. "You're a more reasonable woman than that, Amariah. Don't you remember what happened to your sister?"

Of course she remembered. Her sister Bethany had been kidnapped from the same back alley where Amariah had walked not an hour before, and Bethany had come close, perilously close, to being murdered before William Callaway had saved her. How could Amariah ever forget that night, or the weight of the guilt she'd suffered ever since for her sister's sake?

"That—that was different," she said, turning away from him so her face wouldn't betray her. "This isn't the same situation at all."

"What's the same is that you're being every bit as determined to ignore the facts," he said behind her. "Unless you want to end up with the barrel of a cocked pistol pressed to your temple, as well, then I suggest you stop trying to be such an almighty paragon and call the watch."

"I am not an almighty anything," she said, her voice wobbling upward. "I am Miss Amariah Penny of Penny House, and I'll thank you not to forget it, Guilford."

She squeezed her eyes shut, fighting for self-control. Already on edge, her imagination was fixed on the horrifying image he'd presented of Bethany with the gun held to her temple. She could almost feel the cold metal against her skin, the acrid smell of spent gunpowder, the way the man's arm tightened around her throat to keep her from struggling while he—

"Amariah?" she heard the duke saying as she felt herself swaying forward.

Part of her realized she wasn't fainting with any grace or dignity, the way a practiced lady would, but flopping forward with her legs folding beneath her and her arms flailing like a puppet with clipped strings. Then abruptly she jerked to a stop, caught by Guilford.

"You're all right," said the duke, trying to reassure her. "You'll be fine. Look at me, sweetheart. Look at me. See? It's only your wicked old friend, Guilford, nothing more."

"I *am* fine," she protested weakly, struggling to stand on her own. "It's only because I'm tired, and the wine affected me."

"Oh, yes, the wine," he said softly, turning her around in his arms so they were face-to-face. He was concerned, worried, expressions that she'd never associated with him. "You do know me, then?"

"Of course I know who you are!" She knew she should push away from him and prove she was as fine as she claimed, but the sad truth was that she'd no wish to do so. His arms around her waist were warm and comforting and secure, and though it ran counter to everything she'd believed about herself, she liked feeling protected in this way.

Oh, a pox on it all, she liked him. And this time it had nothing whatsoever to do with the wine.

She frowned down at his rumpled neckcloth, her hand resting lightly on his chest. "How could I not know who you are?"

At last he smiled. "Wicked old Guilford?"

"Of course." If he kept looking at her like this with such unabashed concern she would begin to weep, and she wasn't sure she'd be able to stop. "I would always know you."

His hands slid lightly along her back, no longer merely supporting her. "I should never have let you from my sight. I should never have let you go like that, even for a few moments."

"I left on my own," she said, swaying into him. "You didn't 'let' me do anything."

"Then I should have followed sooner," he said. "How could I have lived with my conscience if anything had befallen you?"

"Ha, your conscience could survive any peril," she said, but the scoffing she'd intended came out instead as a breathy whisper. "You said yourself you were wicked."

"But you're not," he said, and kissed her.

She let him, then kissed him back, feeling light-headed all over again. She closed her eyes, letting herself tumble into the pleasure he was giving, and with a rumbly sigh she circled her hands around the back of his neck to steady herself.

And she needed steadying. Because he'd already kissed her once tonight, in the chaise, she'd thought she'd known what to expect when his lips sought hers again. But this was different. He kissed her gently, with a tenderness she'd never suspected he could muster.

He kissed her as if he cared.

She sighed and settled more closely against him, accepting this moment for what it was…

"Ah, Miss Penny!" cried Pratt, too shocked for his usual reticence. "Pray forgive me, I did not mean to intrude!"

She jerked away from Guilford as fast as if he'd been hot

coals. Pratt was standing in the doorway at the bottom of the service stairs with a candlestick in his hand, clearly ready for bed in a white nightcap in place of his usual wig and a black linen dressing gown instead of his livery.

"Forgive me, your grace, forgive me, miss," he said again, bowing to the duke, "but Boyd told me he thought he'd heard voices in the kitchen even though you hadn't returned, and I thought it best to investigate, never knowing that you'd—that is, that I'd—"

"You're forgiven, Pratt," Amariah said, clasping her hands before her as she worked to compose herself. The shock that still lingered on the manager's face was all the reminder she needed of how selfishly she was behaving here with Guilford, and how grievously she was ignoring her responsibilities to everyone at Penny House, from Pratt down to the poor new mother who'd given birth in the cook's office here earlier in the day. "You did the proper thing by coming here."

She didn't dare look back at Guilford. Would he be angry at the interruption, or laughing at the foolishness of their situation? For it was foolish; she'd never been caught like this before with a gentleman, in what the world would surely relish calling a "compromising situation."

But for Guilford himself, why, clearly this was nothing new to him at all.

"You're absolutely in the right, Pratt," he said with considerably more heartiness than Amariah judged proper. "Better you worry about the lady's safety than her reputation, though as you can see, there's been no harm done on either account. But this broken glass here's a hazard. I'd have someone sweep that up directly."

"Yes, your grace, I will," Pratt said, grateful for the diversion. "Ah, I see now, your grace. The window's been broken."

"Doubtless the work of some local miscreants," Guilford said, giving the broken shards an idle poke with the toe of his shoe. "But I'd summon the watch regardless, just to be sure that—"

"His grace is leaving, Pratt," Amariah said, interrupting before he'd say more and alarm Pratt, too. "Leaving *now.*"

"Are you certain you wish me to leave, Miss Penny?" he asked, his smile at its most charming. "By my reckoning, the night's still young, and I'm sure you've no wish to spend what's left of it alone, not when—"

"Good night, your grace," she said with an indignant curtsy. She'd welcomed his sympathy when she'd been upset, true, but did he honestly believe that sympathy was enough to entitle him to stay the night here with her?

He held his hand out to her, a graceful gesture that could mean either an invitation or a farewell, whichever she chose. How had he ever learned to be so *good* at this?

"Thank you, no, your grace," she said, wishing she didn't sound so wretchedly prim.

He cocked one brow. "You are certain, Miss Penny? You know I'm most skilled at checking beneath beds for stray bugbears and hobgoblins."

"Good *night,* your grace," she said, refusing to be charmed again. She'd already let herself depend on Guilford too much. Penny House was her responsibility, not his, and she owed it not only to her sisters but to her father's memory to keep it that way.

"Forgive me if I plead weariness," she murmured, "and do not see you out myself. Pratt, please show his grace to the front door and his chaise."

And with her head high, she started up the back stairs alone, and somehow did not give in to the considerable temptation to look back.

* * *

Westbrook hurried down the alley toward the street with his head down and his shoulders bent, keeping to the shadows so he wouldn't be noticed. At least he prayed he wouldn't be noticed. He wasn't sure of anything, not after a close call like this last one.

Why the devil was Amariah Penny wandering about her club at this time of the night, on a day they were closed? Worse still, why had Guilford been there, too?

All he'd meant was to leave another little calling card. All he'd wanted was to plant another tiny seed of doubt, a fresh rumor to rumble through the foundations of Penny House. The last thing he'd wanted was a witness or two to identify him.

He turned on the street now, slowing his steps so he wouldn't be noticed. They hadn't noticed him, either. If they had, they'd be following him now, and he was quite alone. His breathing slowed, then his heart. He was safe this time, and he smiled. He *was* safe.

Too bad for Penny House that Amariah Penny couldn't say the same.

The next morning, Guilford was in the foulest of foul moods. It was so exceptionally, notably foul that he not only retreated to the farthest corner of White's front room, but also turned his tall-backed armchair so he faced the wall. He needed time to think, and to berate himself, and to consider everything he should have done differently last night with Amariah. If he'd hung a painted signboard from his neck he could not have made his humor any more clear, and only a madman would have dared to disturb him.

A madman, or, more likely, one of his friends.

"So this is where you've hidden yourself away, Guilford."

Henry, Lord Stanton settled his elbows across the top of Guilford's chair and peered down upon the top of his head. "But then, I'll grant that mourning requires privacy."

Guilford closed his eyes, wishing he could make his friend as easily disappear. "As usual, Stanton, you are speaking like an ass. Why in blazes would I be mourning, except for having my peace disturbed by you?"

"Don't be dense, Guilford," Stanton said with relish, leaning down lower so he could make a stage whisper in the general area of Guilford's ear. "You're already mourning the wager you're going to lose to me."

"The hell I am!" Guilford twisted around in the chair so he could glare at Stanton more efficiently. "What gave you a ridiculous notion like that?"

"The fact that you're no more closer to Amariah Penny's bed than I am," Stanton said with a satisfied smirk. "Perhaps farther, from what I hear."

"You haven't heard a blasted thing, because there isn't anything to hear!"

"My point exactly." Stanton stepped around Guilford's legs so he could face him, leaning against the wall with his arms folded across his chest. "There's nothing to hear, because you've made no progress with the lady fair."

Irritated, Guilford drummed his fingers on the cushioned arm of his chair. "That's for all you know."

"What I know, Guilford," Stanton said with maddening assurance, "is that you and Miss Penny were so busy feeding the beggars that you never did show your faces at Carlisle's last night."

"That's because I decided to avoid the crowds at Carlisle's, and took her to the Golden Fawn near the river instead," Guilford answered. "Not that it's any of your affair."

"The Golden Fawn?" Stanton repeated, incredulous. "That's a sorry old haunt for seduction."

"It served us quite well," Guilford said, remembering how merry and willing Amariah had been in the chaise as they rode home. If only he'd let the wine go to his head, too—or at least to his damned conscience—then he could have pressed his advantage then and there, and be claiming his stake from Stanton even now. "Remember that Miss Penny isn't some gaudy cheap actress eager to display herself to an audience even while she dines."

"True enough," Stanton said. "She's some poor parson's ginger-haired daughter, jumped up to counting out the markers for gentry in a gaming house."

"Watch what you say about Miss Penny, Stanton," Guilford snapped, surprising both his friend and himself.

Stanton's eyes widened with interest. "So you have had her, haven't you? I can't fathom why you'd defend her otherwise."

"No, I haven't," Guilford said sharply, "so you can end your cheap speculation directly."

Stanton smiled, waving one hand languidly through the air. "My dear Guilford, what else *is* this wager but cheap speculation?"

"What's cheap speculation, Stanton?"

Guilford closed his eyes again and sighed with exasperation. Stanton was provoking enough without adding Alec, Baron Westbrook, as well. Guilford had never cared much for Westbrook; he'd always found him as shallow as a puddle, with a wearisome habit of echoing the opinions of whomever he was with. But then, he'd always been more Stanton's acquaintance than Guilford's, anyway.

"It's the wager over the proprietress of Penny House, Westbrook," Stanton explained with obvious delight. "The fine, tall piece with the red hair who stands just inside the door."

Guilford's eyes flew open, his irritation blossoming into full-fledged anger. "Miss Penny's not a 'piece,' Stanton. I thought we'd made that clear before."

"But she *is* a virago, Guilford," said Westbrook, as cheery as a robin, and looking like one, too, in a scarlet waistcoat stretched too tightly over his brandy-fueled belly. "You wrote that in the betting book yourself. I've seen it with my own eyes. You predicted she'd never marry because she was a virago, and no man would have her."

Now Stanton elbowed in, his pale eyes bulging with excitement. "But that's only the half of it, Westbrook! Guilford's made another, more private, wager with me that, virago or not, he'd seduce her within a fortnight."

"Now I'd like a share of *that* sport." Westbrook patted the front of his waistcoat, leaning forward to leer into Guilford's face. "What's the stake, eh? We'll expect details, you know, and proof that you've—"

"Shove off, Westbrook." Guilford rose abruptly, pushing his way past the other two men. "And keep your damned money. You're not part of this wager."

But Westbrook only laughed, trailing after him. "You won't win, you know. Not with this woman. Miss Penny doesn't have time even for a great handsome buck like you, Guilford, not when she's got some rascally cheat on the prowl in her club."

Stunned, Guilford wheeled around to face him. The last person Amariah would want to know of her trouble was a busy body gossip like Westbrook.

"Where in blazes did you hear that?" he demanded in a furious whisper, hoping no one else around them would overhear. "Don't you know a scandal like that could break Penny House?"

"It's—it's common knowledge throughout the town," stammered Westbrook, trying to bluster even as he backed away. "I can't say exactly where I heard it. Damnation, Guilford, it's only a wretched gaming house, as eager to empty our pockets as any other pack of petty thieves. You know it's the truth, as well as I do myself."

"The truth, Westbrook?" Guilford repeated with disgust. "A bastard like you wouldn't know the truth if it flew through that window and bit you on the nose. The *truth!*"

He was still fuming as he stalked down the steps of the club to the street where his chaise was waiting. The truth, hell. Westbrook was an ignorant idiot. It was a damned pity that Amariah couldn't take every last club member who whined about his bad luck down to St. Crispin's with her to see how she turned their losses into food enough to feed a—

"Halloo, guv'nor, your grace."

Guilford stopped, frowning down at the boy standing in path. "Billy Fox," he said. "What the devil are you doing here?"

The boy grinned, and turned his head so he could look squarely at Guilford with his one good eye. Clearly he'd made a serious effort to improve his appearance for this meeting: his face and hands were scrubbed clean, his hair was combed, and even his old black hat had been brushed free of dust and straw.

"Good day t'you, your grace," he said as he touched his hand to the front of his hat. "I come about that place you was offering me, the one with th' horses."

"But why here?" Guilford asked, forcing himself to be more calm. He couldn't be cross with the boy, too, not after yesterday. "Why didn't you go to Grosvenor Square as I told you?"

His grin grew stiff, guarded. "I had my reasons, guv'nor," he said defensively, "and good ones, too."

Guilford nodded, wanting to reassure the boy so he wouldn't try to bolt again the way he had yesterday.

"You haven't changed your mind about the position, have you?" he asked softly. "Or perhaps you've found another place that might suit you better?"

The boy gasped. "Oh, no, guv'nor, it don't be like that! 'Course I still want th' place!"

"Then why did you follow me here?" Guilford asked. "Why didn't you go directly to my stable master, as I'd told you to?"

The boy shook his head and didn't answer, his mouth twisting with words he didn't want to say—words that, Guilford realized, he wanted very much to hear.

Heedless of the curious—and disapproving—passersby around them, he bent down, his face now level with the boy's. "Tell me, Billy Fox. If you still want to tend my horses, I want to know."

"Because I wanted t' make sure o' you, guv'nor," the boy blurted out in a rush. "I wanted t' make sure you wasn't just offering on account o' Miss Penny, to make her happy an' kiss you an' such, an' that when she wasn't there t' see, you'd have me tossed out, same as the rest."

"You thought I'd asked you only to impress Miss Penny?" It was a low, mean thought, and knowing there was more than an uncomfortable kernel of truth to it made Guilford feel lower and meaner still. "Is that it, Billy?"

The boy made a quick, miserable nod. "That's the nub o' it, aye."

Guilford sighed, and rose. He wasn't going to make the same mistake as Amariah, and believe he could change all

London himself, but he could at least begin with a tiny scrap of good and this boy.

"I never go back on my word, Billy," he said, reaching out to clap his hand on the boy's bony shoulder. "Never. Now tell me—do you like kidney pie?"

Billy gasped, his eyes bright. "Oh, aye, guv'nor! Who don't?"

"No man in his right mind," said Guilford, nodding with satisfaction. "I know a tavern near here that makes the best pies imaginable. We'll eat, and we'll talk about horses. And mind you while we do, Miss Penny will be absolutely nowhere in sight."

Chapter Six

"Good evening, my lord." Amariah bowed her head and bent her knees to the precise calculated degree required for a curtsy to a viscount. "We've missed you here at Penny House while you've been in the country."

The viscount smiled back, pleased to have been missed, especially before his friends, and with his pride well burnished, he sauntered away toward the card room. He'd wager high tonight, thought Amariah; she'd have to be sure to stop by his table to give him an extra measure of encouragement, and preserve that satisfied glow.

She turned toward the next group of gentlemen through the door, her smile now warm for them. Strange to think of how difficult this had once been for her, and not that long ago, either. Strange to think how remembering all the names and titles had once been her greatest worry, and what was that compared to the concerns that plagued her now?

"Everything is as it was earlier in the hazard room, Miss Penny," Pratt said behind her, his voice scarce more than a whisper so no others would overhear. "Nothing has changed. The tables are busy, but no one player is winning more than

any other. No gentlemen has been intemperate, or unduly excited. Mr. Walthrip and his men see nothing amiss, nor have
the footmen or guards."

"Thank you, Pratt," she murmured, and heard him glide
away behind her, back to his other duties.

She thought again of the letter that had come through the
window with the brick last night, the warning and threat and
the forced unwelcome familiarity of it. She'd shown it to
Pratt, but no one else on the staff, and though he, too, had
urged her to go to the watch, she'd refused him just as she'd
refused Guilford. Unless she had more proof than the letters,
she was not going to plunge Penny House into a disastrous
scandal. She would weather this like the club had weathered
every other crisis, large and small: with steadfast grace and
resolute courage.

That trial was easy compared to the other one that faced
her. She'd kissed a club member once last night, then es-
caped, only to kiss him again a second time. She'd always
thought she was beyond this sort of behavior, stronger and
more in control of herself than to be so weak. Blast Guilford
and his charming ways! No wonder she'd lain awake until
dawn, sighing with frustration as she'd tossed and twisted the
sheets.

The footman opened the front door again, and before she'd
seen any more of the newcomer than the crown of his hat, she
knew it was him.

Blast the man for making her heart race like this over
nothing—nothing!

"Good evening, your grace." Somehow willing herself not
to blush, she swept her fan to one side and made her best full
ducal curtsy. "How happy we are for you to join us here at
Penny House tonight."

"What nonsense, Miss Penny," he said, smiling as he took her hand and raised it just high enough to kiss the air above it. "After last night, you'd rather I'd never show my face in this club again."

Gracefully pulling her hand free of his, she made herself smile in return, so sweetly it would have overflowed a sugar bowl. "You misjudge me, your grace. You play so badly and lose far too often for me ever to wish you gone from our door."

Still smiling, he came to stand beside her, the way he'd done so many times before that no one seeing them together would notice this night as any different.

"Then you have a powerfully strange way of showing your mercenary affection for me, Miss Penny," he said. "Even a highwayman on the heath confronts his victim eye-to-eye when he demands his loot, but you—last night you couldn't even hold your stand long enough to bid me sweet dreams, let alone to pick my pocket."

She bowed to two more arriving gentlemen, her smile fixed pleasantly in place. "It had been a long day, Guilford, and a longer night. I was so weary I could not keep from my bed another moment."

"I would have carried you upstairs and settled you into bed myself," he said, his fingers brushing against the side of her arm, so lightly that it could have been by accident. "You'd only have had to ask."

"But I didn't." She inched away from his hand. "And how unfortunate that there's no place for any settling by you in my bed!"

"I know," he said. "That's why you so enjoyed my chaise."

"So help me, Guilford, if that is all you can—"

"Did you go to the constable this morning and tell him what happened last night?"

She glanced up at him quickly. "Guilford, I told you then

I wasn't going to do that, and I'll tell you the same now. We've taken considerable precautions to secure the hazard table against cheating. I don't even have any real proof that anyone has cheated, except for the letters."

"Letters?" he said sharply. "Have you received another, Amariah?"

"I told you, I'm not going to the constable, and that's an end to it," she said, avoiding answering his question by ignoring it. Guilford was clever; it had always been one of the things she liked about him. Of course he was sure to catch even a tiny slip like that. She turned back toward the door, holding her hand out to the next gentleman through it. "Good evening, My Lord Westbrook! Why, you've been quite a stranger here at Penny House. How grand for us to have you return tonight!"

"The grandness is mine, Miss Penny, to see you again." Westbrook smiled so widely that his ruddy cheeks almost swallowed up his eyes. With his round face and rounder body, he'd always reminded Amariah of some mischievous elf. "Only tedious family matters have kept me away from visiting this lucky place."

"Then I welcome you back myself, my lord." She'd do that warmly, too; Lord Westbrook was a true golden goose, blessed with family interests in coal and tin and cursed with an absolute inability to master even the easiest games of chance or skill. Money flowed so freely through his hands and into the club's bank that Amariah would have offered him lodgings beneath their roof if he'd wished to stay and play longer. "Come, I'll show you to a chair at the hazard table myself."

But as she offered her arm to Westbrook, Guilford stepped between them. "He can find his own chair, Miss Penny."

"Why should I refuse her kind offer, Guilford?" Westbrook

asked, hooking his thumbs into the watch chain slung across his waistcoat. "Miss Penny's not a lady I'd wish to offend. Nor should you, considering."

"No offense is taken, my lord." Amariah looked curiously from Westbrook to Guilford. The tension between the two men was unmistakable, but also inexplicable. Being peers of nearly the same age, they would certainly be acquainted, yet each had such a different circle of friends she'd never seen them together before this. "It's as I said, my lord. You'll always have a warm welcome here."

"No matter what game I choose to play, Miss Penny?" asked Westbrook, his expression insinuating. "You'll always welcome me no matter what wager I make, or on what cause I lay my money?"

"That's enough, Westbrook." Guilford grabbed the smaller man by the arm, and before Amariah realized what was happening, he was half dragging Westbrook back out the door and into the street.

"Guilford, what are you doing?" she shouted, trying to follow through the pack of other men that now crowded in the door to watch. "Excuse me, if you please, excuse me!"

"Oh, let them go, Miss Penny," said Lord Henry Stanton, who'd arrived with Westbrook. "It's a small private matter between them, after all."

"But what are they doing?" she demanded, unable to see past the others. "They're not fighting, are they? I will *not* tolerate brawling in the street before this house!"

"They're not fighting," another man said, craning his neck. "It could never be a contest. Guilford would murder Westbrook outright."

"I won't allow it!" she cried, waving frantically to the footmen stationed on either side of the door. She didn't want anyone murdered, or hurt, or generally bleeding anywhere near her white marble steps. "Boyd! Cary! Go out there at once and make sure those gentlemen are not fighting, not—"

But her words were drowned by the cheers and applause of the men in front of her, parting to allow Guilford to come swaggering back into the club alone. He stopped before Amariah, smoothed his hair back from his forehead, and bowed, his grin wickedly knowing.

"Lord Westbrook regrets that he will be unable to play here tonight after all, Miss Penny," he said while the other men quieted to listen. "He was taken with a sudden indisposition that required him to return home directly to his bed."

Amariah gasped at his audacity while the others hooted and shouted and stomped their feet as if they were drunken sailors in the lowest rum shop near the docks, and Guilford the greatest conquering bully.

"Your grace," she said tartly, forced to raise her voice over the foolish din. "Your grace, a word in private, *if* you would be so kind as to oblige."

To agree, he swept his hand through the air with a courtier's flourish, or maybe an actor's, given how well pleased his audience was by it.

But Amariah wanted none of it. "This way, your grace," she said, indicating the small private room off the hall as emphatically as any drill sergeant. *"Now."*

He followed her into the room and waited for her to shut and latch the door, his arms folded across his chest. "Are you going punish me, my dear Miss Penny? Scold me? Chastise me with every strident word in your vocabulary? Am I going to be sent from the schoolroom with only dry bread and sour milk for tea?"

"Hush, Guilford, please!" She'd clenched her hands into

tight fists at her side as she resisted the temptation to whale into him with a highly un-Christian fervor. "You're a charter member of this club. You're on the membership committee. You know I must enforce all rules for every member equally."

"Oh, yes, you must *enforce.*" He sighed happily. "What a delightfully stern governess you'd make, Amariah Penny."

"Hush, hush, Guilford, and once in your life, just *listen!*" she ordered, feeling far too much like that stern-voiced governess. "You *know* that our governing laws so strictly forbid fighting on the premises that such grounds are cause for instant and permanent expulsion from the membership roles, and yet you—"

"We weren't on the premises," he interrupted. "We were near them, but not on them. There aren't any rules regarding nearness. And we weren't even fighting, either. Not exactly."

"You were fighting sufficiently to excite the blood lust of every male ninny crowded into that door!"

Guilford shrugged extravagantly. "All I did was explain to Westbrook why he wasn't wanted here at Penny House."

She made a small shriek of impotence. "Guilford, the man once lost *twenty thousand pounds* here in a single night's play! Of course I want him here, as often as he can be coaxed to visit and play!"

"You shouldn't," he warned, his expression losing its playfulness. "Not for twenty thousand pounds, and all the tea in an East Indiaman."

"And I say I should," she countered, unable to keep from jabbing his chest with the blades of her closed fan any longer. "I'll take Westbrook and his twenty thousand and all that tea besides. What possessed you to think I'd do otherwise? After yesterday, I thought you'd understand. The entire purpose of Penny House is to be as profitable as possible. If we are to succeed, we absolutely *need* members like Baron Westbrook who will—"

"Damnation, Amariah, I did it to protect you!"

"Protect me?" She stopped and stared with disbelief. "From Westbrook?"

"Yes, from Westbrook," he said, his voice a rough, defensive growl. "You don't know him the way I do, and a good thing, too."

Merciful Heavens, she thought, he was serious about this. "I don't need a watchdog, Guilford, especially not to keep gentlemen away from Penny House."

He swept his hair back from his forehead with the palm of his hand. "It's not that simple, Amariah."

"Yes, it is," she said, and it was, as clear as water to her. "Because you kissed me last night, now you believe you have the entitlement—no, the *obligation!*—to keep away all other gentlemen, no matter how harmless their intentions may be."

"Amariah, please," he said, reaching for her.

She stepped away, shaking her head, and his mouth settled in a hard line.

"So that's how it is," he said. "The same damned stubbornness again."

"Not stubbornness, Guilford, but common sense," she said warmly. "You have no right to 'protect' me, nor do I wish it."

"You said yourself I'm on your membership committee," he said. "You're the most important person in this club. It couldn't continue as it does without you. Isn't that reason enough to want you safe?"

Had she really guessed that wrong about him? Was his interest in her really not as personal as she'd suspected? Not that she wanted him interested in her, of course, not like that...

"That's no reason at all, Guilford." She snapped her fan

open, giving it an angry flutter. "And it doesn't mean you can tell me what to do or whom to see, and I won't—"

"Don't bother," he said curtly. "It doesn't matter, does it?"

And when he slammed the little room's door shut after him, the glass panes in the windows rattled, and he didn't look back.

"Hush, hush, little man," crooned Amariah as she walked with baby Sammy in her arms. "Hush, hush, now, there's nothing to be gained from crying."

She reached the end of the kitchen and turned back again, walking the same path that she had for the last half hour. Only walking like this seemed to soothe the baby into quiet and rest, and Amariah had come to take her turn among the kitchen maids, giving the exhausted new mother—Janey Patton was her name—a chance to sleep. As soon as the young woman's strength returned, she would be sent to the country, to a place Amariah had arranged for her and her baby with a dairy farmer in need of a milkmaid. There had never been any mention of the baby's father, and Amariah had not asked.

"Hush, hush," she murmured, turning again. Though there were plenty of others on her staff willing to do this chore, she'd been happy enough to volunteer herself. There were few things in life as perfect as a tiny baby, and while Amariah was supposed to be comforting him, the mere act of holding the swaddled infant in her arms was comforting her, too, and helping her clear the tangle of her thoughts.

As soon as she'd risen this morning, she'd sent a conciliatory note to Lord Westbrook, with enough general apologies to soothe any man's bruised pride and the warmest of personal invitations for his return to the club. She hoped he accepted it, and she hoped even more that he'd come back.

What to do with Guilford was much harder to decide.

She still believed she'd been right, that he shouldn't have taken Westbrook outside. She'd learned later from the footmen that there'd been no actual fighting, not much more than a few shoves and heated words before Westbrook had retreated in a huff, but she still wasn't pleased by Guilford's presumption. Yet she couldn't afford to have him wounded any more than she could afford to offend Westbrook. Guilford might not be an ostentatious player, but he was a powerful man of high rank, and his regular presence alone was an endorsement for the club and its exclusivity. If he stopped coming, his absence would be noticed, and noted.

Lightly she stroked Sammy's tiny hand, his fingers flaring, then tightening instinctively around hers. If she wrote to Guilford, it would only be for the sake of the club. She wouldn't mention anything beyond how she hoped to see him at Penny House soon, with a couple of prettily composed bits of flattery. But nothing more: no references to shared kisses or laughter, or how strangely miserable she'd felt when he'd left her last night without saying goodbye.

"Would you like me to take the little fellow for a spell, Miss Penny?" Letty, the head cook while Bethany was on her wedding trip, held out her hands. "I've a few minutes to spare while that broth simmers."

"Thank you, Letty." With the greatest care, Amariah transferred the sleeping baby to Letty's arms. "I have a pile of bills waiting for me on my desk upstairs, anyway."

Yet still she lingered, watching the baby yawn and nestle more comfortably against Letty.

"Oh, he's a dear little lamb, isn't he?" crooned Letty, her weathered face wreathed with a contented smile. "There's nothing quite like having a sweet new babe about the house, is there?"

Amariah smiled wistfully. She couldn't deny that she'd miss Sammy, as well, when he and his mother left. Once again she reminded herself that Penny House was all she needed for a fulfilling and productive life, her days and nights filled with a blend of responsibility, amusing company and useful charity. What time would she have to spare for a husband, let alone the demands of a baby like this one?

But wasn't that the gist of the wager that Guilford had told her was in the betting book at White's, the one that had made her so furious? That she'd be the only Penny sister never to marry, an old maid as well as a virago?

"Miss Penny, here you are!" Boyd the footman came lumbering down the stairs, and was immediately *shushed* by both women. Contritely he tiptoed into the kitchen and set the large bundle he was carrying onto the table.

"This came jus' now from His Grace the Duke o' Guilford," he whispered, giving the bundle an extra pat with the flat of his palm. "His man said t' bring it down here directly."

"Did he." Amariah sighed. How many times must she return Guilford's peace-offering gifts before he realized she wouldn't accept them? At least this one wasn't another piece of jewelry, not in a bundle this large, and at least he *was* asking for forgiveness. "Well, whatever it is, I'll send it directly back to his grace as soon as I write a little note to go with it."

Uncomfortable, Boyd cleared his throat and glanced down at the floor. "I'm sorry, Miss Penny," he said. "But the package isn't for you. It come for Janey Patton an' the babe."

"Not from his grace, Boyd?" Frowning, she bent over to read the card tucked into the twine, just to be sure. "Let's see here."

Written in the shopkeeper's tidy hand, the message was unmistakable. Boyd had been right: it wasn't for her.

For the New Mother at Penny House
& Her Child,
with Happy Wishes &
Joy upon Her Safe Delivery
His Grace, Duke of Guilford

Amariah tucked the card back in place. No peace offering, then. Without looking, she sensed that the others were watching and waiting for her reaction, unsure whether she'd been angry or pleased that Guilford's package was not for her, as she'd expected.

To be honest, she wasn't quite sure herself.

"So this is for Janey and Sammy," she said as cheerfully as she could. "How very kind of his grace."

Almost as if on cue, the baby opened his eyes and wailed, a long, hungry wail that no amount of cooing and rocking from Letty would quiet. The door to the kitchen office that had become the makeshift nursery opened, and Janey came hurrying out, rubbing the sleep from her eyes as she took the baby from Letty.

"I'm sorry he cried, Miss Penny," she mumbled as she unlaced her bodice. "Sammy don't mean it. He jus' be hungry."

"He's a baby, Janey," Amariah said softly. "He's supposed to cry. Why, we see plenty of grown peers of the realm who still cry when they're vexed, or don't get their supper right away."

But the girl didn't laugh or even smile, sitting on the edge of the chair with her head bowed over her nursing son. Each day Amariah thanked God that Janey had found her way to Penny House; she was so painfully shy, it was a miracle she'd survived in the rough-and-tumble London streets as long as she had.

"Here, Janey, this package came for you while you were asleep," she said. "It's a gift from the Duke of Guilford."

The girl gasped; her eyes were full of confusion. "For me, miss? Why'd a duke give me gifts?"

"The card says it's for you and the baby," Amariah said. "I told him about you, and he must have remembered."

"You open th' package, miss, if you please," Janey said warily. "Go on. Th' duke knows you, not me."

"Very well." Amariah cut the twine and opened the stiff brown paper, then gasped with delight. "Oh, Janey, look what he's sent you! *Look!*"

Nestled in fine milliner's paper lay a score of tiny baby garments: caps and stockings and gowns and wrappers, the white linen exquisitely stitched and turned, and yet serviceable enough for use by any squirming baby.

"Oh, lud," whispered Janey, tears in her eyes. "Why'd the duke send such things to my Sammy?"

"Because his grace wished to be kind," Amariah said, tears stinging her own eyes. First Billy Fox, and now this. She hadn't given Guilford nearly enough credit. He'd listened to her, and he'd understood. She wasn't foolish enough to believe he'd chosen these sweet baby things at a milliner himself, but he had realized the kind of peace offering that she'd never refuse. The proof was here on the table before her. "Because his grace is trying to be generous with his good fortune."

Janey touched the little cap nearest to her with awe, tracing her fingers along the long satin ribbon strings as if she feared they'd melt away.

"He's a good gentleman, miss, t' do this for me an' Sammy," she whispered. "He's a *great* gentleman."

"Perhaps he is, Janey," Amariah said, and there was only a hint of irony in her voice. "Perhaps he is."

* * *

Guilford sat in his favorite mahogany armchair, his legs sprawled before him as his manservant, Crenshaw, deftly swept the razor across his jaw. The day was warm, the windows to his bedchamber open, and with his eyes closed, Guilford basked in the familiar routine that began his almost-noon-morning: the spicy scent of the shaving soap, the cup of thick hot chocolate with the folded newssheet on the table beside him, the luxurious slide of his silk dressing gown over his bare chest, the faintly audible humming from Crenshaw as he went about his work. Every part of the routine helped ease him from sleep into day with the least effort possible, and woe to anyone who'd dare suggest he change any detail of it.

Had his package arrived at Penny House yet, he wondered? Directed as it was to the poor woman who'd dropped her baby on their doorstep, he knew there was a chance that Amariah wouldn't learn of its existence. But as he'd made the arrangements, he'd realized he didn't particularly care. True, he did hope to impress Amariah with a show of generosity, but even if she never learned of it, he'd still be doing a good turn for someone in grievous need—rather a form of evening the scales in the eternal balance.

Crenshaw began to wipe away the last flecks of suds from Guilford's face with a warmed cloth, then paused, glancing out the open window.

"There appears to be a hackney at the door, your grace," he said. "Were you expecting a caller at this hour?"

"A hackney here, Crenshaw?" Guilford asked, sitting upright in the chair so he could look, too. "At this hour?"

The footman riding on the back of a hired cab was a curious enough sight, enough to catch Guilford's attention. The footman hopped down and went to the window to take a card from the lady inside—a lady who leaned forward just far enough that the sun glanced off her bright copper hair inside the wide brim of the most elegant, impractical bonnet imaginable.

"What in blazes?" muttered Guilford. "Amariah? *Here?*"

He pushed himself from the chair and from Crenshaw's ministrations, striding from the bedchamber and into the hall. He'd never dreamed she'd come here herself. Ladies, even unconventional ladies like Amariah, didn't call on bachelor gentlemen. Likely she thought she'd leave her card and escape, counting on him still being abed at this unfashionably early hour. Not that he was about to let her escape as easily as that, not when she'd actually come to call on *him*.

He raced down the white marble stairs, his dressing gown sailing out behind him. Who would have known that a pile of clothes for a nameless brat would be such a powerful lure?

"Your grace!" Standing at the front door, his own startled footman was just holding out the silver salver to accept Amariah's card from *her* footman. Both men were staring, as if they'd never seen a bare-chested, barefoot duke come running toward them with daubs of shaving soap still spotting his face and a paisley dressing gown billowing around him like a scarlet cloud. "Forgive me, your grace, I was only—"

"Step aside, Parker!" Guilford ordered. "I must see the woman in that hackney!"

"Guilford!" cried Amariah, her head jutting from the hackney's window. Why was it that today, when she'd been counting on not seeing him, she'd worn this hat, bright green straw with an arching brim that set off her face and hair like a flower inside a curling leaf? "Whatever are you doing?"

"I might well ask the same of you, sweetheart," he said,

coming down the steps to stand before her, his hands on his hips. "I never expected to see you here."

"I'm not really here, as you know perfectly well," she said. She couldn't help but keep looking from his face to his bare chest and back again, growing more flustered by the moment. "I came to drop my card, that is all, and…and…Guilford, you are not *decent!*"

He grinned, enjoying himself immensely. "Of course I'm decent."

"Not for London!" she sputtered, blushing. "Not for Grosvenor Square! You look more like some pagan pasha than a proper English lord!"

"Ah, but there's your mistake, Amariah," he said, taking a step closer. "I'm a lord, true, but I never have claimed to be proper."

She pulled back, bumping the tall, beribboned crown of her bonnet on the frame of the window, and muttering something that, if she weren't the late Reverend Penny's eldest daughter, Guilford would have sworn was an oath. She fumbled with the hat, trying to disengage it from the window, until she finally tore the knotted ribbons free from beneath her chin and yanked the hat forward. She shoved the door open, and jumped down to the pavement beside Guilford, her hair coming loose and the hat clutched in her hands between them.

"*I* know you're not proper, Guilford," she said, hairpins sticking out of her now-untidy hair, "but that doesn't mean that the entire rest of the world needs to see it, or you, either."

He folded his arms over his chest, feeling very much indeed like the pasha of Grosvenor Square. A nursemaid with two small children in tow walked by, the woman hustling the wide-eyed, fascinated children away from the exotically half-dressed gentleman.

"The world can see what it pleases," he said grandly. "I care not for their humble opinions."

"Oh, hush," she said, giving his arm an impatient poke. "I didn't come here to watch you posture."

"Then why *did* you come?" he asked. "What exactly was on that card that your footman was depositing into the safe-keeping of my footman?"

She sniffed. "I came to thank you. That's what I wrote on the back of the card—'Thank you for your kindness.' You'll see for yourself when you go back inside."

"You could have sent the footman with that," he said. "You didn't have to bring it yourself. Surely by this time of the day, you're already preparing for tonight."

"I am," she said, "or at least I should be. But I thought I should call myself. You earned that much from me."

"Yet you called when you felt sure that I'd still be abed," he said, wagging a scolding finger at her. "Thus you could have the satisfaction of having come to thank me in person, but you didn't have to offend your sense of propriety by actually *seeing* me at home."

She ignored his conclusion, proving absolutely that he'd guessed right.

"All those sweet little baby things you sent," she said. "Janey Patton wept when she saw them. That was most generous and thoughtful of you, Guilford. You surprised me, just as you surprised me with Billy Fox."

"I like surprising you." He did, too. It amused him no end.

"I underestimated you, Guilford," she said. "You did very well."

"Did I do well with you, too?" he asked, unable to resist. "Did you weep with her?"

She raised her head a fraction higher, stray red-gold strands of hair tossing around her face. "As a matter of fact, I did. Baby clothes have that effect on women."

"But not on viragos."

"No," she said, and for one awful moment he was afraid she'd cry now, as well. "But then that was your word, not mine. I never claimed to be a virago."

"So I am not proper, and you are no virago?"

She shook her head, and made herself smile. "Not at all," she said. "I am emphatically not a virago, and you are just as emphatically not proper."

"Then for once we are agreed." He'd come to regret that he'd written that particular word in the betting book—not because he'd tired of teasing her about it, because he hadn't; but because he didn't really want anyone else thinking of her as a virago. It was wrong, and someday he'd have to apologize to her for using it.

Someday, that is, after he'd confessed that he'd been the one to first use it.

He bowed slightly, and reached for her arm. "Come inside with me for a dish of tea, or a glass of brandy, or whatever else you please. Then you can continue to thank me as you see fit."

Her smile grew unexpectedly soft, like the morning mist on spring grass, his thoughts waxing far more poetical than they usually did regarding women, but then Amariah inspired such foolishness.

"I cannot do that, Guilford," she said. "You may be improper, but I'm not. I've already erred by standing here with you dressed like—like *that*."

He caught her glancing down again to his mostly bare chest, and laughed.

"Oh, hush," she said, her cheeks flushed. "Can you imagine what our world would say if I were next seen going into your house unattended?"

"The world would say you were a fortunate woman, and I the luckiest man alive."

"But after that, the world would say a great deal more that was not as savory, and none of it useful to the reputation of Penny House." She eased her arm free of his hand. "Besides, I do have much to prepare for tonight."

"Stay, Amariah," he said. He might regret calling her a virago, but he certainly hadn't forgotten the wager about bedding her. How could he, especially when she was looking at him like this?

"Please," he said, coaxing gently. "Come with me. What could happen in the middle of this bright and sunny morning?"

"It's afternoon," she said softly. "And with you, the time of day would not matter one whit."

He flung his arms out from his sides for emphasis, the full sleeves of the dressing gown fluttering like red silk wings, which made a passing horse shy away and its rider swear with annoyance.

"If it doesn't matter with me whether it's morning or midnight," he said, "then it shouldn't matter to you, either. Come with me, pet."

But she only shook her head one more time. "Don't ask me again, Guilford, for I'll only say no. Besides, I've been warned that Lord Alistair is bringing a large party of his cousins from Edinburgh tonight, and the staff and I must be prepared for the worst kind of clannish revelry."

"May we all be delivered from reveling Scotsmen, especially if they bring their infernal pipes." Yet when he smiled, it had nothing to do with the visitors from Edinburgh, and everything to do with her. "Will I be welcome at Penny House tonight?"

He felt the warmth of her smile, knowing it was meant for him.

"You're always welcome, Guilford," she said. "You know that."

"I still like to hear it," he said. From the way she was smiling, he considered kissing her, then thought better of it. There'd be plenty of other times later, when they'd have more privacy for everything that he intended to follow that kiss. "But what welcome will I have from you tonight, I wonder?"

"Your welcome, Guilford?" Her eyes bright with the old familiar challenge, she settled her hat back onto her head, the ribbons dangling over her cheeks. "I suppose you'll just have to wait until tonight to find out, won't you?"

Amariah was still smiling as she climbed the steps to Penny House. She'd been impulsive going to the duke's house, and she'd been foolish lingering with him so long before his front steps. She'd been courting scandal, almost begging for it. Anyone seeing them together, with him dressed—or half dressed—as he was, and she with a hired cab, would have guessed they were saying the most touching farewell after a night of illicit sin.

And yet, to her own amazement, she had absolutely no regrets. Strange how he'd barely touched her, and yet because they both liked to play with words and tease each other, he could make her feel more deliciously wicked than another man might with a kiss. No wonder she was in such a splendid mood now. He'd made her smile, and laugh, and feel generally better about herself and the rest of the world on this fine sunny day. He could do that for her, with an ease that no one else ever could. How could she have any regrets after that? Except, perhaps, that she hadn't had the nerve to go inside with Guilford.

"Good day, Boyd," she said as the footman opened the door to her. "Would you please send Pratt to me upstairs directly?"

But Pratt was already here, hurrying toward her across the checkerboard floor. His face was even more solemn than usual, and on the tray reserved for mail and cards he was bearing a folded newssheet as if it were a casket on a bier.

"At last you are back, Miss Penny," he said. "Have you seen this yet?"

He held the newssheet out to her, and she took it. The pages had been carefully folded open to the middle, highlighting the page with social news and gossip.

"What dreadful news am I to learn, Pratt?" she asked, half teasing as she began scanning the long columns. The good feeling from her conversation with Guilford still remained, making it impossible to share Pratt's gloom. "What horrible wickedness will I—oh, no. *No!*"

She'd only read the headline, but that was all she needed to know. While she'd been dallying with Guilford, *this* news had been spreading through every aristocratic drawing room in London:

Blue-Blood Cheat Finds Sanctuary at Penny House

Chapter Seven

Guilford could not remember a greater crowd outside Penny House. The crush of carriages waiting in line along St. James Street stretched so long that at last he'd finally climbed out and walked the last blocks, his impatience—and his curiosity—too demanding for such a wait. Whatever effect that spurious bit of anonymous rubbish in the scandal sheet today might prove to have upon the club, it certainly wasn't keeping back the members tonight.

Yet when he finally made his way up the steps and through the door, he was greeted by Pratt, not Amariah.

"Where's Miss Penny, Pratt?" he asked with concern, still scanning the jostling heads for a glimpse of the white plume she always wore in her hair. "She's well, isn't she? Not hiding from the dastardly press?"

"She's quite well, your grace," Pratt said with a bow. "I should even venture to say she's exceptionally well. You know Miss Penny's character, your grace. There's nothing she likes more than a challenge, except, perhaps a fight."

"That she does, Pratt," Guilford said, remembering the extra spark in her eye as she'd said goodbye to him earlier.

There must have been out-and-out flames shooting from her eyes once she'd read that bundle of lies. "Did she hunt down the rascal who wrote that story and throttle him in the middle of the Strand? You'd think we had a Tyburn hanging from the crowd here tonight. Or is Miss Penny playing Jack Ketch?"

Pratt's mouth twisted and contorted its way into something like a smile. "In her present humor, Miss Penny could be capable of such a rash misdeed, yes, your grace."

"But she hasn't done it yet?"

"No, your grace," Pratt said. "She is in the hazard room at present, if you should wish to join her."

Guilford grinned, and clapped the manager on the shoulder. "Why, thank you, Pratt. Always good to know the best viewing spot for the fireworks, eh?"

"If you want fireworks, Guilford, you'll come with me." Lord Stanton suddenly appeared beside him, looping his arm over Guilford's shoulder. Even without the half-empty glass in his hand, it was clear Stanton had been drinking, his face too ruddy and his greeting too fond. "Westbrook's having such a run o' luck with the dice, you'd think he was this famous ol' cheat."

"Westbrook's not clever enough to cheat a flea," Guilford said, supporting more of Stanton's weight than he wished as he tried to steer him toward the stairs. "Any luck that finds him is true."

"Then come with me an' judge for yourself, Guilford." Stanton winked broadly, emptied his glass and dropped it onto the tray of a passing footman. "Your ladylove's there, too. Prettier than June and colder than December. Colder-*er.*"

"If you mean Miss Penny," Guilford said, "then she's hardly my ladylove, or anyone else's."

"But that's not true!" Stanton pushed free, his face screwed up with surprise as, unsupported, he swayed gently back and forth. "I *know* that's not true, so don't pretend it is. A mos' reliable acquaintance told me he'd seen Miss Penny leaving your house today in a compromising manner, *if* you understand me."

"Not possible, Stanton," Guilford said, "and a good thing the lady herself didn't hear you say so. She wasn't leaving my house because she'd never come inside it, and the most compromising thing she did was try to knock me to the pavement."

"The devil she did!" Stanton eyed him suspiciously. "You're not telling me th' truth, Guilford. I can tell. You've already had the chit."

"I haven't had so much as a cup of tea from Miss Penny," Guilford said. "She's a paragon of virtue. And that *is* the entire truth."

"She can't even see you, Guilford," Stanton said doggedly, making a weak attempt to strike him on the arm. "You'll never win the wager now. All she's considering is this damned cheat."

"Then I must begin cheating, too, to capture her interest." Guilford smiled, already edging away. Amariah had enough on her plate tonight without having to deal with a contentious drunk like Stanton, especially not when he was so determined to discuss that wager. "Now if you'll excuse me, Stanton, I'm off to view some fireworks."

He turned and made his way through the crowd, determined to escape. He didn't think Stanton was capable of following, not up the polished stairs, and he didn't, instead wandering off to find someone else to lean upon.

But the crowds in the street and on the steps were nothing compared to the crush outside the hazard room, with descriptions of each play at the table inside shouted out and relayed to the others with oaths and cheers. Suddenly a great roar of voices drowned out everything else: if Westbrook were still the caster, he'd either just won enormously, or lost everything outright. Guilford managed to shoulder his way through the doorway and into the room itself, squeezing past the others to find a place along the wall where he could watch.

Even with the tall windows thrown open, the heat from so many male bodies in evening dress pressed together was nearly unbearable. Because the stakes, and the losses, in hazard could run so high, the game always had a nervous energy to it, but tonight that energy felt magnified a hundredfold, the excitement and anxiety vibrating in the too-warm air beneath the low, shaded lamps.

Quickly Guilford scanned the room, looking first for Amariah. She was easy to find: not only because she was the only woman in the room, dressed in bright blue with the white plume nodding from her copper hair, but because she was standing beside Mr. Walthrip, the director of the hazard table and the overall master of the hazard room. Walthrip was bent and trollish, with errant wisps of white hair sprouting above his oversize ears and the long-handled green rake that was the mark of his trade clutched in his fingers like a scepter. His rule of the table was never questioned, his authority absolute.

Allied with Walthrip beside his tall chair, Amariah stood in the safest place in the entire room, perhaps in the club itself. Her expression was a mirror of the director's, too, an emotionless mask that observed all and betrayed nothing. Her gaze glided restlessly over the faces lining the table and walls behind it, watching, judging. When she reached Guilford, he smiled, and though he thought he saw a moment's recognition flicker through her eyes, it was gone just as quickly as she moved on to the man beside him.

Damnation, why didn't she smile back?

"Look at that Penny woman," the man beside him said.

"She's as cool as old Walthrip himself. Westbrook just dropped twelve thousand pounds and the cast with it, and she didn't even flinch. Imagine a woman with so little feeling for that poor bastard's suffering!"

But Guilford *could* imagine, because he knew the woman who'd done it. Amariah wasn't cold, and she certainly wasn't without feeling for another's suffering; but she did understand how disastrous it would be for her to show even a hint of empathy for any player at the table. Guilford's admiration for her rose again. She was already facing rumors of the club harboring a cheat. What would the scandal sheets say if she favored Westbrook, or even Guilford himself?

"Poor, poor bastard," the man beside him continued. "Hope he doesn't blow his brains out over a loss like that."

"Westbrook?" Guilford said, his thoughts pushed back to the game before him. Westbrook's loss would make for a profitable night for the house. Amariah must be pleased, though she was also wise enough to keep that emotion, too, from showing on her face. "Oh, his pockets are so deep, he could lose double that and still look his uncle in the eye tomorrow."

The man beside him snorted. "Better him than me, I say."

Westbrook sat hunched at the table still, glowering as the play continued, his mood as black and menacing as a thundercloud hovering over him. As crowded as the game was, the other men around him took care to give him space, as if his bad luck were contagious. The green tablecloth beside him was conspicuously bare. Ten minutes before, there must have been a small mountain of fish-shaped pearl markers to count his winnings. With one cast of the dice, he'd been left with nothing, and all those pearly fish had been raked away by Walthrip.

But across from him was a young gentleman that Guilford didn't recognize, a young gentleman that fate was now smiling upon. The pile of markers before him proved it: surely this must be the twelve thousand that Westbrook had just lost, or most of it, anyway. The young man's broad, freckled face was shiny with sweat, his eyes bulging with excitement, and he rattled the dice in the wooden casting box with frantic nervousness.

"What main, m'lord?" droned Walthrip. To him every man who played at Penny House was a lord; it was a convenient assumption, and one not far from the truth. "What main?"

"Seven," the man answered, his voice ripe with the burr of Edinburgh. He must be one of Lord Alistair's guests tonight, the reveling Scotsmen that Amariah had been preparing for. "That's the number o' pups in my favorite yellow bitch's last litter."

Around him others sniggered or laughed outright, as if they were schoolboys mocking another who'd been caught giving a blatantly wrong answer.

"Quiet," Walthrip ordered. "What main, m'lord?"

"Seven," the young Scotsman said contritely, now all too aware of how he'd erred by saying too much. He pushed the pile of markers forward, signifying he'd wager them all, and one of his friends whistled low beside him. "Seven."

"Seven it is, m'lord," Walthrip said. "Main is seven."

Although Guilford seldom played hazard—he preferred games with more skill and cunning, where less was left to chance—he knew that seven was a beginner's call, chosen for its lucky reputation or, for that matter, for the number of yellow pups in a litter. But it was a difficult number to match for a winning toss, and the rumble that passed among the others at the table acknowledged it.

The Scotsman nodded, and gave the caster's box one final

rattle as he mouthed a silent prayer for his luck to continue. The whole room seemed to hold its breath together as he finally shook the dice free, the little cubes dancing and skipping across the green cloth before they settled to a stop.

A four, and a three. Seven. The lucky devil and his yellow pups had just nicked it outright, and won. The silence exploded, with the Scotsman's clansmen cheering and clapping him on his back so hard he nearly toppled forward onto the table, while the others cheered and shouted and swore and marveled and stamped their feet.

"Seven, m'lord," Walthrip said, not deigning to raise his voice over the din. "Chance wins, m'lord."

"You mean chance *cheats*." Westbrook stood so abruptly that his chair crashed back to the floor behind him. "No one, sir, has that kind of luck without help, *sir.*"

The Scotsman looked up, startled, his fingers buried deep in the huge pile of markers before him. "What did you say, my lord?"

"I said that chance helped luck, sir." Westbrook leaned across the table toward the other man, biting off each word. "I said that chance cheats."

The Scotsman smacked his hand down on the table, his face livid. "No one calls me a cheater, not even some puffed-up English lordling! I used the same damned dice as you did, and if—"

"Silence, m'lord!" Walthrip's liver-colored lips quivered with outrage. "Please recall that in this house, we obey the rules of genteel society."

Incredulous, the Scotsman shook his head, appealing to Walthrip while his friends tried to calm him. "But you heard what that petty little fool called me! You all heard what he said about—"

"Check the damned dice, Walthrip," Westbrook ordered. "Ten to one they're weighted in the Sandy's favor."

"That's enough, Westbrook," Guilford said, not caring how many others turned to stare at him. "You don't need to say more."

Westbrook glared back. "Mind your own affairs, Guilford, or I'll settle with you later."

"My Lord Westbrook," Amariah said, her voice ringing clear. "Recall yourself. Mr. Walthrip inspects every pair of dice that is used at this table, and a new set is introduced hourly."

What a first-rate woman, Guilford thought. *No shrieking, no hysterics, only plain common sense in a voice fit not for a virago, but an avenging angel.*

Her smile was grim, a warning that most men would heed. "Control your temper, my lord, I beg of you, or I will have no choice but to ask you to leave Penny House."

His puckish face mottled with fury, Westbrook struck his fist on the table.

"If the dice aren't rotten, then check the damned caster's box, *Miss* Penny," he snarled. "If you won't take my word against some wretched, puling cheat of—"

"Oh, aye, shoot your mouth at the lady!" jeered the Scotsman, yanking his arms free of his coat sleeves. "What a brave bonny man you are, to—"

"I'll show you what kind of honest Englishman I am!" shouted Westbrook furiously, shoving and knocking other men aside as he tried to charge at the Scotsman. "You damned filthy cheat!"

But the Scotsman's cousins were already plunging into the crowd toward Westbrook, shouting like Highland warriors swooping down upon their hapless enemies. Not that the English members of the club stood still: they, too, jumped into the fray, shouting and swearing and shoving and swinging fists and breaking glasses. The guards and footmen began grabbing whomever they could to try to break up the brawl.

"Amariah!" Guilford shouted, trying to find her over the flailing arms. Walthrip's tall chair was empty, the director and his green rake vanished. Then for one quick second he glimpsed the top of her head, the white plume nodding above the rest of the crowd. *"Amariah!"*

He plunged through the churning mass in evening dress, fighting to carve a path toward where he'd last seen her. No woman belonged in here now, especially not the woman that some of these well-bred gentlemen might resent or begrudge or even simply desire.

"Amariah!" he shouted again, roaring to be heard. More guards and footmen were pouring into the room, while other, more levelheaded gentlemen were now struggling to get out. "Amariah?"

"Guilford?" She popped up suddenly, her plume gone and her face pale against so many dark superfine coats. "Guilford!"

Then as quickly as she'd appeared she vanished again, and Guilford pushed forward, desperate to find her. "Amariah, Amariah!"

"Here!" She grabbed his hand as if she were drowning, and he pulled her close, shielding her with his body as together they forced their way into the hall.

"Are you all right?" he demanded as soon as they were clear, turning her in his arms so he could see her face. "You're not harmed?"

"Of course I'm not!" she sputtered, twisting to look back into the hazard room. "I cannot believe they've all done this! Look at them, Guilford! They're worse than a pack of raving hyenas, they are, and they'll ruin everything I've worked so hard to do—*everything!*"

"No, they won't." He was trying to calm her, even as he himself was more relieved than he'd thought possible that she wasn't harmed. "Everything will be fine."

"How can you say that?" she demanded, her face flushed with frustration and fear, too, though she'd never admit it. She tugged against his hand, wanting to return. "I should go back in there and make them understand that—"

"You can't tell them anything, not now," he said. "But tomorrow you will. Westbrook and Alistair will be tossed out for good, and—"

"Neither of them is the cheat," she interrupted. "No matter what they said about each other, they're wrong. Neither of them were here before tonight, so they couldn't be the one I've been warned against."

"Don't worry about that now," he said. "You and Pratt must have the place settled and put to rights by tomorrow night. You will, too. No one will know that anything happened here tonight. Though you may have to find Walthrip hiding under the table."

"I'm glad you're so confident." She reached up to her hair, and seemed to wilt, sagging against the wall. "Oh, blast, Guilford. They stole my feather, too."

"I'll buy you another," he said. "I'll buy you an entire flock of ostriches from Africa. But you and Penny House will survive this, Amariah. You *will*."

She watched the guards hauling away peers with blackened eyes and torn waistcoats, and sighed dramatically. "I know I will," she said, and sighed again, "just as I know I'll win in the end, too."

He smiled, and thought again of kissing her. "Now who's confident?"

"I am, and with good reason, too." She raised her hand, and opened her fingers so he could see what she'd kept squeezed in her fist. "Because these dice were rigged, just as Westbrook said, and may God help the rascal who brought them into my house once I find him."

The next morning was bad, perhaps the worst that Amariah had experienced since she'd first come to Penny House. The actual damage to the hazard room was surprisingly slight. A few chairs had been broken, a few glasses smashed and the shards ground into the floorboards, a few sleeves on livery jackets torn, but that was all. The total expenses came to less than a hundred pounds—that is, not counting the loss of revenue from the early end of play for the night—but as Guilford had predicted, everything had been put back to rights by noon. The bumps and cuts and bruises to her footmen and guards were more extensive, but there'd been no broken bones or other lasting damage, and the men themselves had all seemed to treat the brawl like a great lark.

So had the club's members, who'd staggered from the door last night alternately groaning and bragging, and puffing out their collective chests as if they'd each won the main fight at Donnybrook Fair. She'd been so angry with Guilford the night before for pushing and shoving and knocking heads with Westbrook in the street, and yet here it seemed he'd only been doing exactly what every other man wished to do, too. This sort of male tomfoolery was incomprehensible to Amariah, and so appalling to her that, in the darkest hours of the night, she'd actually questioned whether she possessed the patience and fortitude to continue running a gaming club for the most ill-behaved half of the species.

Now she sat at the table in her quarters with Walthrip and

Pratt, watching as Walthrip prodded one of the dice she'd retrieved last night with a thin-bladed knife and a surgeon's delicacy.

"This was not the work of a schoolboy amateur, Miss Penny," he said, squinting down at the dice in his hand. "This individual knew precisely what to do, and how to do it. Observe the process, if you will. Each of the dice was drilled through the center dot of the trey, filled with lead, then patched over where it would not be noticed. There's the patch, there."

"But I noticed the difference at once in my hand," she said. "It didn't balance the way it should."

"That's their beauty." He rattled the dice gently in his baby-pink hand, then rolled them across the table. They stopped with a three and four: seven. He scooped them up, and repeated the toss five more times, with the same faces always showing. "They never falter."

With a little *harrumph,* Amariah tried the dice herself, with the same result. Seven, always a seven.

The same seven that the young Scotsman had needed to nick the game.

"But they're our dice," she said. "I recognize them."

"They are," Pratt said, leaning closer. "Or they were."

"True enough," Walthrip said sadly. "But somehow one of our pairs was spirited away from the table, treated and reinserted in the course of play. Given the number of watchful eyes, I cannot fathom how it was done, but done it was, with sorrowful results."

Pratt tossed the dice, and Walthrip grabbed at his wispy white hair with both hands and groaned as the same seven turned up. "I cannot apologize to you enough, Miss Penny," he said. "In my entire career, I have never had such a mishap at one of my tables. If you release me from my duties, I will understand entirely."

"Oh, hush, " she said gently, reaching out to pat the old director's arm. "I'll do nothing of the sort. We shall solve this together."

"So you believe it's young Alistair that's our cheat?" asked Pratt, tapping the dice with his forefinger. "How else could he do so well on every toss?"

Amariah shook her head. "He couldn't be, Pratt. Last night was the first time he'd ever come to Penny House, let alone played hazard here. Someone else must have switched the dice, and he was only the fortunate beneficiary."

Pratt cupped the dice in his palm. "Even a neophyte would notice the difference in how these feel."

"But he never held them in his hand to feel them," Walthrip said. "The dice were always in the caster's box. He would have had to have been an expert player to feel any difference at all with the dice inside. No, another introduced these dice to the game through some sleight of hand that went unnoticed by us all."

"And so we are back to where we began," Amariah said with a discouraged sigh. "If nothing else came of that foolishness last night, I thought at least we'd learned who the cheat might be."

Pratt tossed the crooked dice one last time, and left them with their seven facing up.

"That was what His Grace the Duke said, as well, miss," he said. "He said that right away, quick as can be. He said that we'd have to know less now than before, and that we must—"

"You're speaking of Lord Guilford, aren't you?" Amariah asked warily, though she already knew that must be whom Pratt meant. What other duke among the club's members would discuss such a matter with Pratt or the others behind her back, as if he'd every right? Why wasn't he like all the others on the membership committee, who happily left everything to her? It seemed as if he were growing more and more interested in the club's affairs, to the point that he was almost—almost—meddlesome. "When did his grace say this to you, Pratt?"

Pratt pursed his lips, immediately contrite. "Last night," he said carefully. "When everyone was leaving. His grace told me how you'd been so clever to seize the dice from the hazard table, but how in the end it would be of no use."

"That is all?" she asked, unsure whether to believe him or not. Pratt worshipped Guilford, the same way every one else in London seemed to. At least he'd deigned to give her a bit of credit by calling her clever. "His grace didn't tell you what to do next, or give you any orders?"

"No, Miss Penny," Pratt said primly. "His grace has only the greatest admiration for you. His Grace would never compromise you, or your position here at Penny House."

Oh, yes, he would, thought Amariah, but let it pass. "At least his grace and I came to the same conclusion."

"Yes, Miss Penny," Pratt said quickly. "And if his grace said that—ah, that must be Mary with the newssheets."

As he rose to answer the knock on the door, Walthrip took the opportunity to bow his goodbye, and flee. With a sigh, Amariah sat back in her chair, folding her arms over her chest as she braced herself for whatever the gossipmongers had launched onto the streets today. She felt almost like a playwright waiting for first reviews, and she didn't doubt for a moment that last night's events would receive notice. With so many blue-blooded combatants, how could they not?

"Please give me the *Advertiser* first, Pratt," she said.

"They'll be the kindest. You take the *Morning Chronicle,* and I'll save the *Tattle* here for last."

"The best for last, Miss?" asked Pratt as he opened the *Chronicle* to the page with news of society.

"Only the best if one considers being the least truthful, tactful, and most scandalous as worthy qualities." Quickly she scanned the report in the *Advertiser.* Buried behind the news of a brilliant new actress's debut in a plum role—and, more importantly, hints of her place in the prince's bed—was a short mention of "intemperate altercations" at Penny House last evening.

"Here we are," she said, reading aloud. "According to the *Advertiser,* 'an emotional response by a small party of Lord A*******'s relatives to suggestions that they were perhaps more fortunate than other gentlemen at the table.' That's rather accurate, really."

"The *Chronicle* is finding fault with Lord Westbrook, miss," Pratt said, tipping his sheet toward the window for better light as he began to read aloud.

"As is always the case among those who joust with the dice over the green cloth, luck will smile more warmly upon some than upon others. On the evening last at Penny House, the peace and gentility of that place was disturbed by the unhappiness of a certain Baron, having learned that the Fate of Hazard can take away her favors as readily as she might grant them. His response led to considerable unpleasantness in the room, and closed play for the remainder of the night."

"Nothing to fault in that, either," Amariah said, daring to hope that perhaps her fears were unfounded.

Pratt nodded. "Lord Guilford said that none of the gentlemen will tell the writers exactly what happened, miss. His grace said that they'd rather their ladies didn't know about it, and that they'll keep mum."

"His grace speaks from personal experience, Pratt." Amariah sipped the last of her tea, trying not to remember Guilford's self-satisfied swagger from the other night. "Are there any other pearls from the lips of Lord Guilford that I should know?"

"No, Miss Penny," Pratt said. "Not in particular. Though his grace did liken last night's effect upon Penny House to the difference between a bland dish brought to table, and one spiced to perfection, as if Miss Bethany were in the kitchen."

"Then his grace should likewise recall the perils of an overspiced dish," she said, "when too rich a seasoning can result in such unpalatable results that it is scorned by all."

"Yes, Miss Penny," Pratt said quickly. "As you wish."

But Guilford was right, of course, as Amariah knew perfectly well. It had been the unique spice of three young ladies from the country inheriting a gaming house that had made the club so popular from its inception. Could he be right, too, about them growing too bland and complacent?

She sighed, and reached for the last paper, the *Covent Garden Tattle,* holding it disdainfully out between her thumb and forefinger. "Now, if we can only survive the wretched ink from the *Tattle.*"

She spread the paper out on the table, patting the creases flat, and began to read.

Under the heading of A Dishonorable Night At Penny House, she found more than enough spice for the hottest East Indian curry imaginable.

"HONESTY & HONOR must be the mark of any private gaming club with pretensions to welcome the Best Company, but such was not the case on the evening last at Penny House, in St. James Street. With whispers of a CHEAT already in the air, one noble member of the Club felt compelled to challenge the win of a visitor from the North, a young Scots gentleman whose quick change of FORTUNE much improved his state with one toss of the dice, while Baron W***b***k was left with the emptiest of pockets."

"Forgive me, Miss Penny," interrupted Pratt indignantly, "but that is not what happened, not at all!"

"You know the *Tattle* will never let the truth confound a good tale, Pratt," Amariah said grimly. "But listen, the lies grow more outrageous.

"No aid was forthcoming from the Club officiaries, all of whom chose to side with the Scotsman against this LORD, & what is more, they stood by while the friends of SCOTLAND savaged him & laid waste to his person. Doubtless this lamentable Affair will end shortly in a Meeting of Honor between the two in some distant corner of the this town, leaving the Red Queen of Penny House to dissemble the Question of Unfair Advantage viz., the work of the GREAT CHEAT, & leave him to wreak his evil again at her table for their mutual PROFIT."

Too angry to speak, Amariah made a wordless sound of pure fury, then flung the paper into the grate, the pages flapping as they fell into the flames. "I do not care what Guilford told you, Pratt. *That* is not spice, but pure, hellish venom!"

She shoved back her chair from the table. "Those people mean to ruin us, Pratt, and I will not sit here and let them do it. If they dare call me the Red Queen on account of my hair, why, then I shall be a queen, and teach them what comes of defiling my kingdom!"

"No, Miss Penny," Pratt said, his voice quivering with shared outrage. "That is to say, yes, Miss Penny, you shall not sit by."

"No, I will not." She struck her fist so hard on the table that her teacup danced in its dish. "Call a hackney for me, Pratt. It's high time I paid a visit upon the editor of the *Tattle* myself."

Chapter Eight

G uilford paused on the pavement, squinting up at the small signboard swinging over his head. The paint was peeling, the name as faded on the sign as it was on the door to the small office before him: strange how such a shabby enterprise could cause so much havoc among so many of London's finest families. Not that Guilford himself was intimidated; he didn't care a fig for what was said or written about him.

But for Amariah's sake, he'd done the unthinkable. He'd seen the early editions of the newspapers before he'd gone to bed last night, and that had been enough to make him rise this morning nearly with the sun. He hadn't been awake at such an obscene hour since he'd reached his majority, but for Amariah he'd done it. And for her he'd gone and called upon two bruised and groggy gentlemen who hadn't wanted to see or hear him, though see and hear him they had. And finally, for Amariah again, he'd come to this grubby part of the Strand to do battle with the scribblers of the *Covent Garden Tattle* on her behalf, and it still wasn't even noon.

"I've come to see your master," he announced to a pudgy apprentice with ink-blackened fingers, sitting on a tall stool to sort the box of type in his lap. The *Tattle*'s office was small, narrow and dirty, with flyspecked political prints tacked onto the bare walls and the leavings from last night's supper still sitting on a tall desk near the front window. "We've business to discuss, business that needs his attention directly. Go on, fetch the rascal."

The boy slid from the stool, wiping his hands on his apron. "What name, sir?"

"My name?" Guilford smiled, determined to play this out exactly as he'd planned. "The Duke of Guilford."

The apprentice ducked his head and scurried off to the back room, returning with a man who, from the amount of belly spilling over the sides of his own apron, must surely be the pudgy boy's father.

"Simon Dalton, your most humble servant," he said with a flourish of his black-fingered hand that was dangerously close to mocking. "I cannot tell you how honored I am, your grace. You grandees seldom favor me with your presence."

"Most gentlemen don't find it necessary, Dalton." Guilford tossed his copy of the day's *Tattle* onto the desk. "But that pack of lies you've strung together today has left me no choice."

Dalton pursed his lips, his round cheeks contracting around his mouth. "Strong words, your grace. Strong words indeed."

"Truthful words," Guilford said, keeping his own expression impassive. "Not that you'd recognize the difference."

Dalton bowed, his eyes rolling up to watch Guilford. "I must beg you to recall, your grace, that my humble trade is to sell papers, not truths."

"At least you don't deny it," Guilford said with disgust. He didn't have to pretend that at all. "Are you the author of that calumny about last night's events at Penny House?"

Dalton bowed again, and smiled. "You admire my work, your grace?"

"All I'd admire is your insolence," Guilford said, "and I've more than my fill of that. You weren't even there at Penny House, not that they'd ever admit the likes of you. How the devil could you write such lies?"

Dalton shrugged. "I have my agents, my reporters, to act as my eyes. The public has a right to know what passes behind those tall doors on St. James Street."

"Then the public should be shown the truth, not your twisted version of it."

"Truth, your grace, is like beauty, and always decided by the eye of the beholder." Dalton smiled archly, as if with a single clumsy aphorism, he'd settled everything. "But I fail to understand your displeasure, your grace. You were not mentioned, not even in passing. Are you perhaps acting as second to one of the dishonored gentlemen?"

"There's no need for a second, because there will be no duels," Guilford said sharply. "I've spoken with the two gentlemen myself this morning, and dissuaded them from even considering such outrageous and unwarranted behavior."

"Oh, your grace, I am sorry you did that," Dalton said peevishly. "There are few things so good for my sales as a duel!"

"There are also few things less legal, or more deadly, Dalton." Guilford's patience was growing thinner by the second, and if he weren't here for Amariah's sake, he'd simply thrash the wretch and be done with it. "What the devil gives you the right to incite murder like that? Don't you care how many lives you ruin by your slanders, or how your careless words can destroy even the most respectable establishment?"

"Penny House." Dalton's eyes glittered above his doughy cheeks. "That's it, your grace, isn't it? You don't care at all about Westbrook or the other fellow, or whether they splatter each other's brains about on the morning dew. You only care about how a duel or a cheat would affect Penny House, and the lovely Miss Penny."

Guilford grabbed Dalton by the shoulder straps of his apron, nearly hauling him off his feet. "You are never again to speak of Miss Penny, Dalton. Not here, not in your vile newspaper, not anywhere."

Dalton wriggled, struggling to free himself as his toes scrabbled across the floorboards. "You—you can't bully me, your…your grace!" he gasped. "I won't be threatened, or…or bought!"

"You won't, Dalton, because you'll do as I say." With an extra shove, Guilford released the printer. He couldn't afford to let his temper get the better of him, and ruin his plan. "No more of your slanders about Penny House, or else I shall take you to court for libel and slander."

Dalton scuttled backward, his hand to his throat.

"I could have the best counsel in the world, your grace, yet I wouldn't have a prayer of winning," he said indignantly. "That's not fair play, and you know it. I'm not rich or titled like you, nor connected to the high judges. You'd scarce have to say a word against me, and I'd lose my press and my paper. You'd break me, you would!"

"I would indeed," Guilford said. "But isn't that exactly what you try to do to the lives and reputations of others every day?"

Dalton's mouth worked furiously. "I don't hurt your kind, your grace. Great lords and ladies—nothing I say hurts them."

"But it does if it drives them to pointless, idiotic duels," Guilford said. "And it does if you say that Penny House harbors cheats."

"I'll not give up writing about Penny House, your grace,"

Dalton said indignantly. "I can't, not with all you fine noble-men dawdling there, losing your fortunes and your good names. It wouldn't be fair to my trade."

Guilford frowned down at Dalton. "You can write about Penny House all you wish, Dalton, so long as you're honest about what you say."

"Honest," Dalton said with a mix of disgust and contempt. "Who'd pay to read that, your grace?"

"You won't know until you try it." Now was the time for Guilford to play his trump—the only sure way he'd come upon to keep Amariah's name from the scandal sheet. He turned his back toward the other man, idly studying a grimy old print of James Charles Fox and the Duchess of Devonshire. "You said you had your sources. Make them tell you the truth for once."

"Bah," Dalton said, spitting out the syllable. "Lackeys and potboys, ready to spill what they know for the few shillings I can spare! What truths can they give me, your grace?"

Guilford didn't answer, pretending to concentrate on the print before him. He suspected that Dalton was following his usual path, and not being entirely truthful. Though his stories were filled with lies, there were enough honest details to prove that his informant must have more access to the work-ings of Penny House than any mere lackey could. A greedy footman, perhaps, or one of the hired guards overseeing the play; how unfortunate for him that this morning Guilford intended to put that informant's betrayal—and his extra in-come—to an end.

"I'd venture you must pay more for your information, Dal-ton," he drawled without turning. "At least you shall if you don't want me to—"

"Guilford!" Amariah exclaimed. "Whatever on earth are you doing here?"

Guilford waited and didn't look, hoping, praying, that she wasn't really there to spoil everything.

She was.

"Guilford?" she asked, his name now a question. "It *is* you, isn't it?"

With a reluctant sigh, he finally turned. She was standing in the open doorway, the sun spilling around her: considering everything that had happened last night, she looked exceptionally lovely.

"Good day, Miss Penny," he said, bowing. "I trust you are well."

"Of course I am, Guilford." With only the most cursory of nods to spare for him, she turned at once toward Dalton. She was wearing the hat with the extravagant plume, cocked forward over her brow like a helmet for battle. A copy of the *Tattle* was rolled tightly in her gloved hand and fury glowed like a bright swath of paint across her face.

No wonder Guilford almost pitied Dalton.

"You are Mr. Dalton, sir?" she demanded, coming to stand directly before him with her heels squared together. "You are the printer and primary writer of the *Covent Garden Tattle?*"

"I am indeed, ma'am," Dalton said, his hand over his heart with gallant expectation. "And your name, ma'am?"

"I am *Miss* Amariah Penny, sir." She struck the rolled newssheet down on the desk with the force usually reserved for exterminating large, determined insects. "And I am surprised you do not recognize either me or my name, *Mr.* Dalton, considering how many times you have defiled both in your hideous excuse for a journal."

"I am honored, Miss Penny!" Dalton exclaimed, though his eyes were popping with surprise. Clearly the man hadn't expected her to be so young, or so beautiful, or most important, so vengeful. "Please, please, let me welcome you. Shall I send my son around the corner for tea?"

"You'll do no such thing, Mr. Dalton," she said, and struck the rolled paper again with an emphatic crack. "I'm here for answers, not for tea. How dare you write what you did about my establishment, sir? To say my staff condones dishonesty, and that we give no care to our members' welfare? How dare you print such lies?"

"It's entertainment for the masses, Miss Penny, nothing more." Grinning like a nervous idiot, Dalton cleared a stack of papers from the only chair in the office and drew it forward like a peace offering. "The amusements of the gentry are always of interest to the rest of London."

Amariah glanced down at the offered chair with the same disdain she'd shown the tea from around the corner, and remained standing. "You make it sound so simple, Mr. Dalton. Don't you realize that in the process you risk ruining me?"

Sweat glistened on Dalton's broad, red forehead. "I assure you, Miss Penny, my only intention is to earn an honest living for myself and my family, and to entertain and edify my readers in the process."

"Since when are lies edifying, sir?" She swept the newspaper through the air, making Dalton instinctively jump to one side. "Penny House is not only a diverting haven for the best gentlemen, but also an establishment whose profits fund charities throughout London. If you hurt our profits, then you rob the food from orphans and widows and cripples who have no other source of sustenance. Is that diverting to you, Mr. Dalton? Is that amusing?"

Dalton drew himself up. "That's your business, Miss Penny. You can spend your profits where you may. But I do

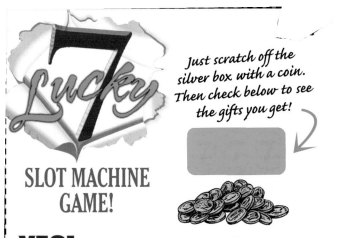

Just scratch off the silver box with a coin. Then check below to see the gifts you get!

SLOT MACHINE GAME!

YES! I have scratched off the silver box. Please send me the 2 FREE books and mystery gift for which I qualify. I understand I am under no obligation to purchase any books, as explained on the back of this card. I am over 18 years of age.

H7KI

Mrs/Miss/Ms/Mr _____ Initials _____

BLOCK CAPITALS PLEASE

Surname _____

Address _____

_____

Postcode _____

7	7	7	**Worth TWO FREE BOOKS plus a BONUS Mystery Gift!**
🍒	🍒	🍒	**Worth TWO FREE BOOKS!**
♣	♣	♣	**Worth ONE FREE BOOK!**
🔔	🔔	🍒	**TRY AGAIN!**

Visit us online at www.millsandboon.co.uk

NO STAMP NEEDED!

THE READER SERVICE™
FREE BOOK OFFER
FREEPOST CN81
CROYDON
CR9 3WZ

NO STAMP
NECESSARY
IF POSTED IN
THE U.K. OR N.I.

not see why my family and I must suffer so that you may play at Lady Bountiful."

Amariah sucked in her breath, a sign of her anger that Guilford recognized at once. But he'd give Dalton credit for bravery for calling her "Lady Bountiful" to her face.

"I am not asking you to suffer, Mr. Dalton," she said, biting off each word in turn. "Only that you never write another word about Penny House again."

"Not you, too!" Dalton cried, his blue eyes popping with outrage. "I won't do it, miss. That's the same as I told his grace. You can't make me obey you, and I won't do it."

Amariah wheeled around to face Guilford. "Is that true? Did you really ask him to stop writing about Penny House?"

"I did," Guilford said. "That's why I'm here. I saw what he'd printed about last night's, ah, festivities, and came at once to speak to him."

"Why, Guilford." He couldn't miss the change in her expression, the softness that was meant for him. It was the baby clothes all over again, and he freely basked in the warm admiration of her smile. "It's so early in the day, too. How *honorable* of you."

Guilford sighed, the truth now weighing upon him, too. "I asked Dalton, yes," he admitted. "Which is not to say he agreed."

"I didn't," Dalton said, folding his arms over his chest. "I can't agree to some half-cocked demand like that."

Amariah gasped, all that fine, warm admiration gone in a flash. "What are you saying, Guilford?" she asked suspiciously. "Whose side are you on?"

"Yours," Guilford said. "Penny House's. The side of truth and honor."

"Truth, my—ahem," Dalton said. "My readers would be

bored to tears if I printed only the gospel. I'd be ruined if word of it got out."

"But you'd also be ruined if I took you to court for libel." Guilford smiled at them both. "This is where we'd left off when you arrived, Amariah. Dalton had decided that he needed a new, more reliable informant for his news of Penny House. Someone with full freedom of the club, as it were."

Amariah's eyes narrowed. "If any of my staff dared be so untrustworthy as to betray the members of Penny House by selling their most private secrets, why, I'd dismiss him on the spot, and without references, too."

"I know," Guilford said solemnly. "Which is why I am going to be Dalton's new informant."

"You, your grace?" Dalton was shaking his head so hard that his jowls swung back and forth. "A peer providing information to the *Covent Garden Tattle?* Spilling the secrets of your own kind? How would I trust you, your grace? How would I know you weren't lying to me?"

Guilford smiled and smoothed his hand across the front of his shirt, relishing the irony of the printer's complaint. Perhaps it was better that Amariah was here to witness this after all. This way she could see for herself what he was doing for her, saving her club's reputation by putting his own on the line.

"How indeed, Dalton?" Guilford repeated. "I suppose you must rely upon my word of honor as a gentleman that I wouldn't mislead you."

"But you've already misled me!" cried Amariah, hitting him so hard on his arm with the rolled-up newspaper that he yelped. "How could you do such a thing, Guilford?"

Surprised, he stepped back, rubbing his arm. "Because it makes perfect sense, Amariah. What better way to make certain that only the truth is printed than to give this man exactly that?"

"But you'll be a spy!" she said, furling the paper more tightly in her hands. "Penny House is supposed to be a refuge to our membership, not a place where they'll be spied upon by a turncoat like you!"

"They'll never know," Guilford said, warily keeping his eye on the paper in her hand. She was usually so reasonable about Penny House; he'd never expected she'd react like this. "No one will, except for you and Dalton."

"I won't tell," the printer said quickly. "If his grace don't want it known, why, then I'll be as still as the grave. 'As observed by a celebrated gentleman of the town.' That'll make them guess, your grace, won't it?"

"They *will* guess!" Amariah cried, the plume on her hat quivering. "The gentlemen will be so busy suspecting and mistrusting one another that we'll have nothing but accusations and quarrels the whole night long!"

"Then I'll be as honest as can be, and let Dalton use my name," Guilford said. Why in blazes didn't she see the perfection in such a scheme? "Whatever works best for Penny House."

"And you believed this—this vile arrangement was for the best?"

He smiled, trying to reassure her. "All I want is to help you, Amariah. You must know that."

"Did I ever ask for your help, Guilford?" she said, the sparks fair flying from her eyes. "Did I ever ask for you to meddle in my affairs like this?"

"You didn't have to," he said, wishing he didn't sound so damned defensive. "I saw the paper myself."

"So did I," she retorted. "And I could have handled this perfectly well on my own!"

"No, you wouldn't, Miss Penny," Dalton said smugly,

clearly feeling victorious enough that he could afford a little of his usual cockiness. "Not at all. You're a lovely enough creature to gaze upon, my dear, but I'll listen to his grace."

Her lips tightened with frustration, her cheeks flushed.

"You see what you've done, Guilford," she said, her anger now tinged with a forlorn kind of resignation. "Why, if I were a gentleman, I'd challenge you to a duel myself!"

Dalton laughed. "There's your first tale, your grace," he jeered. "The infamous virago herself, calling out a gentleman to the field of honor!"

Oh, hell, thought Guilford. *Now even a worm like Dalton had heard about that.*

"Now I didn't say it, Amariah," Guilford said swiftly, holding his hands up before him. "You know I'd never call you anything like that."

Her gaze met his and held it for a long, wounded moment, a moment that made him feel like the greatest idiot in the world.

"No, Guilford, you wouldn't," she said slowly. "But then so long as you have your toadies, you don't have to, do you?"

"Amariah, please," Guilford began, but she was already through the door, nearly running for the hackney waiting for her.

"A virago indeed, your grace," Dalton said, still chuckling with his thumbs hooked into the straps of his apron. "You couldn't have coined a better word for a she-devil like that one, eh?"

"To hell with you, Dalton," Guilford thundered, his gaze never leaving Amariah. "Go straight to hell, and don't come back."

For what must have been the hundredth time since they'd opened for the evening, Amariah glanced up at the face of the tall clock in the front room: nearly midnight, and still no sign of him.

"Pratt, here," she called as the manager passed by her in the hall. "Tell me, if you please. Have you seen the Duke of Guilford yet tonight?"

"No, Miss Penny," Pratt said. "Not tonight."

"Thank you." She kept her expression emotionless, without any reaction. Yet was that sympathy she saw in Pratt's carefully composed face? Had he somehow sensed her disappointment, her misery, with how this day had gone? Was Pratt pitying her because Guilford had yet to show his handsome face at the club tonight?

Blast him for doing this to her!

"Good evening, my lord," she murmured, smiling warmly at a peer whose name and title seemed to have completely vanished from her head. That would be Guilford's fault, too, making her squander so much of her brain on his infuriating self that she kept forgetting the more important things she needed to remember. "How happy we are to have you joining us tonight!"

Lord Whatever-His-Name-Was smiled in return, brushing back the neat oiled wings of his hair from his temples.

"After last night's row, who'd want to keep away?" he said. He held up his right hand to show her his grazed and swollen knuckles, as proud as any prizefighter. "I haven't had such grand sport since I was sent down, Miss Penny, and that's a fact."

Her smile froze on her lips. "I should hope we won't have that kind of excitement here every night, my lord."

The gentleman winked. "I shall be ready whenever I'm called to the field of honor, Miss Penny."

"Indeed, my lord," she said, ushering him along. "You'll find several of your acquaintance already gathered at the whist tables."

She still could not believe that the dreadful things written about Penny House in the papers were only making membership and attendance more desirable, not less so. There'd been a score of men before this one who'd said exactly the same thing.

But that still didn't make Guilford's new role as the *Tattle*'s informant any more palatable to her. It wasn't just that she didn't trust Dalton, or what he'd do with the information that Guilford gave him. It troubled her that the duke seemed to believe he'd done a great and noble thing by volunteering to spy on his friends, and then report what he'd seen to the world. Worst of all, he seemed to believe she'd wanted him doing this—almost as if he'd *rescued* her.

Yet wasn't that exactly how she'd felt when he'd told her that he'd come to the *Tattle*'s office as soon as he'd awakened? He'd told her, and he'd smiled at her, and she'd felt exactly like a fairy princess saved from a fire-breathing dragon.

And then—oh, she wasn't sure what exactly had happened then, except that he'd joined with Dalton against her and against Penny House and against everything honorable and true that he claimed he'd respected, too. It felt like a pact with a devil, a pact that pointedly excluded her. No more being the princess rescued from the dragon, and no more believing that Guilford was smiling only for her, either. Likely he'd smile the same way at the dragon itself.

She turned away from the crowd in the front hall for a moment, rubbing at the tension knotted in her forehead. She wasn't sure if she wanted him to come to the club tonight or not, and if he did, she wasn't sure what she'd do, either. Ordering the footmen to keep him out would make for an even greater scandal, but if she let him in as usual, who knows what he'd decided to tell Dalton for tomorrow's *Tattle?*

If he came through that door now, would she smile at him as if nothing had happened, or should she give him only the chilliest of greetings?

And would she ever be able to trust him again?

With a disgruntled sigh, Lady Frances Carroll poured fresh tea into Guilford's cup. She was his oldest and most respectable sister, which made her entitled to voice her disapproval however and whenever she deemed necessary, including now.

"Truly, Guilford, you must be the most vexing brother in all Christendom," she said, the powder from her hair dusting across her velvet-covered shoulders as she shook her head. "For weeks, you've sent me nothing but empty excuses and regrets, and when finally you do deign to visit me instead of your clubs or your mistresses, I can scarce get an interesting word out of you."

"I don't have 'mistresses,' Fan," Guilford said wearily, wishing that he'd sent one more regret tonight instead of being dutiful. "I cull the herd frequently, to keep things interesting. In fact, at present I haven't a single one in the paddock."

"They're not cattle, Guilford," Frances said sternly. "You are being uncharacteristically disrespectful. They may be a low sort of female, not quality, no, but they're not dumb beasts."

"You say that only because you've never met any of them." Now Guilford sighed, too, resting his chin in his hand as he stared down at the steam rising from the tea he did not want. "If you had, you'd have an entirely different notion of disrespect."

His sister shuddered, and looked down her celebrated nose. "Then it's a good thing I haven't."

"True enough." He sighed again. Why in blazes had he

come here tonight, anyway? Not that he didn't appreciate Fan or her family, but coming to her house had more to do with not going to Penny House than with his sister. He wasn't exactly avoiding seeing Amariah. It was just that, after this morning in the *Tattle*'s offices, he hadn't the slightest idea of what to say to her when she came into sight.

"So what is this one's name, Guilford?"

He started, and blinked. "This one what, Fan?"

"The new lady-bird." She smiled shrewdly, studying him with the same knowing intensity as a philosopher with an insect. "I know you, Guilford, and I know you are incapable of living without at least one woman in your life, no matter how much you deny it."

"She's not a lady-bird," Guilford said, on the defense. "You can't lump her in with all the others."

Frances sat back in her chair, her hands clasped in her lap.

"Well, good!" she declared happily. "Then you have finally found a lady worthy of yourself, and your rank! A match at last, and high time, too! And here I'd been worrying over those nasty rumors about you and that creature from the gaming hell!"

Guilford frowned. "She's not a 'creature,' Fan. She's Miss Amariah Penny, and though she wouldn't fit your requirements for a lady, she's more noble than most of the noblemen I know."

His sister's happiness popped like a balloon. "Oh, Guilford. Not again! Here I thought I might dare to hope for a summer wedding, and an heir nine months after, the way that Mother and Father would have wished!"

"Miss Penny's not like the others, Fan," he said, trying, even though he knew his sister would never understand. "She's the daughter of a country vicar."

"A vicar's daughter?" Frances's expression turned as sour as if she'd stuffed every lemon wedge on the tea plate into her mouth at once. "And yet she runs a gambling house?"

"She inherited it, with her sisters," he said, warming to his subject. "They turn all their profits to charity, you see. She's good and kind, but she has spirit, too, and wit. She entertains me no end."

"I suppose she's beautiful, too?"

"Exceptionally so," Guilford said, smiling as he thought of Amariah's many qualities. "She has the most glorious red-gold hair, and bright blue eyes, and—"

"No title, no fortune, no future." Frances sighed again. "My only consolation is that she'll soon go the way of all the others."

"If she does," he said, remembering the wounded look on her face when she'd fled this morning, "then it will be her doing, and not mine."

"Hers!" Frances scoffed. "Why, it's never the woman's doing! What woman would ever toss you onto the rubbish heap?"

"Miss Penny would," he said, "if she thought I deserved it."

He stopped, realizing what he'd just said. Since when had he become a coward around women, anyway? When had he begun worrying what he deserved or didn't from them? Not even that infernal wager would matter compared to this. He should be the one in charge. If he cared as much about Amariah as he was now claiming to Frances, then he owed it to himself to try to patch things up between them. If she'd felt he'd wounded her somehow—which he didn't think he had—why, then, he'd just have to set her to rights. Hiding himself away here at his sister's house wasn't going to accomplish anything.

"Miss Penny, Miss Penny," Frances said with renewed dismay. "I think you should treat this Miss Penny exactly as she deserves."

"You are right, Fan," he said, rising from his chair to kiss his sister on the cheek. By Penny House's hours, the night was still young, and he could be there in next to no time. "Absolutely, indisputably right. I mean to treat Miss Penny exactly as she deserves, and as soon as possible, too."

Slowly Amariah climbed the stairs to her quarters on the top floor, leaning heavily on the banister. Her head hurt so much that the pain nearly blinded her, making her wince at the brightness of the candles and the loudness of the men's voices all around her. She'd had the apothecary make her a special draft to ease the headache and nausea the last time she'd been stricken, and she hoped now it would work for her, as well.

If either of her sisters had been here, she would have had one of them take her place at the door hours ago, and retreated upstairs to her bed. But she was the only Penny sister at Penny House, and considering all that had happened in the last few nights, she could not afford to disappear, no matter how ill she might feel.

She paused at the stop of the stairs, surprised to find no guard at his usual post, keeping her private quarters private. Then she remembered that last night she'd had Pratt shift the guard downstairs to the hazard room as a reinforcement. Well, no matter, she thought; there'd never been any trouble this far upstairs before, and besides, she was past caring.

She unlocked the door with one of the keys she always wore, then moved through the apartments to her bedchamber without bothering to light a candlestick, not wanting even that much more brightness to hurt her poor head. She was familiar enough with the shadowy rooms and furniture that she needed only the light that came from the banked coals in the grate, and the moonlight filtering through the curtained windows.

She found the draft in the drawer of her dressing table, mixed it with water from the pitcher on the washstand and drank it down, pinching her nose against the smell as the apothecary had instructed. Still the taste was awful, and with her eyes squeezed shut she gasped and shuddered, fighting with her stomach to keep down the vile concoction. She swallowed, then swallowed again, and took a deep breath. She'd be all right. She had to be, for she'd no real choice. She splashed water on her face, repinned the plume in her hair, then headed back toward the staircase.

In the doorway between her bedchamber and the parlor that served as both drawing and dining room, she stopped, holding her breath. She hadn't locked the door when she'd come inside, had she? Something wasn't right. Something was different: something was *wrong*.

She could sense it, someone there in the shadowy shapes that had suddenly ceased to be so familiar. That could be a footfall, the shuffle of a shoe across the bare floor. Amariah didn't move, her ears straining for another clue. In the distance below, she could hear the usual voices from the club, the usual laughter, carrying on as if nothing was amiss.

"Who's there?" she demanded hoarsely. "What do you want?"

No answer, not that she expected any. But whoever it was now realized that she was in the same room, and was holding his—or her—breath, too.

What if this were the man who'd thrown the note through the kitchen window, what if he'd come now to carry out his threat against her?

Slowly Amariah reached to her left, groping until she found the piecrust edging of a small mahogany table. She slid her fingers along the rippling wood until she found the heavy pewter candlestick that she knew would be there. She slipped the tall wax candle free and left it on the table, then brandished the candlestick in both hands. She'd never considered it as a weapon before, but now the weight of the pewter and the heavy, old-fashioned knurls and flourishes were oddly comforting.

"Whoever you are, you must go," she ordered with more confidence. "You're trespassing, and you don't belong here. Go, go now!"

She stepped away from the security of the table and into the middle of the room, the candlestick clutched tightly in her hands.

"Go *on*, you villain!" she shouted. "Go now, now, before I—"

She saw the shadow, a half second of darker darkness, and then she was being knocked sideways, gasping from surprise and hitting the floor hard. She tried to swing the candlestick and found only empty air, tried to struggle back to her feet and her legs tangled in her skirts.

She managed to roll to her knees and pushed herself up, only to be clipped across the side of her head and sent sprawling across the floor again, the wind knocked from her chest. Gasping for breath where she lay, she could see only her attacker's legs, thick ankles in stockings and heavy shoes. Somehow she still held the candlestick in one hand, and with her last effort she swung it at the man's ankles.

The man swore, and kicked hard at Amariah. Shards of pain splintered through her arm, driving all other thoughts from her head. Whimpering, she rolled away from him, clutching her arm and curling into a ball of agony.

Light sliced across the room from the open door, and she closed her eyes and turned her head to block it out. She felt the man's hand on her shoulder, and weakly she tried to pull away.

"Look at me, sweetheart," the man ordered in a hoarse, urgent whisper. "Look at me!"

She knew that voice; she knew the man. With a broken sob, she turned her face toward his, and opened her eyes.

Chapter Nine

"Wiggle your fingers for me," Guilford said, crouching beside her chair. "Please. For me."

Amariah's mouth crumpled, and he was sure she'd begin to weep again. By the candlelight, her face was swollen from crying and from the bruise that was already blossoming on her temple. Her hair was tangled and loose and her gown was torn, but what worried Guilford was that she'd seemingly lost her will, her fight—the one part of her that most made her Amariah.

What would have happened if he hadn't come when he did? Damnation, what if he hadn't been in time to save her?

"I don't think I can do it," she whispered miserably, still cradling her forearm in her other hand. "It will hurt."

"Try," he urged. "If you can't do it, then the bone's broken for certain, and I'm calling the surgeon whether you agree to it or not."

"No!" she cried. "I told you, Guilford! A surgeon will tell the constable, and I can't have that!"

"Then do this," he said gently. "Wiggle your fingers, and prove to me you're as fine as you claim."

She took a deep breath and slowly straightened her arm.

In ugly contrast to her delicate puffed sleeve, her forearm was swollen and red where she'd said the man had kicked her, and Guilford couldn't help muttering another oath to himself. He'd make sure the man who'd done this to her would pay for her suffering, and pay handsomely.

"Show me, Amariah," he coaxed. "If any woman's brave enough to do this, it's you."

That made her give him a tremulous smile through her pain. She concentrated on her hand, and cautiously began to move her fingers, one at a time as if she were playing a pianoforte.

"Can you twist your wrist, too?" he asked. "Carefully now, nothing sudden."

She took another deep breath, and turned her wrist back and forth, curling and uncurling her fingers to be sure.

"There you are," he said, relieved. "I'm no surgeon, but odds are if you can do that, then the bone's not broken."

"I told you." She lowered her arm, wincing. "But it still hurts, Guilford. It hurts like—like Hades."

"I'm sure it does." He rose, going to the table to pour her a glass of brandy from the decanter. "Here, drink this. I won't send for a surgeon, but I will call for someone in the kitchen to bring you ice. They will have ice, won't they?"

She sighed forlornly. "Of course we do. Letty uses it to chill the jellies and charlottes, and to put around the fish."

"You'll use it to help with the swelling." After he rang for the kitchen, he lit three more candles for light, and began looking around the room. He meant to speak to Pratt, too, but not until she'd had time to calm herself. "Could this have been the same cowardly bastard who threatened you in that note?"

"I'd thought of that myself," she said, looking down so he wouldn't see the fear she knew must be in her eyes. "But this man didn't come here to find me. He would have…followed me into the bedchamber if he had. He only came after me after I'd swung the candlestick first."

Guilford's expression was black. "So you have no notion of who the man might be?"

"None," she said unhappily. "All I saw of him were his feet, and that in the dark. He wore shoes with plain oval buckles and thread stockings, so he must have been either a footman, or a gentleman."

"A small start." Very small indeed, considering how that description fit nearly every man in Penny House that night. The stairs had been empty when he'd come up himself, meaning that the man had already either fled the house or blended unnoticed back among the others. "I know you keep these rooms locked. He must have had a copy of the key, or—"

"I—I'd left the door open," she admitted, looking down into the glass of brandy. "I only meant to stay long enough to take a draft because my head ached, and I didn't bother to lock it. And before you ask, the guard on the landing wasn't there, either, since I'd sent him to help watch in the hazard room. I was wrong and I was careless, and I'm sorry, Guilford, but that's the truth."

"I'm sorry, too, but only because you had to suffer." He sighed, wishing she hadn't been so dangerously careless, and held the candlestick over her desk. "Look here. You didn't leave it like this, did you?"

"Of course not!" she exclaimed, her face more somber as she surveyed her usually neat desk. The top was covered with papers dumped from their files, with letters and open ledgers scattered haphazardly over the top. "What was he hunting for, I wonder?"

"Money? Gold?"

She shook her head, her gaze immediately shifting to a

painting of a bucolic landscape on the wall. So that was where the club's strongbox must be hidden into the wall, not that he'd call her on it now.

"Where do you keep the promissory notes from wagers?" he asked instead. "He could have been looking for one of those, hoping to steal away the evidence of some ruinous loss."

Again she shook her head. "The promissory notes are all kept with the coins and banknotes," she said, "and even so, everything's taken to the bank by Pratt with two guards with guns each morning. Most times there's very little of value here."

"Value or not, there was something the bastard wanted." In a way, Guilford was glad that robbery seemed to be the man's motive, and that the harm to Amariah had been more incidental than planned. "Drink the brandy. It will help you sleep. In the morning, you can sort through this mess and see if anything's missing. Then, too, you can decide what to do next."

"I told you. I've already decided. I want no constable, no scandal, no—"

"You ignored the brick through your kitchen window, too."

"That was entirely different!" Yet the fear in her eyes proved she'd already thought the same. "There's no connection at all!"

"You don't know that for fact, Amariah," he said. "It could be the same man who—enter!" Guilford paused to beckon the servant to the door.

A drab little scullery maid came into the room, her gaze beneath her white cap darting from Amariah to Guildord and back again.

"Fetch us a wide dish of ice at once," Guilford said. "Miss Penny slipped on the stair and hurt her arm, and needs the ice to soothe it."

The girl bobbed her curtsy, and hurried off to obey.

"Pratt will be here as soon as he learns of that," Amariah said miserably, and he could hear the tears returning to her voice. "He knows everything that happens in this house, and he won't be as easily fooled. Oh, Guilford, what am I to do? Not just with Pratt, but with all this—mess?"

"Pratt doesn't have to see any of this until morning, not if you don't wish it," he said, rejoining her. Tomorrow he'd also make sure Pratt sent for the constable, but she didn't have to think about that now. "He already knows you weren't feeling well. Take to your bed. Can you undress yourself, or do you need help?"

She narrowed her eyes at him. "I can manage well enough, Guilford."

"Ah, and here I was ready to play your abigail!" He grinned and winked, hoping to make her smile back, but she was already trying stiffly to stand on her own.

Quickly he slipped his arm around her waist to support her, feeling how gratefully she leaned into him as he guided her into her bedchamber. "You *are* hurt, Amariah. I'm calling the surgeon."

"No, you're not," she said, more forcefully than she'd said anything else. "And you won't speak a word of this to Dalton, either. If I read it in the *Tattle,* so help me, I'll come for your head myself."

"That would almost be worth it," he said. "Where's your night rail?"

"In the tall chest. There's a yellow wrapper beside it. You promise you won't tell Pratt tonight?"

"Tonight, no." He found the soft linen gown, trying hard to be noble and not to imagine her body inside it. "But tomorrow you must do it."

"I will," she said, taking the gown. "There's Deborah at the door with the ice."

"I'll get it." He watched her standing there, wondering how in blazes she was going to get herself out of the gown that buttoned up the back and into the night rail when she kept holding one arm like a wounded bird. "I can send the girl to help you if you—"

"No," she said, trying to square her shoulders in the old familiar way. "I'll be fine. Now shut that door, if you please, and let me dress in peace."

Most likely she *would* be fine, he thought as he went to take the ice from the maid. There was a thin line between stubbornness and will, but for tonight it was going to be all will that saw her through this. She was a strong woman, as strong as they came, and he admired her for it. But tomorrow, she'd have to be strong enough to admit that she needed help, and summon the constable. This wasn't just scandal; this was a crime. Though Guilford doubted the intruder would be caught, at least she'd have sent the message that she'd taken him seriously.

The little maid was waiting in the hall, holding a wide wooden bowl filled with chipped ice and two kitchen cloths folded over her arm.

"Thank you, lass," he said, taking it from her. "That will be all."

"Beggin' pardon, y'grace," the girl said, her words shaking with nervousness, "but Mr. Pratt said t' make sure Miss Penny don't need nothing more. For her arm, that is."

"Thank Mr. Pratt for his concern," he said, "but all Miss Penny needs now is to rest."

The girl nodded and curtsyed—what else could she do, really?—and fled, leaving Guilford with the ice. It was clear that the ever-discreet Pratt must suspect something else more romantic was occurring between him and Amariah, or he would have come marching up here himself. Well, let Pratt think what he would for now, and let Amariah sleep in peace. There'd be plenty of time to set the manager straight in the morning.

He shrugged out of his coat and tossed it onto a chair before he tapped on the bedchamber door. "Ready to receive company, Miss Penny?"

"Not yet, Guilford," she called. "In a *moment*."

Even through the door he could hear the frustration in her voice, and guessed how much she must be struggling both with her clothing and her pride. Yet he waited, knowing that, for her sake, he needed to be patient. By the time she finally called him to open the door, the ice in the wooden bowl had begun to melt into a sloppy puddle.

She was sitting on the edge of her bed in the night rail, the discarded blue gown folded over the back of a chair with surprising neatness. But instead of wearing the yellow wrapper with its narrow buttoned sleeves, she'd pulled the coverlet from the bed over her shoulders like a cape, and the look in her eyes dared him to notice.

"How does your arm feel now?" he asked, the safest question he could consider.

"Well enough." She was pale beneath her coppery hair, her face taut with pain and exhaustion, and he still couldn't fathom how she'd been able to undress herself. "Look at my poor arm! I'll have to wear long gloves for a month to stop everyone from gawking."

"One winter when I was a boy, I toppled from my horse and twisted my ankle." He pulled a small table over to where she was sitting, and set the bowl of ice on it. "Father and his physician insisted I sit with my foot in a bucket of snow. My foot turned bright red and I swore like a sailor because of the cold, but it did help keep down the swelling. Now it's your turn."

"At least I won't swear." She pushed the coverlet back from her elbow, leaned forward, and gingerly placed her arm into the ice. She didn't swear, but from the way she grimaced, he suspected she was coming awfully close.

"This had best help," she said through gritted teeth. "I feel like a fillet of cold salmon."

He laughed softly. "It will feel better after a while. I promise."

"I'll hold you to that, Guilford." She sighed, not entirely convinced. "And in turn I promise not to tell your friends that his grace has had to play my nursemaid."

"I won't quarrel with that." It did feel strange to be waiting on someone else. From the cradle onward, peers never did, as a rule. His sister would be mortified.

"I didn't think you would." Her mouth twisted in a wry little smile. "Might I ask you to do one last little favor for me?"

"Name it," he said, feeling an unfamiliar little jolt of joy that she was asking him. Whatever the favor was, he'd do it for her.

"Ah, you're such a fine gallant, Guilford, that I feel like a perfect fool." She looked back down at her arm, the wry smile turning charmingly sheepish. "If you don't wish to do this, then I'll understand entirely, but—would you please brush my hair for me?"

"Oh, sweetheart, of course," he said, secretly relieved that her request was such an easy one. He rolled back the sleeves of his shirt, to show he was ready to work. "That's not a favor, but a pleasure."

Dubious, she turned to watch him. "You might say otherwise once you've begun. My hair snarls into a mare's nest at next to nothing. If I don't brush it out before I go to bed, it's all knots in the morning."

"I'll be as adept as any French coiffeur." He took the heavy tortoiseshell brush from her dressing table and came to sit beside her. "But tell me if I pull too hard, mind?"

She'd stiffened, her shoulders tight, not quite trusting him. "You'll have to pull the pins out first. Most have fallen out, but I can still feel a few left."

"I remember watching my sisters and mother have their hair dressed for a ball, the season my oldest sister, Frances, first came out," he said, gently feeling for the pins in the thick, tangled curls. "I couldn't have been more than eight or nine, to be allowed to watch. The style then was for huge, stiffened clouds of hair, and as a treat Mother had hired the most fashionable hairdresser, an Italian named Fortebello. One by one, like a parade, he gave the females in my family towering puffballs of powder-dusted hair, draped with huge bows and strands of false pearls. They were enchanted by the effect, but I thought they looked like dandelion heads, and so I told my sisters."

She laughed, relaxing. "That was most unkind of you."

"It was the truth," he said. "I think that's the last of the pins."

She shook her head. "Don't be so confident. The worst is still before you. But if you begin brushing from the ends and don't rush, you'll have no trouble."

"So little faith, Miss Penny," he said, but she was probably right. Her hair *was* tangled, the once-artfully curled lovelocks snarled into knots. Tentatively he began as she'd advised, brushing from the ends upward, and to his relief the snarls began to slip free. By the light of the single candle, her hair glowed like fire, falling over his bare arms. He'd lost all notion of the time, yet he could still hear horses and carriages and voices rising from the street below.

"Only once before have you spoken to me of your family," she said, "and now you've done it twice in the last quarter hour."

"I suppose I don't because they're not terribly interesting to anyone else but us," he admitted. "I've no dark secrets or terrible tragedies in my childhood. My parents were as fond of us as we were of them. No one was ill, in debt, or away at war. It was a fine, comforting way to be a boy, but likely most boring to anyone else."

"I like hearing about it," she said, her voice both husky and drowsy. "It's not boring in the least, not to me."

"Then I must not be telling it the right way," he said, chuckling. "I must be exaggerating for dramatic effect."

He could feel the tension easing from her, too, her head slipping back toward his chest as he pulled the brush through her hair. The knots and tangles were gone now, yet he didn't stop. He could smell her fragrance, lilacs and lavender mingled with her own scent, and as she relaxed, her grip on the coverlet had loosened, too, letting the woolen cloth and the linen night rail slide from her bare shoulders. Her skin fascinated him, as pale and luminous as a South Sea pearl, and he longed to run his fingers along it, lightly, to see if it was as velvety soft as he'd guessed it must be.

Nothing boring here, that was certain.

She sighed, and shifted her arm in the bowl, the remaining chunks of ice clicking together in the melted water. "I'm numb," she said. "How much longer must I keep this here?"

"As long as you can bear it," he said. "As long as you wish to."

If it were his decision, he could stay here for all eternity. She was drowsy and soft and warm and achingly vulnerable, and he'd no wish at all to let her go. Dressed in a wool coverlet, a plain linen night rail and a dish of ice water, she was tempting him far more than all the other women in his past who had relied upon silk and French lace. With her here in the circle of his arms, he felt he could protect her, keep her safe, in the way that he hadn't earlier. It was similar in a way to how he'd felt when he'd given the groom's job to Billy Fox, a good, useful feeling. What he felt now was like that, only better, because the one he was rescuing was Amariah.

She pulled her arm from the ice, blotting it dry with one of the kitchen cloths, then sighed and leaned back a little farther so she was nestled against his chest.

"I have a confession to make, Guilford," she whispered. "I was not entirely truthful with you."

"No?" Damnation, what was she about to tell him? That she was married, or that the man who'd struck her was her lover, or something else a thousand times worse?

"No." She sighed again, her wistfulness palpable. "When I said I'd only one favor to ask of you, I wasn't telling the truth. I've one more."

He dropped the brush on the bed beside him, linking his arms around her. "Only one?"

"Only one," she said, her voice dropping to a whisper. "And you can refuse this one, too. I know I'm being a weakling coward, and too tired to think straight. I should be brave, but after what happened earlier, Guilford, I—I'd be most grateful if you'd stay and keep me company until morning."

"You wish me to stay here with you?" he asked, not believing what he'd just heard, or how much he wanted to believe it was true.

"Yes." She put so much sadness into the single word that he was sure she believed he was going to refuse. "I do not like to admit it, but I—I'm frightened, Guilford. There, I've said it. I'm frightened, and I don't want to be alone."

"Then of course I'll stay." He brushed his lips across the top of her hair, so lightly that she wouldn't realize it. How had she become so impossibly dear to him? Did he really have to have come this close to losing her to realize he couldn't imagine her not in his life? "What kind of friend would I be if I did otherwise?"

"Thank you," she whispered, curling closer against him. "Thank you."

He drew her close and held her, just held her, until she closed her eyes and her breathing slowed, and he knew she slept. Then he held her still, long after the candle had guttered out, long after the street outside had quieted, until he slept, too.

Exhausted, Westbrook sat braced in the corner of the swaying carriage, his hat pulled low over his eyes while he wondered vaguely if he'd be sick again here with Stanton before he reached home. It was the oversweet perfume of that yellow-haired whore that had made him retch the first time, that and the cheap Madeira passed off by Mrs. Poynton as the first-rate smuggled stuff. If he'd any sense, he would have spewed it in her face as a lesson, and left her and her whores with the reckoning unpaid.

But a gentleman had to present a proper face to the world, and squabbling with the keepers of overpriced brothels didn't qualify as polishing his reputation. Besides, that yellow-haired whore had the most cunning tongue imaginable, and having both her and the little French doxie bouncing together with him on the same bed had made the night worth the ticket.

Whores never failed him the way gaming did. Westbrook couldn't forget that. At Mrs. Poynton's, he always won. And when word of how he'd satisfied both whores made the rounds among his friends tomorrow, why, then, no one would ask about how he'd fared at Penny House, or even if he'd been there at all when—

"My God, Westbrook, look at that!" Stanton exclaimed, kicking his leg to get his attention. "Wake up, and tell me I'm not dreaming!"

Without lifting his hat, Westbrook kicked him back. "Why the hell should I do anything you say? Why should I care, anyway?"

"Because he won," Stanton said, and the note of undeniable envy in his voice finally caught Westbrook's interest. "Damn Guilford, he's won."

"Guilford?" That was enough for Westbrook to sit upright, squinting as he pushed his hat back from his eyes. "What's that lucky bastard won now?"

It was nearly dawn, and he could see they were on St. James Street, not far from the Square. They weren't far from Penny House, either, not that Westbrook wanted to be going back there any time soon. The last yawning linkboys were dousing their lights and trudging home, while the earliest milkmaids from the country were carrying the milk cans to their first deliveries.

But it wasn't either the linkboys or the milkmaids that Stanton was pointing to.

"Slow, I say, slow!" he shouted at the driver, thumping on the roof of the carriage. "Look there, Westbrook. Am I blind, or isn't that Guilford's blue chaise, standing in the selfsame place at the curb as it was when we left for Mrs. Poynton's?"

Westbrook leaned from the window to stare at the chaise with the sleepy driver and footman dozing on the box, forcing his bleary eyes to focus on the gold-picked arms painted on the chaise's door. "It's Guilford's, all right. Not that it matters to me."

Stanton reached out and shoved him hard. "Don't be a damned idiot, Westbrook! We saw Guilford arrive just before we left, and we saw him go upstairs and never come back down. We never did see the Penny woman—recall how her people told us she wasn't well, and had retired to her rooms?"

"What of it?" Westbrook shrugged elaborately, as if he didn't care, as if his mouth weren't dry and his heart thumping. He didn't want to think of a man as intelligent as Guilford upstairs with Amariah Penny, asking her questions, putting facts together.

He didn't want to think of them together at all.

"Because of the wager," Stanton said morosely. "I was so blasted sure not even Guilford could bed the virago that we'd made a little wager of five hundred pounds that he couldn't do it in a fortnight. A bloody *fortnight!* He scarcely took a week to get between her legs, and now he'll expect me to pay! You can afford to drop that kind of money easy as your handkerchief, but I cannot."

Still Westbrook stared at the chaise, unwilling to let Stanton see the guilt that must surely be on his face. "Just because his chaise is here doesn't mean he's in her bed, or even inside the house. He could've left, and come back. He could be in one of these other houses, too."

"That's true." Stanton nodded, thinking. "I did ask for proof, real proof. For once you're right, Westbrook. The chaise alone doesn't mean a blasted thing, any more than him being wherever she isn't."

"They say her rooms are kept closer than the Tower of don," Westbrook agreed, reassuring himself as muc ton. "Everything's under lock and key. How w get to her, anyway? It's not as if a woman like that would be slipping him the key with a kiss."

"True, all true," Stanton said, and rapped on the carriage's roof to continue. "The wager's not done until Guilford shows me the proof."

Westbrook nodded eagerly. "You don't even have proof that anyone else was in those rooms last night except the Penny woman herself."

But Stanton wasn't really listening, his thoughts elsewhere as he slumped back against the squabs.

"I should've known better than to make such a wager with Guilford," he said with a sigh. "It's not enough that the women all tumble for him, and always have. The man's a duke, a peer, as rich as Croesus himself. There's no justice to it."

Now Westbrook sighed, too, drumming his fingers absently on the crown of his hat, sitting on the seat beside him. Everything went Guilford's way. Hadn't Guilford humiliated him in the street before Penny House, then again over the duel he should have fought with that damned Scots cheat? But that was all: he remembered how Amariah Penny looked at Guilford, melting-soft like butter in the sun, and how every time Guilford sat down at the table to play, luck was on his shoulder, no matter what the game.

Stanton was right. There was no justice. Luck was never Westbrook's friend, the whores only moaned when he'd paid their mistress first, and for all of her false, fawning pledges of admiration, Amariah Penny still looked over his head as if he weren't there.

But even justice could be changed if one were clever enough, and luck with it. He had proved that tonight, hadn't he? Westbrook rubbed his hand over his mouth, hiding his smile. Stanton could weep and whinge all he wanted. But *he* had gone and changed his bad fortune to good, and he'd certainly made his own justice, not just for him, but for Guilford and Amariah Penny, too.

The next time when he sat down at the hazard table, maybe luck would come to his shoulder instead.

It was the snoring that finally woke her.

Amariah lay curled on her side, still halfway between being asleep and awake. She wasn't ready to pull herself the rest of the way into the day, not just yet. Every part of her seemed weary and aching, and begging for more rest, and with a sigh she turned her face into her pillow, trying to blot out the sunlight that streamed into her bedchamber.

But she couldn't blot out the snore: a great, deep, rumbling, male snore, the kind she hadn't heard since Father had died.

The kind of snore she'd never heard in her own bed, and with a start she was instantly awake. She pushed herself up, grimacing at how much it hurt, and turned toward the snorer.

"Guilford!" she exclaimed in a horrified whisper, pulling the coverlet tightly around her shoulders. "Oh, merciful heavens, what are you doing here in my *bed?*"

He frowned, and grumbled, and stopped snoring, but he didn't exactly awake. He wasn't technically in her bed, either, but lying on top of it. His neckcloth was gone, his cuffs rolled back, and the top buttons of his shirt were undone; his coat was on the floor and his shoes kicked off somewhere else, but otherwise he was still as decently dressed as any gentleman ever was at this hour. His waistcoat was still buttoned, as were— most merciful heavens of all—his breeches, and even the gold chain of his watch was draped elegantly across his belly.

"Guilford, wake up!" she whispered again, with more urgency than horror. She began to reach out to shake him, and whimpered. Her forearm ached, a dull, constant ache, with a fearsome, mottled bruise like an oversized plum between her wrist and her elbow. In a rush she remembered last night— how she'd tried to stop the intruder, but he'd struck her instead, how frightened she'd been, how Guilford had come to her rescue when she'd needed him most.

And how nothing untoward had happened between them in this bed.

She frowned down at him, lying on his back with his head settled quite blissfully on her second pillow. His dark hair was tousled against the white linen, and his beard had grown overnight, a peppery shadow over his mouth and along his jaw. He looked different when he was asleep. Younger, more boyish, less wily and knowing and flirtatious, which, she supposed, meant he looked less like the Guilford she'd always known before last night.

But then that Guilford wouldn't have brushed her hair for her, or tended her with the gentleness she'd needed. For as long as she could remember, she'd been the one who'd taken care of others, but last night, he'd been the one looking after her, and she'd liked it. She'd liked *him,* too, for understanding her. This new version of Guilford had smiled, and told her stories of his boyhood to help keep her fears at bay, and held her until she'd fallen asleep. This must be what mornings were like for her sisters, waking with their husbands beside them: peaceful and protected and secure.

Not that she'd any right to think of the man beside her in that way. He'd really been quite nice, this other Guilford, and she sighed wistfully. It was hardly his fault that her own foolish heart longed for more from him, more that she'd no right to expect and he'd no inclination to give. What a pity it was that either version of him would still ruin her reputation and Penny House's with it if he were discovered here in her bed.

With her left hand, she took his shoulder and lightly shook him. "Guilford, please. You must wake now. Guilford!"

With a little snort he finally woke, rubbing his hands over his face. He opened first one eye, then the other, saw her, and smiled.

"Amariah," he said, his voice thick and groggy. "How wondrous fair you are in the morning!"

"No, Guilford, please, we've no time for that," she said, sitting back on her heels. "It's late, and you must go."

He pushed himself up on his elbows, his hair sticking up every which way from his head and his smile irresistibly sleepy. "How is your arm, sweetheart?"

"Ugly," she said, "but better. Guilford, I mean it. You must go, now, before anyone realizes you're here."

"So soon?" He reached down to the front of his waistcoat and drew his watch from the pocket. "It's not even noon. The club won't open for hours and hours yet. Surely no one's about yet to see me one way or the other."

"Noon!" She scrambled from the bed and grabbed the little brass clock that sat on her bedside table. "Oh, Guilford, it's past eleven! The maids will have already swept out the public rooms and cleaned all the grates, and everyone in the kitchen will be working on the food for tonight!"

"So they'll all be too busy to notice me," he said. "Or you with me."

"No, no, no!" she cried with growing despair. "What it means is that every last one of them has noticed that I've not yet come downstairs. It means that they're all whispering and guessing and making jests, and because Deborah saw you here last night, they'll say you're the reason!"

"Then they'll be entirely right." He leaned forward, frowning a bit as he looked higher on her face. "The bruise on your temple looks ugly, too. Come here so I can see it properly."

"They won't be right at all." She smoothed her hair back from the bruise on her temple so he could see it better. "Is this truly that bad? I can wear gloves over my arm, but I've never worn paint on my face in my life."

"You may have to tonight. Come here, closer." He took her jaw in his fingers, holding her face steady. "You can still have a surgeon look at that, you know."

"All he'd do is try to bleed me, and I won't have that." She didn't move, more anxious for his opinion than she wanted to admit. "I could put ice on it, too. You said that would help."

"The swelling, yes, but not the purple." The shadow of his beard made his smile seem more rakish. "Most women don't mind having their names linked with mine."

"I'm not most women," she said, but she didn't pull her chin free of his hand. "Especially not 'most women' linked to you."

"I've noticed," he said softly, "and I approve of your difference."

She sniffed, and at last began to draw back, away from him.

"Wait," he said, slipping his palm over the curve of her cheek to bring her back. "I'm glad you're better this morning. Being here with you gave me mountains of time to consider how precious you are to me, Amariah. I've never known any other woman like you, nor likely will I."

"You—you just don't look in the right places," she whispered.

"What, under the willows and hedgerows?" he asked. "When I think of what happened to you last night, and what could have—"

"But it didn't," she said, feeling oddly breathless. She'd never seen him smile quite like this before, as if nothing else mattered to him except for her. "It's over, Guilford, done."

"No, it's not," he said, his face coming closer to hers. "I'd say it's only begun."

He kissed her, and she realized she'd been expecting him to kiss her ever since he'd found her in the dark last night. She kissed him hungrily in return, as if she needed this reassurance, too, of life, of pleasure, of his desire for her and hers for him. For these few minutes, she could put aside the burden of her responsibilities, and simply be herself.

She slanted her head to deepen the kiss, letting her hair fall around them. She liked how he held her face, his fingers strong yet his touch so light, and she savored the wicked pleasure of kissing him here, on her bed. His hand slid down from her jaw to her shoulder, easing beneath the coverlet, beneath the loose neckline of her night rail, lower, lower.

When he finally found her breast, she realized she'd been holding her breath with anticipation, and when his fingers caressed her bare flesh, her nipple tightened at once. Her shuddering sigh of pleasure and joy vibrated between their mouths. Mindful of her bruised arm, he still found a way to turn her and ease her back against the pillows, his body settling over hers as if it had always belonged there, as if—

"Guilford, listen, someone's at the door!" She tried to wriggle free, wincing as she bumped her arm against his back. "Most likely it's Deborah with my breakfast tea. I have to answer."

"No, you don't," he said, feathering kisses down her throat. "You're the mistress of Penny House. You don't have to answer to anyone, especially not some little maid with your tea."

"But I do, for exactly that reason," she said, trying to ignore the persuasive chills those feathery kisses were giving her. "Every question comes to me, and not even Deborah will go away until I answer."

He sighed, rolling to one side. "Then sack them all," he said. "They deserve it, and you deserve me."

"Neither of us deserve this," she muttered, her bare feet landing clumsily on the floor. The knock came again, more insistent, and she once again gathered the coverlet around her. "If I shut the door, will you promise to stay in here until I send them away?"

"I've hidden from husbands and fathers and a vengeful brother or two, but never from a pot of breakfast tea." He grinned, but there was something bittersweet in his eyes as he watched her leave. "Hurry back, love. Please."

She smiled and closed the door, her body tremulous and on edge from his caresses, her heart racing with what he'd just said. *Hurry back, love.* Had he meant that as one lover to another, or simply as the most careless of endearments? Which Guilford had she left in her bed?

There was another knock, and she forced herself to compose herself and answer the door as she usually did. By daylight, she could see exactly how the intruder had rummaged and tossed her belongs: in addition to the scattered heaps of papers, the drawers had been yanked from her desk and their contents scattered, and the old painted tin box where she kept her sisters' letters had been pried open, emptied and tossed aside, crumpling one corner. Her eyes filled with tears as she paused to retrieve it from the floor, running her fingers over the chipped paint and dented tin. What *would* have happened if Guilford hadn't come when he had?

"Miss Penny?" Deborah's shrill voice came from the hall, and even through the door Amariah could smell the scent of the steeping tea. "Miss Penny, are you within?"

"Coming, Deborah," she said, setting the box back on her desk. It would take her most of the day to sort through the mess, and decide what, if anything, had been taken. She tried not to think of how much more she'd rather spend that time with Guilford.

Determined not to give the maid anything more to discuss downstairs, she shook her hair down over her forehead, and hid her bruised arm beneath the coverlet. Then, at last, she opened the door.

"Your tea an' toast, Miss Penny," Deborah said, holding the tray before her.

"I trust you are better, miss," Pratt said beside her. Another gentleman was beside him. "When you did not answer before, I thought it best to accompany Deborah here myself, and with Dr. Hislop and Mr. Green, too. Mr. Green is a constable, Miss Penny."

Pratt gently pushed open the door, and the girl and the two other men squeezed their way past Amariah.

"That's not necessary, Pratt," she protested. "None of this is. No physician, no constable. I'm perfectly fine, perfectly. You can see for yourself."

But Pratt had already seen enough, from the way she was favoring her arm to the emptied drawers and scattered papers on her desk, and even, she feared, to the closed door to her bedchamber.

"As you say, Miss Penny," he said gently. "As you say. But now, if you please, it's time you told me the rest."

Chapter Ten

"There is nothing more you can recall of the man beyond that he wore stockings and heavy shoes with oval buckles?" the constable asked incredulously. "Nothing more at all, Miss Penny?"

"No, sir, I cannot," Amariah said defensively. Although she was sitting in her favorite high-backed armchair, after so many questions she felt far less like a queen and more like a prisoner in the docket at the Old Bailey. The bandage that the physician had insisted be tied around her forehead did not help make her more agreeable, nor did the splint the man had used to bind her arm—only, she was sure, to merit a large fee for his unnecessary service.

"It was dark, Mr. Green," she continued, "and he'd knocked me to the floor. What else was I to see?"

"I'd hoped for some peculiar feature that might help us identify the culprit, Miss Penny." The constable was a very thin young man in a long gray coat that made him look thinner still, and he had a strange way of swaying back and forth as he spoke. "But to say only he wore shoes and stockings— that is of no use at all."

"Then neither are you, sir." She stood, ready to dismiss him, and eager to do it, too.

"I've heard rumors that you've had a cheat here in the club," he said, ignoring her obvious hint that he should leave. "A cheat is only a different kind of thief. Could he have come up here intending to rob you, too?"

She thought again of the threatening note, and at once decided not to speak of it to the constable. Guilford had agreed with her that the note had had no bearing on what happened here last night, and she saw no reason to confuse the issue more.

"There were rumors of a cheat, but no proof," she said firmly. "We dealt with the issue ourselves."

When there'd been other trouble at Penny House earlier in the year, when she'd worried about her sister Bethany and a citywide poisoning plot, she'd contacted a private agency to investigate. She'd kept things discreet. She certainly hadn't called in the parish constable as Pratt had done. She didn't want to answer any more of this prying man's questions, especially not while it meant she was keeping Guilford waiting in her bedchamber.

"This matter is better tended by ourselves, as well," she continued. "Pratt, if you'd be so kind as to show Mr. Green to the—"

"I shall be happy to do so, Miss Penny," Pratt said with the same patience he'd already shown her, "once you have finished your explanation. We still have not heard of His Grace the Duke of Guilford's part in the drama. Deborah said he was the one who sent for the ice, and who opened the door to her."

Amariah felt herself flush. She should have known Pratt would ask after the duke; it would have been impossible, really, for him not to. But was Guilford himself listening from her bedchamber? Would he hear Pratt's question, and her reply? And what would it matter if he did?

"I had come upstairs because I wasn't well," she said, choosing her words with great care. "His grace wondered at my absence, and followed me to inquire after my health."

"But these are your private apartments, are they not, Miss Penny?" Green persisted. "Is his grace often in the habit of visiting you here?"

Pratt clucked his tongue. "Please, sir, consider the lady, and the indelicacy of your question!"

"Thank you, Pratt, but if Mr. Green feels such a question has a purpose, then I'll answer it," Amariah said, determined to marshal her Penny House authority, even in a coverlet. "Last night was the first and only time that his grace has come to these rooms. I believe that he frightened away the intruder, and saved my life."

Green clapped his hands together, so lightly that they made no sound. "That may well be true, Miss Penny. Most likely it *is* true. But why would his grace have chosen this particular night and time to follow you upstairs? How could he have known you were in such peril?"

"He didn't!" Amariah protested. "That is, there was no way for him to know. It was only coincidence that drew him here to save me, no more."

"Coincidence." Green clasped his hands behind his back, his gaze drifting around the room until it stopped on Guilford's coat, still hooked haphazardly over the back of the chair where he'd tossed it last night. "Does his grace like to play for high stakes, Miss Penny?"

"Not at all," Amariah answered, unable to look away from that black superfine wool proof of Guilford's presence. "Although he is a charter member of the club, he comes more for the company than the gaming, and plays for modest stakes, if at all."

"And yet he is here nearly every night?"

"I told you, Mr. Green," she said as firmly as she could. "His grace comes to Penny House for the company."

Green smiled. "*Your* company, Miss Penny?"

"Mr. Green, if you please!" sputtered Pratt.

"Very well, very well. Then let me ask another question of the lady," Green said, undeterred. "Why would his grace come to these rooms if not for the sake of your company? What other reason would draw him here?"

"I—I do not know," Amariah said, fighting the panic that threatened to seize her. She had wondered this herself, and that wondering had made her feel so disloyal and suspicious toward Guilford that she'd tried to dismiss the notion from her thoughts. But having the constable raise the same question unsettled her, making her doubt herself as well as Guilford. "I cannot say, though I am most grateful that his grace did."

Green nodded, considering, and smiled at her. "Then surely you will know the answer to this question, Miss Penny. You greet each of your club's members at the door. You speak to them as favored acquaintances, and often compliment them upon their accomplishments, honors or appearance."

"That is true," answered Amariah warily, unsure of where this was headed. "It's part of my role as owner and hostess of Penny House to recognize each of our members and their tastes."

"Then tell me, Miss Penny," Green asked, his voice rising for emphasis. "Does His Grace the Duke of Guilford follow the new fashion for gentlemen's dress of long trousers, or does he remain true to wearing stockings for evening?"

"Damnation, judge for yourself!" The door to the bedchamber flew open, and Guilford came striding into the parlor to stand beside Amariah's chair. "I'm sorry, Miss Penny, but I couldn't leave you alone any longer. If this meddling scoundrel has questions to ask me, then by God, he should be a man, and ask me to my face!"

Her heart racing, Amariah didn't dare look up at Guilford, fearing her face would betray her. He was wearing his rumpled clothes from last night, his jaw dark with his unshaven beard. There was no mistake that he'd spent the night here, any more than her being dressed in her night rail and a coverlet could say anything other than that she'd been roused from her bed.

Except, of course, that she was ruined. Utterly, utterly ruined, and every one of them in the room knew it.

"Your grace, this is Mr. Green, the parish constable," she said as evenly as she could. "Mr. Green, His Grace the Duke of Guilford. And yes, your grace, I do believe Mr. Green has questions for you about last night."

"Your grace, I am honored." The constable bowed, his lanky frame folding in half. "But my eyes have already answered my last question. You still do favor stockings and breeches."

"I do," Guilford said sharply. "The same as ten thousand other gentlemen and their servants in this city."

"Yes, your grace," Green said, refusing to back down, even with such a difference in rank yawning between them. "But because Miss Penny has provided so few facts, then I am forced to rely on what she has given me."

"And the best you can do is to choose me as your villain?" Guilford asked imperiously. "Recall who I am, sir, and recall my honor with it. Then explain to me why coming to this lady's aid is so grievous a crime."

Green's smile veered perilously close to a smirk. "It's also the unfortunate truth, your grace, that many a woman who suffers at the hands of her lover will still protect that same man from the punishment of the law."

"Don't," Amariah ordered swiftly, one word of caution before Guilford said more than was wise, more than he could ever take back. She twisted in her chair to face him, laying her hand upon his sleeve to stop him. "Please—please don't."

She'd never seen such cold fury in his eyes before. Knowing it was there in her defense didn't reassure her, either.

"Do you understand what this bastard's saying about you?" he asked, his voice low and urgent. "About me?"

She nodded, and swallowed. She couldn't count on him to keep his temper, and not make a bad situation even worse. Instead it was up to her, and she turned back toward Green, and the now-horrified Pratt.

"I understand, your grace," she repeated. "And I understand that however sordid and scandalous Mr. Green's allegations may be, I need not fear them, for they are based on falsehood and suspicion, not truth. How can the charges he makes about lovers stand when we are not linked that way, not last night nor ever?"

"Forgive me, Miss Penny," said Green, "but circumstances suggest otherwise."

"Circumstances may suggest many things, Mr. Green," she said. "These circumstances were that I was too shaken to wish to be alone, and his grace kindly obliged me with the reassurance of his company. You may not be aware that his grace serves on our membership committee, and as such often advises me on every aspect of the club."

"As you say, Miss Penny." The scornful cast of Green's brows showed how little he believed her, just as she'd expected. But what she'd say next could change the constable's mind—at least it could if he'd admit she was right, and he was wrong.

"As she says," thundered the duke, "and as I say, too. Unless you should like to question my word of honor, Green?"

"The constable is merely making his case, your grace." Amariah rested a restraining hand again on his arm, though this time she let the coverlet slide higher over her own wrist so he could see the splint—a reminder that would likely be far more meaningful to him than any mere words. "I don't believe Mr. Green sees any of this as a question of honor. At least not yours or mine."

She lifted her head, holding it as high as if it were still crowned with one of her favorite white plumes as she tried to regain her usual confidence. Didn't Guilford himself believe enough in her to take her side? Wasn't he valuing her word and reputation as much as his own? She'd rise above this— this *foolishness*.

She smiled at the constable, stealing a quick glance at Guilford. Stony anger still clouded his face like a mask, but in his eyes she saw the spark of something else—surprise, bemusement, maybe even a dare—that showed he recognized what she was doing.

"Just as I must be observant to the tastes of my club's membership, Mr. Green," she began, "I should think that keen observation would be a most necessary skill to possess in your trade, as well."

"That it is, Miss Penny," he said, falling into the false comfort of her smile. He held up the small pocket notebook in which he'd been making his notes. "I must observe everything to learn what has happened here. How those drawers have been emptied, what might be missing, how you were injured. Each detail is like a piece of a grander puzzle, Miss Penny.

What first seems most insignificant may in time prove most crucial."

She smiled winningly, on familiar ground now with Green preening and overconfident like every other man.

"Even though the villain's stockings and shoe buckles were all I could recall?"

"It's all in here, Miss Penny." Green's smile was smug as he opened the little notebook, flipping the pages until he found the entry about the shoes. "'Thick-set male legs in stockings, heavy shoes with plain oval buckles. Those are your own words, Miss Penny."

"You are certain, Mr. Green?" she asked, tipping her head to one side. "I know sometimes I speak too fast."

"I am certain, because I wrote it down exactly as you spoke it," Green said, patting the cover of the notebook. "Details, Miss Penny, details."

"Indeed." She smiled again, and waved her uninjured arm gracefully toward Guilford's feet. "Then surely you must observe the detail of his grace's shoes. To be sure, he *is* wearing stockings and shoes, as you observed, but his buckles are not plain, as I told you, but cut steel, with an incised pattern to the cutting. Details, Mr. Green, details, and I should venture that his grace should no longer be considered one of your suspects."

Green's face went very sour, staring down at the duke's feet, and for once, he seemed to have nothing to say.

Amariah gathered up her coverlet one more time, and rose. "If you shall excuse me, your grace, gentlemen, I must dress for the day. Mr. Green, I'll send word to you if anything of value is missing once I have tidied my desk. And I must also ask you to keep everything you may have seen or heard in the strictest of confidence. The membership of Penny House includes the most powerful and highly ranked gentlemen of London, and they would not take kindly to their affairs being discussed by you."

"Or course, Miss Penny, you have my word on that, but if you please, I don't believe I'm done here," Green said doggedly. "For your own safety, I'd advise that I stay, and help you sort through these papers, to be sure that nothing is overlooked."

"Another lost detail, Mr. Green?" She smiled beatifically. "Thank you, but no. I believe I can tend to it sufficiently myself."

The constable had no choice left now but to bow and leave, and Amariah turned next to Pratt. "Please send one of the maids upstairs to help me sort through this wreckage. Whomever you can spare."

"Yes, miss." Even with his customary solemnity, Pratt's anguish was palpable. "If I might say, miss, I'm most relieved to see that you've suffered no lasting injury from last night, and how sorry I am that such a thing was permitted to occur here at Penny House."

"It's hardly your fault, Pratt, when I was the one who'd sent away the guard and left the door unlocked." She smiled ruefully, and reached out to pat his shoulder. "And I appreciate your concern for me. I truly do."

He couldn't help making another small bow, his response to everything. "You are essential to Penny House, miss. The club could not exist as it does without you."

"Thank you, Pratt," she said softly. She wasn't vain enough to believe she was indispensable, but she understood what he meant: that she was the one guiding Father's wishes and keeping true to his spirit through Penny House's peculiar marriage of gaming and charity, without which the club would never be the same. "But no more surgeons, and no more constables, please, especially no more of that odious Mr. Green."

"Yes, Miss Penny." Pratt's forehead wrinkled with distress. "But we can hardly let these villains enter in here unchecked, and—"

"We'll take care of it ourselves, Pratt," she said firmly. 'Later this morning, I would like to meet with Mr. Fewler and his guards, and after that we'll call together the rest of the staff. I'll want everyone to be even more attentive, for their own safety, as well as the good of the club."

"But Miss Penny—"

"That is all, Pratt." She pointedly turned toward the desk so that he, too, would leave, and with a momentous sigh, he did.

And left her alone with Guilford.

"So is it my turn to be dismissed, Amariah?" he asked lightly. "Will you send me off the same way, without so much as a by-your-leave?"

"You're not the same, Guilford," she said, "and you know it."

Had he any idea of how truthful that was? She felt oddly uneasy with him now, almost skittish, all the warmth and closeness she'd felt earlier in the morning overwhelmed by cold reason. Maybe it was being forced into the usual bustle of running Penny House that had made the time with him seem like no more than a dream, or maybe it was her customary independence warring with how much she'd needed him last night. Or maybe it was simply realizing that, after last night, they couldn't go back to how they'd been before.

She couldn't make herself look at him, and instead began fidgeting with the bandage that held the splint in place on her arm, her left hand awkward and clumsy with the stiff knots. "Here, help me get this wretched thing from my arm."

He came to stand beside her, also staring down at the splint. "Shouldn't you leave it alone?"

"I don't need it," she said, still fussing. "You know I don't. It's just pure quackery, and a nuisance, too."

"I don't know anything where you are concerned." He came and took her arm, untying the splint as she'd asked. "Except that you notice the buckles on my shoes."

She laughed, letting the triumph she'd kept inside finally bubble up. "He won't dare question you again, will he?"

But Guilford didn't join in her laughter. "You don't really believe that fool of a constable will obey you, and keep his mouth shut about what he saw here, do you?"

Her smile faded. "Not for a moment," she said, rubbing her arm where the splint had been. "He's male, isn't he?"

He tossed the splint and bandages on the chair behind her. "Don't tar all men with the same brush, Amariah."

She looked up at him from beneath her lashes, trying to gauge his mood. "I suppose I'll decide that after I read the *Tattle* tomorrow."

One look at his face, and she realized how badly she'd blundered.

"If any of this is in the *Tattle,* it won't be from me," he said grimly. "I told you I'm doing that for you, and for Penny House. It's a shame you can't believe me."

"Did I say that?"

"You didn't have to," he said. "Where do I stand, sweetheart?"

That sweetheart was no endearment, and she knew it. "We're—we're not lovers, Guilford, no matter what anyone else may think. You heard it in Mr. Green's famous details, too."

"I heard otherwise last night, in your bed." He took a step closer. "Now I want to hear the truth from you. Do you truly feel nothing for me?"

She looked down, avoiding his scrutiny, and didn't answer.

"Since when are you silent, Amariah?"

"Since I don't know what to say," she said softly, understanding his frustration. "I don't, Guilford."

"Damnation, Amariah, this shouldn't be so hard."

"But for me it is," she said wistfully. "I know what will be said of—of this. If I lose my reputation, then the club, too, becomes a bit more tarnished, a bit more tawdry. I know that every gentleman that comes through our door tonight will look at me in a different way, and Penny House with it. They'll eye me and measure me and laugh about how I'm no different now from any actress at the Haymarket who entertains gentlemen in her dressing room."

"Not if you're with me, they won't," he said confidently. "They wouldn't dare."

"Don't pretend otherwise, Guilford," she said, unable to keep the sadness from her voice. "You're far wiser than that. You know how society is. You'll be lauded as the man who finally won my favors, while I'll only be praised for setting my price so high, and selling myself to a duke."

"Don't listen to them," he said, slipping his arm around her waist to pull her close. "You're not some silly miss at Almack's. You're an independent woman with means of your own. What those others say doesn't matter."

She rested her hands lightly on the front of his rumpled waistcoat, trying not to let it remind her of last night, and trying, too, to keep her tears at bay.

"Of course it doesn't matter to you," she said, knowing this must be the last time she felt his arms around her. "You're the Duke of Guilford. Nothing can affect you. All I can do is to try to rise above the talk, to ignore what they whisper and give them no more fuel for their gossip."

"Amariah, that is the most ridiculous—"

"No, Guilford, please," she said, placing her fingertips gently to his lips to silence him. "Forgive me, but this is how it must be. I can't be seen with you ever again outside of the club, and even then I must never be noticed alone with you, or in close conversation."

His fingers wrapped around hers, holding them closer to his lips to kiss them fervently. "Hang them all, sweetheart. Come with me, and you'll never need worry over them again. Better to turn our backs, I say, and please ourselves."

She closed her eyes for a moment, struggling to keep her reasons focused as he kissed each of her fingertips in turn. He was kind and impetuous and full of charm, the first man she'd known who could make her laugh and sigh, too, and the first man who'd been brave enough to show her real tenderness. But he was also a man of great rank, power and wealth; she'd become worldly enough herself since coming to London to understand what it meant when a gentleman set out to "please" himself. Affection, desire, passion, friendship, but not love.

He was asking her to become his mistress.

"If I had only myself to consider, Guilford, only you and I, then it would be different," she whispered miserably as she curled her fingers away from him. "But when I consider all the others who depend on me and Penny House, everyone from Pratt down to little Sammy, to my father's memory and my sisters, too, to all the poor folk in the streets and parish houses that rely upon the food I can provide—I won't turn my back on them, too, Guilford. I cannot."

He searched her face, hoping for another answer beyond her words. "Then what of me, Amariah? You would turn your back on me instead?"

She bowed her head. "I can't help it, Guilford. To sacrifice all those others to follow my own pleasure—I would be failing myself as well as them. It would be *selfish*."

"Very well." He released her so abruptly that she stumbled back. "If that is your decision."

"It is," she said, tugging her coverlet back over her shoulders. "It's the only choice, Guilford."

"For you, Miss Penny. Not for me." He took his coat from the chair, thrusting his arms into the sleeves. "I came here last night intending to set things right between us. No more doubts, no more questions. And it seems you've done exactly that, doesn't it?"

"Yes, Guilford," she said quietly, so quietly she doubted he heard her as he left. "So help me, yes."

Guilford leaned back against the squabs in his chaise, his empty stomach rumbling and his temper foul. He was tired and thirsty and frustrated, and he didn't care who knew it.

What in blazes did Amariah Penny want, anyway? He'd rescued her, and calmed her, and held her the whole night through. Hell, he'd even brushed her hair. He felt differently about her than he had about any other woman, and he wanted to show her that. He'd been so virtuous and gallant with her, never even considering taking advantage of her until she'd begun taking advantage of him, that his friends would never believe it.

He could understand how closely she'd guarded her reputation, and why she'd been so distraught this morning when Pratt had brought in that wretched constable. He had sisters. He knew how reputation was everything to decent women, and he'd grant her a bit of leeway from the shock. But then when he'd tried to make things right by her, offering her his protection against the gossips and the men who'd now come sniffing around her, she'd gone all high-and-mighty with him. He would have given her anything she wanted, whatever she needed to be happy and make a great show in the world, and she'd tossed it back in his face as if it had been nothing.

He swore again, shaking his head at the gross unfairness of *her* decision. How had she been the one to make such a choice for them both, anyway? He didn't consider himself to be a selfish man, but he was a duke, and he'd always had certain…*expectations* of how his life should be. He'd never been denied anything he wanted, especially where women were concerned. Why should he be, anyway, when feminine favor was usually so freely given?

But Amariah had refused him. He'd wanted her and all that creamy-pale luscious body of hers, and she'd wanted him in return, wanted him as much as a woman could want a man. He'd kissed enough women in his life to know what desire tasted like, and he'd tasted hunger, raw and needy, every time Amariah's lips touched his.

Then she'd sent him away. Worse yet, she'd told him, not only that he'd no place in her bed, but in her life. She'd laid out rules as if they were sitting at a hand of whist, telling him how and why and when he could even speak to her, yet her eyes had been full of tears when she'd done it. She wasn't just depriving him; she was depriving herself, as well, and he couldn't begin to find the sense to it.

He couldn't help but think that that wretched wager with Stanton was somehow at fault. What had begun as a careless amusement now felt like a dishonorable curse hanging over him and Amariah, and cheapening what he felt for her. At least it was a curse he could banish. He'd write to Stanton this morning and tell him the wager was off. Stanton would squawk, but Guilford didn't care, not if it might bring him closer to Amariah.

The chaise stopped and as soon as the footman opened the door, Guilford was climbing out and stalking up the front steps to his house. Dishonorable *and* distasteful, and so he meant to tell Stanton if he—

"Beggin' pardon, your grace!" The boy scurried to one side and bowed low, still clutching the broom he'd been using to sweep the steps.

Guilford stared down at the boy, his thoughts jolting back from Amariah. "Billy Fox."

"Aye, your grace, so it is." He grinned up at Guilford, touching his knuckle to the brim of his black felt hat. That hat had been one of the first things Guilford had ordered bought for the boy when he joined his household, and the next, more private order had been that Billy was excused from doffing that hat to his betters, on account of his scar. "You remembered me, aye."

"You're not easy to forget." Regular meals had put flesh on his bones and a bed of his own had brought color to his face, so that the plain house livery he wore made him look almost respectable. "Why are you here? Why aren't you in the stable, with the horses?"

"One o' the regular boys what's a footman took sick, your grace," Billy explained, leaning on the broom, "an' Mr. Cartwright—the butler—asked me t' take his place in the house for today."

Now of course Guilford knew that Mr. Cartwright was his butler, just as he knew Mr. Cartwright would be furious if he heard his substitute footman addressing the duke, let alone addressing him with such good-natured familiarity. But because Guilford had liked the boy from the first, he was more amused than offended, and it wasn't at all because Billy reminded him of Amariah, either.

"Ah, Hop an' Buck surely have a hungry look about them, don't they?" Billy was leaning around Guilford, frowning a bit as he appraised the horses drawing the chaise. "Not that I fault them, from having stayed out all o' the night long with you, your grace."

"Here, Billy, now, and leave his grace be!" shouted the appalled driver from the box. "Now, boy, now!"

Guilford looked over his shoulder. "There is no problem, John," he called. "The boy is fine."

Belatedly Billy squared his narrow shoulders the way he'd been newly taught. "Is there anything else, your grace?"

Guilford nodded. "Do you think the horses suffered last night?"

"They're hungry, sure, but John'll have watered them." The boy's shoulders relaxed, and he glanced curiously up at Guilford. "Was the gaming that fierce last night, your grace, t'make you play until dawn?"

"To be honest, I didn't play a single hand or toss," Guilford said. "I dined with my sister, and didn't arrive at Penny House until late."

The boy tapped the broom on the step. "But I'd wager you did see Miss Penny, your grace."

"I did, indeed," Guilford said, looking at the front door of his house. He suspected that a footman, or even Cartwright himself, was hovering directly on the other side, ready to open it the second his grace showed his intention to enter, but also where that footman was no doubt shamelessly eavesdropping on him and Billy. "You haven't gone to her since you began working here, have you?"

Billy shrugged, noncommittal. "Miss Penny's been kind t'me since she came to town, your grace."

Eliot frowned, recognized a too-careful answer for what it

was. What the devil was Amariah doing, anyway, interfering with one of his people like this? "Have you had word from her, then?"

The boy shrugged again, his expression now focused on something in the faraway distance. "Miss Penny says I must always consider her me friend, your grace."

Guilford sighed with impatience. How many more times would he be confounded today, anyway? "Come inside with me, Billy," he said, and at once the door opened, the footman bowing extravagantly. "We'll talk while I eat breakfast."

But the boy hung back. "Beggin' pardon, your grace, but I'm forbidden the upstairs," he said uneasily. "I'd be in righteous trouble for it."

"Not while you're with me," Guilford said, realizing as soon as he'd spoken that he'd made much the same assurance to Amariah earlier. "Parker, I'll take breakfast in the front parlor this morning. Billy, this way."

Without looking, he knew the boy was following him, and when he turned around in the parlor, Billy in fact was there, standing uncertainly with his hands hanging at his sides. At least he'd left the broom outside.

"Now answer me the truth, Billy," Guilford said firmly. "Have you had word, either spoken or written, from Miss Penny since you joined this household?"

Still the boy didn't answer, and Guilford shook his head. "Billy, if you are unhappy with your position here, then you should be speaking to Cartwright or even to me, not to Miss Penny."

"Oh, but I *am* happy, your grace!" Billy protested, his entire body taut for emphasis. "I wasn't complaining t' Miss Penny, not at all! I went back to St. Crispin's on me day free, an' she was there, an' even before she asked how I liked it here, she was asking after you, your grace, an' that's the Maker's sweet honest truth, may He steal me away now if I'm lying!"

Now Guilford frown covered his surprise. "Miss Penny asked after me?"

"Yes, your grace, she did, she did!" Billy said, nodding vigorously. "An' I told her you were fine, as much as I could see o' you, an' she said she was glad t' learn of it. An' then Miss Penny smiled, your grace, like she really was glad o' it. She smiles like an angel, she does, a very angel. She don't do that for every gentleman, your grace."

"She does it every night at Penny House, to every gentleman that comes through the door." Guilford was still smarting from how Amariah had rejected him earlier, and unwilling to believe that she'd felt otherwise. "She's very good at smiling like that, too."

"I'd warrant she don't smile at them the way she smiles at you, your grace," Billy said confidently. "I've seen it. She smiles special smiles for you. Loverlike smiles, your grace."

"Ha," Guilford said, not bothering to hide his bitterness from the boy. "What would you say, Billy Fox, if I told you that I asked her to be exactly that—loverlike, if you will—to me this morning, and she turned me out for my trouble?"

He'd meant it as a rhetorical question, but Billy answered it anyway. "What would I say, your grace? Why, I'd say you must not have said the words she wished t' hear."

The door opened, and Guilford's breakfast appeared, a footman setting the large tray on the table near the window.

"So what words would you say, Billy?" Guilford asked as he plucked a piece of buttered toast from the silver rack. "How would you make yourself understood to the angelic Miss Penny?"

Billy frowned, and folded his arms over his chest as he considered. "I said she smiled like an angel, your grace, not that she *was* one. She's not. She's too practical for that. Th' way she comes into St. Crispin's, taking charge like a general in the field—oh, aye, she's worrying over this life, not th' next."

"That's true," Guilford said, dropping into the chair at the table as he reached for the pot of peach marmalade for his toast. He was thinking not only of St. Crispin's, but of how she'd rejected the bracelet first. How in blazes had he forgotten that? "She's far more practical than most women."

"That she is," Billy agreed. "I'm thinking you should talk to her that way, too. Practical an' purposeful. *That's* what'll win Miss Penny."

Guilford chewed, reflecting. He was actually considering taking the advice of a ten-year-old stable boy regarding Amariah. Why wouldn't he? Billy was wise beyond his years, and besides, he was right. Hearts and flowers and ruby bracelets wouldn't win Amariah, but if he could find a way to be more moral, more charitable, more practical, than she was herself, then she'd have no choice but to agree to be more passionate, more amusing and entirely less practical with *him*. What better way to give them both what they wanted?

"Practical *an'* purposeful," Billy repeated sagely. "That's th' ticket, your grace."

Guilford smiled. The ticket, indeed.

And Amariah would be his.

With a sigh, Amariah rubbed the ache in her arm, and began to sort the last pile of jumbled papers from her desk for Pratt to put away. So far there'd been no pages torn from any ledger, nothing missing that she could recall. She didn't really expect to find anything gone now, either, but she wasn't about to stop her search now.

The meeting with her staff had gone as well—and as poorly—as she'd expected. Because there were few secrets among them, most had already heard about the intruder last night, but they'd still taken her warnings to be more cautious every bit as seriously as she'd hoped. She'd worn long sleeves to cover the bruise on her arm, but she hadn't used enough face powder to cover the one on her forehead, and she'd caught two of the younger maids staring, their faces intent with fearful fascination. Tonight she meant to wear a ribbon or even a turban, for the last thing she wished was to have the members betting among themselves over who'd beaten her, or something else equally preposterous.

Would Guilford come back to Penny House tonight? she wondered. *Would he appear as he usually did, and pretend nothing had happened or changed, or had he vanished forever from the club, and her life?*

"Have you found anything out of place, Miss Penny?" asked Mr. Fewler, the head of the hired guards. A barrel-chested man with slick black hair, Fewler was a former Bow Street man, and his company of private guards now specialized in prevention of crimes in the better sort of establishments like Penny House. Although Amariah knew that her sisters had never liked nor trusted him, declaring his manner too blunt and brusque, Amariah herself had always found him to be surprisingly accurate in both his judgment and his advice. Though neither he nor Constable Green had yet produced any answers as to who last night's intruder might be, Fewler had none of Green's self-importance, nor would he ever leap to a false conclusion and cling to it doggedly, the way Green had about Guilford.

What sort of mischief was Guilford committing now? she wondered. *Was he writing some dreadful calumny about her for the* Tattle, *or calling on some witty, beautiful woman* who'd be more willing than she ever could be? Or would he simply have retired to his bed, to sleep and laze away the day in preparation for tonight's amusements, his hair dark against the white pillow and the sheets slipping down over his bare chest, while…

"He didn't use force to open any of these drawers," Fewler was saying, running his blunt fingers along the edge of the desk drawers. "Could he have had another key, miss?"

She flushed, embarrassed. First Guilford, then Green, now Fewler: must she keep confessing her carelessness?

"No, the man didn't need a key," she admitted, "because I hadn't locked the drawers any more than I'd locked the door after me. I couldn't have made it any easier for him."

Fewler frowned. "That's not wise, Miss Penny, though by now I needn't tell you that."

"I've learned my lesson, Mr. Fewler, if that's what you mean," she said, still sorting through the papers. "But I'd never thought I'd have to be so careful, not up here. Why, this is strange. Pratt, did you know that Baron Westbrook won at hazard the other night?"

"Lord Westbrook?" Pratt looked up from the box he was packing. "No, Miss Penny, I did not. I don't recall him being long in the house, but then we were very crowded."

"I hadn't seen him at all," Amariah said, "yet as you say, I could have missed him. According to this promissory, he won rather handsomely against Lord Stanton. Good for him! He has such dreadful luck, no matter how high he wagers, that it's good to see him win once in a while. After that foolishness with the Scots, I feared he'd ignore us."

"Might I see the note, Miss Penny?" Fewler asked, and Amariah handed it to him to study. "Don't you generally deposit these in with the cash in the strongbox?"

"Most days, yes," Amariah said. "But as Pratt said, we've been so busy that I haven't sorted through them as soon as I should. They're never alike, you see, with the gentlemen settling their accounts privately between them. These are mostly for our records."

Fewler handed the note back to her. "Westbrook's uncle should be pleased to see the poor bloke win like that. I'd wager the old fellow's tightened the purse strings in the last months."

Curious, Amariah twisted around to face him. "Why would his uncle do that now?"

"Losses," Fewler said succinctly. "He's lost two ships in the sugar trade in a big blow off Jamaica this fall. Loaded with the new crop, and gone in an instant. Total losses. Hurricanes, they call them out there in the Indies."

"How dreadful!" She was surprised that she hadn't heard of this; it was good business for her to keep track of any such large reverses suffered by the membership and their inheritances. "How did you hear of it?"

"I've acquaintance in the insurance houses," Fewler said. "They're always first to know the shipwrecks. Has Westbrook asked for credit at the table?"

"Not yet, no." Amariah set the paper into its own separate pile. Strange how easily the workings of the club continued on, as if what she'd done and said with Guilford hadn't happened at all. "Though I suppose we should be prepared for it. Warn Mr. Walthrip to keep a close eye, and be ready to speak to Lord Westbrook if it becomes necessary."

Pratt nodded, making a note. "The minimum line, I should say if he asks, considering he must wait for his inheritance."

"Given his history, I'm inclined to believe this latest win was a fluke." Amariah sighed. Extending—and withdrawing—credit to members who were financially embarrassed was never pleasant. "No gentlemen with deep pockets likes them shortened. Perhaps that's why Lord Westbrook's been so quick to jump at any offense lately, like a little terrier."

The way he had with Guilford, trying to goad him into a duel, as if Guilford would ever do anything that foolish!

"Let us hope his winning continues, Miss Penny, for all our sakes," Pratt said, glancing down at the note as well. "Winning improves every gentleman's mood."

"True words, Mr. Pratt, true words." Fewler patted Westbrook's promissory note with the palm of his hand, as if it were a good, obedient dog. "Happy gentlemen like this Lord Westbrook never give us any trouble. It's the ones that feel disappointed or denied that you must watch."

Ones like the Duke of Guilford...

Chapter Eleven

"Mr. Bly to see you, your grace."

Guilford put down his pen and shook sand over the last sheet of his notes for Simon Dalton at the *Tattle*. He glanced over them one more time, hoping that he'd given Dalton enough detail about Penny House to use, but not so much as to upset Amariah. He folded the sheet and pressed the seal to close it.

"Have this taken directly," he said, handing it to the footman. "There will be no reply. I'll see Mr. Bly now."

He smoothed his cuffs and ran his fingers back through his hair, as much preparation as he'd make before seeing the solicitor. He already knew what he'd offer, but he needed Bly to put it in the proper legal rigmarole. He wanted everything right to impress Amariah, and he'd no intention of leaving anything to chance.

"This should be easy enough, Mr. Bly," he said, rubbing his hands together with satisfaction as the solicitor entered and bowed. "You've done contracts like this for me before."

Mr. Bly made a wincing smile at him over the tops of his narrow spectacles. "You're very wise to make these arrangements beforehand, your grace. You're a most generous gentleman under any circumstances, but settlements with young women are far more complicated once the initial, ah…ardor has passed, and the cold grasp of greed has come in its place."

"This one will be a bit different," Guilford said as the solicitor opened his leather envelope. "This lady already has a splendid house of her own near St. James Square, and she has no interest in jewels, or a box at the theater, or even an open account at a milliner's."

Bly's wispy brows arched with surprise. "Then your grace is being most careful, requiring a contract when the female party requires neither goods nor funds in return for her company and person."

"Oh, she'll require funds, and a great deal of them, too," Guilford said. He meant to leave no room at all for argument between them. "They just won't be payable to her. She's to have a thousand pounds every month that we remain together, with a final annuity of five thousand upon parting."

Bly peered over his spectacles again. "I must say, your grace, that your great generosity once again astounds me."

"The lady deserves it, and a great deal more," Guilford said, remembering how lush her mouth had been to kiss, how he was sure he could lose himself for hours on end in a mouth like hers. "It's a matter of convincing her, that's all."

Bly dipped his pen into the ink. "If she chooses to refuse your largesse for herself, then might I know the name of the beneficiary?"

"St. Crispin's Church, and the parish surrounding it," Guilford said, liking the sound of such generosity. If Amariah truly did want to put her charity before everything else, then she couldn't deny the benefits of such an arrangement. He'd never feel the pinch of a thousand pounds, but how many no-

ble things such a sum would accomplish in that neighborhood! "Believe me, the lady will approve."

"Then she is a rare lady indeed," Bly said, his pen scratch-
ing over the paper. "I trust she will appreciate you, your grace,
and be suitably generous to you in return."

"So do I, Bly," Guilford said, remembering what it had
been like to lie with her in her bed beneath the attic, and how
much he wished to do it again. "So do I."

That night Amariah again stood in the front hall, smiling and laughing and greeting the members as they arrived.
The elaborate silk turban she wore low on her forehead
gave her a charming exotic cast that drew many compliments. None suspected that she wore it to cover the bruise
that was now the same shape and color as a new plum, or
that the elegant long kid gloves were serving the same purpose for the swelling on her arm. She smiled and laughed
and pretended nothing was wrong, nothing had happened,
and nothing about Guilford's obvious absence tonight could
ever upset her.

"Lord Westbrook, good evening!" she said as the baron
came through the door. "How happy I am that you have decided to visit us again so soon!"

"How can I keep away, Miss Penny, when I'm drawn to
your fair self?" He was even more excited than usual, his face
flushed and his words racing over one another. "Why should
I punish myself that way?"

Amariah laughed. She couldn't help it. Westbrook looked
so supremely happy with himself and the world, from his
ruddy cheeks to the little black curls on his temples to the twin
rows of twinkling marcasite buttons on his waistcoat. The men
kissed by luck at Penny House might as well have their good

fortune written on placards across their chests; it was that evident in how they carried themselves afterward.

"I've heard you were most successful at hazard the other night, my lord." She tapped each of his shoulders lightly with the blades of her furled fan, as if she were a queen granting him a knighthood. "You shouldn't be so modest."

"I'm not a braggart, Miss Penny," he said with such relish that it proved he was exactly that, whenever and however he could be. "I do not believe in blowing one's own horn, not when there's others to do it for one."

"Like me, my lord?" She smiled archly, and cupped her hand around her mouth like a town crier. "Hear ye, hear ye, Lord Westbrook won at hazard!"

"Hush, Miss Penny, quiet now, don't go on so," he said, suddenly uncomfortable at the attention. "I told you, I'm a modest man."

She dropped her hand from her mouth. His attitude surprised her, for in the past, he'd crowed like a bantam rooster over even the tiniest gain at the table.

"I'm sorry, my lord," she said contritely. "Modesty is always more pleasing than pride."

Self-consciously he pulled out his handkerchief, using it to blot away the sweat that had suddenly appeared on his forehead.

"That's what it is, too," he said, glancing around as if to make sure no one had overheard. "Modesty, Miss Penny. I don't have to explain that to a lady like you. Don't want the fellow who lost to me taking offense, you see."

"No, of course not, my lord," she murmured, striving to mollify him. It was never easy to predict how different gentlemen would react to luck, both good and ill. She couldn't at the moment recall the name of the gentleman who'd signed the promissory note to the baron, but perhaps there was more history between him and Westbrook than simply the dice: a woman, a horse, a sister offended. Considering how close Westbrook had come to an out-and-out duel the other night, he was wise to be cautious now. "I can certainly appreciate your discretion in such matters, my lord, and respect it, as well."

"Thank you." He nodded, and took so deep a breath that it threatened to pop those marcasite buttons. "I trust you are well tonight, Miss Penny?"

"Thank you, my lord, yes, I am." Now what had made him ask that at this point in the coversation? She smoothed the edge of her silk turban lower over her forehead, reassuring herself that it was still in place over the bruise. "Quite well."

"I am glad to hear it," he said, so solemnly she almost believed he was. "Most glad. Where's Guilford tonight, eh?"

"His grace?" Now it was her time to glance about the crowded hall, though she knew full well she wouldn't find him. "If the duke hasn't arrived yet, then he will soon."

She tried to smile as if her chest weren't tight with sick dread. Had Westbrook already heard rumors? Had word already traveled through the east end that Guilford had spent the night in her quarters?

"Guilford's usually here by now, right at your side," Westbrook said. "Some nights with him there, it's the very devil just to get a by-your-leave from you."

"Forgive me, my lord, but I do not believe that is the case," she said firmly. "Besides, the Duke of Guilford sits on the membership committee of Penny House, and is intimately concerned with the workings of the club. If you see him in close conversation with me, I can assure you that we are more likely discussing a new dealer at the faro table, or whether we should be stocking a different brand of cognac in our cellar."

Westbrook's nod was quick, almost apologetic. "Maybe Guilford's tiring of the place. He does that, you know. Always the first to discover the new fashion, then the first to discard it, as well."

Or more likely it wasn't Penny House that Guilford had tired of, but her.

"I can't begin to predict his grace's whims and inclinations," she said, trying to make light of the whole question. "But I do know he doesn't join us here every night, any more than you do."

"Guilford's not much of a gamester, either," Westbrook said. "You'd never see him playing for the stakes I did the other night."

"That's true, my lord," she agreed, wondering where this conversation was leading. "His grace has many other interests besides cards and dice. But I'd be the most selfish woman in London to expect all you gentlemen to come here exclusively."

"I would, Miss Penny," the baron said with unexpected earnestness, the sweat glistening again on his brow. "If Guilford leaves Penny House, if he decides he's too grand to continue on your committee, I'd be most honored to be considered for the place."

Of all the possibilities she'd been fearing, she'd never expected this one. "How vastly generous of you, my lord! For gentleman whose days are as full as yours must be, that is a very kind offer."

"I'm not so busy that I couldn't spare the time for Penny House," he said, his bunched handkerchief like an oversized white flower clutched in his hand. "I've played every game you offer in these rooms, which is more than Guilford can say."

"You're most kind, my lord," she murmured without offering any real hope. Westbrook would never have a place on the club's governing committee, no matter how many games he played. He was too low in the peerage for such an important position, too quick-tempered while lacking in wit or style, and with too little influence to do Penny House any good in any way. All he had to recommend him was that he meant well, and he lost frequently, which wasn't nearly enough.

"I know how to win, too, Miss Penny." His confidence— or maybe it was just his will—was making his voice rise. "You saw the proof of that yourself. And I'm honest as the day is long. That cheat that made you bring on extra guards—you'd never have that sort of trouble from me!"

"I should hope not, my lord!" He wasn't clever enough to cheat at hazard, poor man, especially not at any table directed by Mr. Walthrip.

"You wouldn't regret having me beside you, Miss Penny," he continued. "I can assure you of that. I'd make you forget all about Guilford not being here."

As if anyone could replace Guilford!

"I thank you for your offer, my lord," she said gently, not wanting to hurt his feelings, "and I promise to consider it."

"Do," he urged. "I cannot tell you what an honor it would be to spend more time here, and in your company."

Amariah smiled her most polite but unencouraging smile. Westbrook wouldn't be the first gentleman to mistake her welcome to Penny House for something more. Baron or not, he was almost as clamoring and needy as the lowest paupers crowding the steps at St. Crispin's, and though she did feel sorry for him since his fortunes were suffering, she could not afford to spare him any more of her time here in the front hall.

"Now if you'll excuse me, my lord," she said, "I must see to the other—"

"The other members of the club." Westbrook nodded enthusiastically. "Of course you must. They expect your hospitality. You see, I already understand how matters stand here, don't I? But I'll leave you to it. Yes. You know where to find me, as always, in the hazard room."

He cocked his hand in a kind of mock salute before he turned away. Fewler had said that it was the men who lost who were the most dangerous, and predicted that she'd never be troubled by those who won, but then, he'd never met Baron Westbrook.

Amariah sighed, then smiled, as she prepared to greet the next newcomer through the door, hoping more than she'd ever admit that instead of the next Westover, it would be Guilford.

And for the rest of the night, she hoped in vain.

Guilford had never been in the front room of Penny House at this hour of the morning. It didn't seem right, somehow. The curtains to the tall windows were looped to one side, the better to let in both the sunlight and the fresh morning air through the open windows. The chairs were turned upside down on the tables, the cloths stripped away for laundering. The candlesticks were empty, awaiting new candles for the night, and the sideboard was as bare and empty as can be, waiting for the platters of roast meats and fowl to be brought up from the kitchen tonight.

And just as the bright morning sun reveals many a midnight beauty to be gray and haggard, her paint faded and her false hair undone, the flaws and deceptions of the parlor showed clearly now without the softening grace of candlelight. The landscape painting over the mantel was a patent copy instead of the Old Master it pretended to be, the hollowware had the dull sheen of plate instead of sterling, and the tops of the bare tables were humble, battered oak instead of mahogany.

Yet the difference between this and the stylish elegance that Guilford was accustomed to seeing by night made him even more confident that he was doing the right thing. Amariah wasn't a woman fooled by facades, which was one of the things he liked best about her. She'd made Penny House into the most fashionable gaming house in London, but she'd done it without spending a farthing more than was necessary, or compromising her commitment to her charities, either. She was bound to agree to his offer. How could she not?

He shifted in his chair, wishing she'd hurry from wherever she was to here, with him. One night without seeing her, and he was on absolute tenterhooks to see her again.

He looked up as soon as he heard the door open, all expectation.

"Miss Penny sends her regrets, your grace, but she is delayed," Pratt said. "Janey Patton and her baby are leaving us this morning, and Miss Penny is making her last farewells."

"Of course, of course," Guilford said, though it took a moment for him to recall who Janey Patton was. The woman who'd delivered her bastard in the Penny House kitchen—that was it, the one for whom he'd ordered the baby things. Guilford hoped Amariah remembered that, too.

And he hoped she remembered it soon. He drew his watch from its pocket, checking the hour once again. He never had been much good at waiting, and he especially didn't like waiting now, with so much at stake.

"Do you require anything else, your grace?" Pratt asked, and Guilford waved him away. What he required was Amariah, and not even Pratt could make her come if she wasn't ready.

"She'll come, your grace," Bly said sympathetically, drawing the contracts from his leather envelope and squaring them on the little table beside him. "The ladies often have their own concept of time."

"Not Miss Penny." Guilford resisted the urge to look once again at his watch. "She's worse than any man when it comes to squandering so much as a minute. I wonder that she even spares the time to sleep."

"I have every confidence in your ability to change her if you so desire, your grace," Bly said, resting his hand on the contract. "You, and your generosity, and—"

"Your grace, good day." Amariah had begun speaking before she'd even stepped through the door. "You wish to see me, your grace?"

"Yes," Guilford said softly, realizing with a jolt exactly how true an admission that was. It had been less than a day since he'd left Penny House, and yet the hours apart from her had stretched and spun out endlessly. She hadn't bothered to try to hide the bruise on her forehead, a shocking reminder of how close he'd come to losing her. With him, she'd never have to be in danger like that again. She was too precious to put through that kind of risk, not if he could help it.

But that was why he was here, wasn't it? When he looked at her now in the plain linen gown she wore for day, he remembered the pearly glow of her bare shoulder when the coverlet had slipped down her arm, and the soft fullness of her uncorseted breasts as she'd clutched the cloth around her. This morning she wore her hair drawn tightly back into a knot at the back of her head, but he remembered how silky to the touch that hair had been, how it had waved and curled down her back and over his hand as he'd stroked the brush through it. He thought of her scent and touch and her taste, and he wanted nothing more than to hold her and kiss her again, and not let her go.

"Pratt said you had an important matter to discuss with me, your grace," she said. "Forgive me for making you wait, but we are busy here this morning, and I've many matters that need my attention."

She was standing in the doorway, purposefully neither entering the room, nor closing the door. Pratt himself was hovering just behind her, all proof that she'd meant it when she'd said she'd never be alone with him again. Well, good. If she wanted to live by such ridiculous rules, then she'd be bound to agree to the tidy arrangement he was offering.

He rose slowly, smoothing the cuffs of his shirt. "Miss Penny," he began, and cleared his throat to begin again. Having both Bly and Pratt hanging about would keep him from charming and seducing her into compliance, but perhaps formality was the best for establishing what was really a business agreement between them. "Miss Penny, you know the high esteem in which I hold you and your person."

Instantly her face was all wariness, guarded against him. "I know only what you tell me, your grace."

"Then you know that I regard you without peer among the ladies of this town," he said. "Your wit, your intelligence and, of course, your beauty are beyond compare."

"I thank you for the compliments, your grace, however unworthy I may be of them," she said. "But I cannot fathom why you should have come here if that is the sum of your errand."

"Because it's not," he said, coming to stand before her. Even if this was to be a formal business arrangement, he couldn't resist closing the physical distance between them. "I know how different you are from other women, Miss Penny, and I not only delight in that difference, I respect it."

Her eyes narrowed suspiciously. "Guilford, this isn't like you," she said. "Not at all. What are you plotting?"

"I'm not plotting anything," he said indignantly. "Well, at least nothing nefarious, as most plotting usually is. What I'm *planning,* Amariah, is a way for us to be happy."

"I'm happy now," she said, unconvinced. "Why should you have to plan anything else?"

"Because of the other night, sweetheart," he said. "Because of how much we enjoy each other's company."

She lowered her chin, a bad sign. "Guilford, don't. We've already covered this sad, sorry road, and you *know* how I feel—"

"Which is the exact reason I'm here," he said quickly. "You're not the kind of woman who'll be swayed by jewels or a carriage in your own colors."

"How vastly clever of you to realize that!"

"I *am* vastly clever," he said, "as are you. I've considered how your position here precludes any…attachment between us, and for the best of possible reasons, too. All those widows and poor old soldiers and orphans like Billy Fox, not to mention the bast—I mean, babies like the one belonging to little Janey Patton. They depend on you, and what you earn for them here at Penny House. You can't abandon them just because of me, and I'd be a selfish clod to expect you to."

How fortunate that Pratt had mentioned Janey Patton's name! Guilford could see how remembering the new mother had softened Amariah's expression, her chin coming up a fraction at the mention of the baby. Not that Guilford sensed he was being conniving about this. Recalling Janey was simply fortuitous, another good portent for success, and anyway, he'd felt rather good about having sent the clothes to the fatherless baby.

"You have many faults, Guilford," she said, "but selfishness isn't generally among them. At least not any more than other dukes."

"That's just the beginning, Amariah." He reached out for her hand, gambling that she'd let him take it after mentioning the baby. Fortunately, she did. "You've changed me, you know. I'm planning to be even more unselfish."

She smiled, a smile so warm he almost considered kissing her now, before the other men and before anything was truly settled.

"Was it the visit to St. Crispin's that opened your eyes?" she asked. "Or has it been having Billy Fox in your stable, and seeing firsthand what a difference you can make in the life of an unfortunate?"

"It's you, sweet, and your doing. You may take all the credit you please." He linked his fingers into hers. "Now I don't want to interfere with all the charitable things you do, Amariah, but I don't want us to be deprived of each other's company, either, on account of what society might say. This is the best solution imaginable."

Still smiling, she shook her head. "You're making no sense, Guilford. You mean well, I know, but your intentions are garbling your wits."

He lifted her hand to his lips and kissed it. She *was* special, and he couldn't recall ever wanting a woman as much as he wanted her. "One thousand pounds this very morning, payable to St. Crispin's parish, with you named as the administrator. How does that sound?"

She gasped aloud. "How does that sound? Why, that sounds like you are the most generous gentleman imaginable!"

He grinned. "That's because I am," he teased. "I mean to make that a thousand a month."

"A *month?*" Her eyes widened round as saucers. "I've never heard of such—such *kindness!* Are you certain you wish to make such an extravagant offering, Guilford, or are you simply mad?"

"I am mad, Amariah," he said, "mad for you."

"Oh, yes, mad for *me*," she scoffed, her laughter bubbling up in the unexpected, merry way he found so infinitely delicious. "No one is that daft, Guilford! Not for a thousand a month!"

"You're worth every last shilling," he said. "And a thousand for St. Crispin's, or wherever else you please, every month as long as we're together."

The merriment changed to sudden shock. "Together? Together in what manner?"

"The usual one, sweetheart," he said, his voice low, for her ears only. "The same one we began to explore the other night. I want you, Amariah, and you want me, and this way we can be together without your charities suffering in the least."

She jerked her hand away. "Oh, you *are* mad," she cried, "fit for Bedlam and nowhere else!"

"I'm not mad like that, Amariah!" he protested, surprised by her reaction—or, more accurately, her overreaction. "I'm being eminently sensible, the way you are yourself!"

"Sensible?" she repeated, her voice wobbling just enough for him to understand that in some inexplicable way he'd wounded her. *"Sensible?"*

He nodded. "I've arranged things as practically as possible so there will never be any confusion or doubt. Amariah, I care for you. You're like no other woman I've ever known, and I want to make you happy."

She shook her head with wondering disbelief. "First you promised to help me by spying for the *Tattle,* and now this—*this!"*

"A thousand a month as long as we're together," he continued, still plunging ahead, "and five thousand when we part."

Suddenly the hurt he'd glimpsed in her eyes changed. She

was angry now, furious, her jaw set and her hands clasped so tightly at her waist that the knuckles were white.

"A parting gift before I've agreed to the rest?" she asked, biting off each word. "I should think, your grace, that such worries are premature."

"Not at all, Miss Penny," Bly said, unaware of the sudden change in her temperament. He patted the neat stack of papers on the table beside him. "His grace is demonstrating excellent judgment by settling this now, with a nice contract that will stand in any court, and signed before reason is clouded by passion."

"Not now, man," Guilford snapped. "Not *now*."

Amariah peered around the door, seeing the solicitor for the first time. "Who, sir, might you be?"

"That's Bly," Guilford said quickly. "He's my solicitor."

"Your procurer, you mean," she said to Guilford. "I will do what I must to follow my father's wishes, your grace, to aid and comfort those who have less. For you to try to put a price upon my efforts in this way, your grace, is—is *despicable*."

"Then what do you want me to do, Amariah?" he demanded, his frustration boiling over. "Damnation, you scorn every offer I make, reject every gift I try to give you!"

"You could try taking your offers and gifts among the empty stalls at Covent Garden tonight," she said, turning away. "I'm sure you'll find plenty there eager to oblige you."

"Amariah, wait, please!" He grabbed her by the shoulders, holding her steady so she couldn't turn away. "Don't you understand how dear you are to me? Whatever you want, it's yours. It's yours, but all you must do is tell me!"

"Perhaps you should be the one who should be understanding, your grace!" Her face was flushed with anger, her eyes glowing with it. "If you *understood* me, then you'd know that you'll never have enough gold to buy my heart or my body. For the gentleman I love, I'll give them for free, gladly and joyfully, but never in return for any price."

"But I *do* love you, Amariah!" he said. "I love you!"

"Do you, your grace?" For an endless moment, she searched his face with such intensity he felt his cheeks grow warm beneath her scrutiny, and once again he was sure her blue eyes were awash with unshed tears.

What did she discover? he wondered desperately. *What did he lack? What more could she hope to find that he hadn't already offered?*

"I do love you, sweetheart," he said hoarsely. "I do."

"Then I am most sorry for you, your grace," she said, softly, slipping free of his hands. She stepped back, visibly composing herself to curtsy a formal farewell. "I regret having to disappoint a man as fine as you, but I will not be your whore, not even for the price of your love. Good day, your grace, and if you choose not to return to Penny House, I'll understand."

Chapter Twelve

"Look at this, Westbrook," Stanton said, twisting around in his leather-covered armchair. "You've earned yourself a mention by name in the *Covent Garden Tattle*."

"I have?" Surprised, Westbrook snatched the paper from Stanton's hand. "I'm never in these things."

"Why should you be?" Stanton let his hands drop over the padded arms of the chair and sighed dramatically. The club was quiet at this time in the afternoon, which was the only reason he'd gotten first crack at the latest issue of the *Tattle,* anyway. "You're not rich enough, interesting enough, nor wicked enough for anyone to take notice, let alone write about."

"This writer thought so." With unabashed delight, Westbrook immediately spotted his name—edited, of course, with the customary asterisks that neither protected nor fooled anyone. Maybe this would even be enough to claim Guilford's place on the Penny House committee. "Ha, there I am!"

"Read it before you start crowing," Stanton cautioned, his heavy-lidded eyes already filled with boredom. "The

attle doesn't believe in respectful praise to those it skew-
s, you know."

"It begins respectful enough," Westbrook said, reading aloud.

"In our constant pursuit of TRUTH, we revisited the site
of the most recent Disturbance on St. James Street, viz.
the elegant gentlemen's retreat of Penny House. Many a
noble face proudly displayed the wounds of the
previous Battle of Honor, with bruises more worthy
of the Donnybrook Fair than the House of Lords. Included in this newly blooded group were the Marquis of
S*****l**d, the Earl of Fl**t, & the Baron W***b***k."

"Did you see my knuckles, Stanton?" Westbrook thrust his
and into the other man's face, flexing his fingers for the
reatest effect. "But I gave out more than I was given, that's
r certain."

Stanton was unimpressed. "Perhaps you should have the
hole thing engraved on a silver charger for posterity's sake."

"You're just jealous because they didn't mention you,"
Vestbrook said, too pleased with his newfound notoriety to
e offended. He wondered if the girls at Mrs. Poynton's house
ad the *Tattle;* he'd be sure to bring a copy or two of this is-
ue with him tonight, in case they hadn't seen it. "Do they
ention me again?"

Stanton waved one hand languidly through the air to sum-
on a waiter to bring him another brandy.

"Read on, read on," he said. "Though I doubt you'd stop
ven if I wished it."

"Stow it, Stanton," Westbrook said cheerfully, then contin-
ed reading.

"Yet after such an infamous melee, we were surprised to see that all had once again been put to Rights. We likewise observed that extra guards & other officers of justice & peace had been employed to keep the play honest, & a fit Diversion for all Gentlemen belonging to the Club. We are most honored & heartened to see our earlier WARNINGS had been heeded, & the banner for TRUTH & HONESTY once again raised high."

"Well, you're certainly not going to be mentioned there Westbrook," Stanton said. "Not in the same breath as truth an honesty."

But Westbrook had stopped thinking of himself. "Mis Penny was there last night?" he asked uneasily. "Did she, ah did she speak with you?"

Stanton groaned, and stared up at the ceiling. "Of cours she was there. She's never *not* there. You spoke to her your self, you idiot. I saw you."

Westbrook swallowed, trying to keep the anxiety from hi voice. He hadn't meant to strike her, indeed he hadn't, bu she'd surprised him, there in the dark, so that he hadn't ha time to think. "She didn't, ah, say anything curious to you?"

"She was pleasant enough as always, but I wouldn't call i curious," Stanton said while Westbrook held his breath. "Sh was wearing that new silk turban on her head with long curl hanging out along her neck—even you couldn't have misse it—and I told her how fetching it was. Gave her that *harem houri* look. Not that I used those exact words, of course, bu the Turkish fashion does set a man to thinking of all the se cret charms she's hiding away."

"Do you believe that's why she was wearing the turban To hide something?" Westbrook hadn't even considered tha

He knew he'd caught her on the head when she'd come after him with that pistol, or club, or whatever it was in the dark. Could he have wounded her so badly that she'd needed to hide it? "She could hide all sorts of secrets under all that silk."

Striking a woman, even unintentionally, was a grievous crime. How much had she seen of him, anyway? Was it enough to identify him to the constable? And what if they'd linked him to that promissory note he'd forged and left on her desk? He should never have babbled on to her about winning, reminding her like that. He'd tried to disguise his handwriting, but what if they compared it side by side to the letters he'd sent before about the cheat in the hazard room? Oh, he'd be in it then, up to his neck with no way clear!

"What was she hiding in her turban?" asked Stanton, exasperated. "The Crown Jewels that she'd stolen from the Tower. What the devil do you think I meant, you idiot? I meant what she had beneath her gown and shift, not under her damned bonnet!"

Westbrook scowled back down at the newssheet, praying he hadn't betrayed himself. It was a powerfully good thing that Stanton wasn't half the genius he thought he was. And Guilford hadn't been there, either. If Guilford had been sticking his clever nose into this, then he'd likely be in real trouble by now.

Now he went back to reading, determined to distract Stanton before he started thinking again.

"We must also pause to praise the SUPREME RULER of Penny House, who must be praised as much for her wisdom as for her beauty. To single out & honor one lady is a dangerous practice, for fear of slighting all the others, but the RED QUEEN—Queen of Hearts, Queen of Diamonds, Queen of Penny House deserves such distinction for her swift judgment against the nefarious CHEATS, her grace in the LINE OF BATTLING GENTLEMEN, & her Bravery & Strength in the bold face of MENACING DANGER at the hands of him who wished her ill. We wish only the best to this Gallant Lady, & would that she could serve as a Proper Model to others of her Sex."

"Well, now, that's a pretty slice of pie for Miss Penny," Stanton said with fresh interest. "I wonder who she paid for that?"

"Everything's for sale if the price is right," Westbrook said, striving to sound sage instead of panicky. She must have told the *Tattle*'s editor about what happened in her rooms two nights ago. What else could that rubbish about the "bold face of danger" mean? Would his name appear in the next issue: Baron W***b***k, who'd attacked the brave Red Queen herself?

"She's a clever one, that Miss Penny," Stanton continued, taking his brandy from the waiter's tray. "What with the rumors of a cheat and that fight you started with the whole clan—"

"I didn't start it!" Westbrook protested. "I was provoked!"

"Whatever you please," Stanton said, serenity filling his face as he sipped the brandy. "You'd think most of members of Penny House would've stayed away from the place after scandals like that, not wanting to be tainted themselves, but she's turned it all to her advantage. I've never seen the place more crowded than it was last night. I'll gladly do what the old *Tattle* advises, and lift my glass to the Red Queen herself."

He raised his glass in tribute just as the waiter returned, a letter on a salver for him.

"Here now, what can this be?" Stanton said, putting down his glass to crack the seal on the letter. "Who'd write to me here?"

"Whichever one of your friends knows how to write," Westbrook said, nervousness turning him belligerent. "And he being here, I'd say the possibilities are limited."

"It's from Guilford," Stanton said, his voice full of amazement. "Can you fathom it?"

"Guilford wrote to you?" Westbrook's voice squeaked upward with distress. What if she'd told Guilford, too, and now Guilford was telling Stanton? "Why'd he do that?"

"See for yourself," Stanton said, tossing the short letter into Westbrook's lap. "He's calling off the wager about Amariah Penny."

Westbrook seized the note, relief flooding over him. "You mean he's failed to bed her in the allotted time?"

"He still had another week," Stanton said, swirling the brandy in his glass. "No, I'd say he's had all the success he could hope for. Recall that we saw his chaise before Penny House the other night."

"Then why'd he call off the wager when he won?"

"Because the duke's in love with her, that's why, and he doesn't want the world to know any of it. So much for the saintly Miss Penny's precious reputation!" Stanton's mouth curled into a lascivious grin. "I say, Westbrook. You're always up for sport. Why don't we share Guilford's good news, and give a little information of our own to those rascals at the *Tattle?*"

"You mean tell them that the Duke of Guilford has a new mistress?" Westbrook asked eagerly. This was far, far better than any little scandal he could concoct, far more certain, too, and sure to make everyone forget any suspicion that might be pulling toward him. "The Red Queen turns scarlet whore?"

"Something like that, Westbrook," Stanton said, and laughed. "And all for sport, you understand. Something very like that indeed."

Alone upstairs in her rooms, Amariah sat at her desk with her bruised arm sitting in a pan of water with ice, trying to concentrate on reading the newest letter from her youngest sister, Cassia. Cassia had not been back to Penny House since Bethany's wedding, and with Amariah's added responsibilities as the last Penny sister at the club, she in turn had been unable to visit Cassia and her husband, Richard, at Greenwood Hall, their home in Hampshire.

It was especially difficult not seeing Cassia now, while she was expecting her first child, and as Amariah read Cassia's descriptions of her changing body and temperament, she tried to picture her little sister with a baby of her own. For as long as Amariah could remember, she'd been the one who'd looked after her younger sisters, taking the place of their own mother. It was strange to think that now Cassia would be a real mother, and likely Bethany soon after, while Amariah would be the one who might never have children at all.

Who would have guessed her life would turn out like this? She'd always imagined herself wed to one of the young men from the county, most likely another cleric, as her father had been, with a cottage full of children. She'd thought she'd lead a useful life in whatever village she lived near, perhaps even teaching in the parish school. She'd gotten to do the good works, true, but she'd never dreamed she'd run a fashionable gentlemen's club in London, managing a large staff and mingling with lords and other powerful men every night while great sums of money frivolously changed hands all around her.

And she'd never once thought—not once—that she'd still

e a spinster at twenty-six and destined to become everyone's favorite old aunt. It wasn't even that she wanted a husband, for most husbands would make her give up what she
did at Penny House, and she didn't want that, either. What she
wanted was simple enough: she wanted love.

She sighed, turning her arm gently in the chill water. It was
a warm and sunny afternoon, warm enough that she'd opened
the windows, and the ice had melted into tiny little pellets in
the water. Guilford had promised her ice would make her
arm feel better, and he'd been right. If she were honest, he'd
been right about a great many things, from recognizing how
much Billy Fox loved horses to seeing there was something
a bit peculiar about Lord Westbrook, even to suggesting to
Pratt a better—and less expensive—Madeira to serve.

But when he'd finally told her he loved her, she'd been absolutely certain he was wrong.

She groaned, and bowed her head. Why had he gone and
ruined everything? What they'd had wasn't perfect, but it had
been better than what he'd proposed, and infinitely better
than not seeing him at all.

As shocked as she'd been by his offer, the more she'd
thought about it, the more reasonable it seemed. Not that she
would take money in return for her body, of course—her self-
respect ran too deep for that—but she could understand how
she'd so perplexed Guilford that he'd believed this was the
only way. In his world, it likely was.

He'd been right about much of the rest, too. She'd refused
lie with him in her bedchamber because she hadn't wanted
scandal to lessen the club's earnings, and he'd volunteered
to make up the losses. He couldn't offer marriage, but he'd
offered the next best thing he could, fortified with the legal-
ity he knew she respected. He'd realized how different she was

from other women, and that had made her more, not less, at-
tractive to him. High-ranking as he was, he'd still made rare
gifts of himself to her, coming with her to St. Crispin's, even
brushing her hair when she hadn't been able, while she realized she had given him very little in return. He'd known that
even a woman as strong as she tried to be would need an even
stronger male shoulder to lean upon. And when he'd said she
wanted him as much as he wanted her, he'd been so right she
could have wept from it.

She missed him already.

She heard Pratt at the door, and called for him to enter. She
lifted her arm from the water and was blotting it dry with a
cloth as Pratt joined her.

"Forgive me, miss, but I still believe you should have left
the splint in place," he said, managing to be at once scolding
and concerned. "It doesn't look well at all."

"It looks like a bruise, nothing more or less," she said,
turning in her chair to face him. "A bruise always looks worse
before it looks better. What is that you have tucked under
your arm?"

"The latest issue of the *Covent Garden Tattle.*" Pratt hesitated,
keeping the paper out of her reach. "Do you wish to read it?"

She held her hand out, her heart racing. Part of her wanted
to toss the paper directly into the fire, without tormenting
herself by reading whatever Guilford had written. The other,
braver part of her demanded to read it, and be ready to con-
front the worst.

The braver part won, and she snapped open the crackling
sheets. "Do you know what's in here, Pratt?"

"No, miss," he said. "Not the details, anyway. But the boy
who brought it to the back door said that Penny House was
mentioned."

"And he got you to buy it from him, too." She sighed impatiently, scanning the columns of type until she found Penny House's name. Quickly she read the story, then read it again to make sure she'd seen the words as they were printed, and not as she'd wished them to be.

"Is it that bad, Miss Penny?" Pratt asked anxiously. "It's worse than last time, isn't it?"

She looked up from the paper, struggling to keep her emotions from her face. "Why do you believe it's worse, Pratt?"

"Because last time you were a very fury, miss," he said, "and this time you're pale as death. I'd rather see the fury."

Carefully she folded the page to highlight the story. She was the only one who'd know that Guilford had written this, and written it for her, too. He'd done exactly as he'd promised, repairing the Club's reputation and correcting all the errors that had been in the last issue, and he'd done it for her. But that wasn't all. Queen of Hearts, Queen of Diamonds, Queen of Penny House: nearly every drawing room in London would have this paper on a tea table by nightfall, yet she would be the only one who'd understand what it meant.

There were, she realized now, a great many ways for a man to say *I love you.*

And Guilford—without a doubt, Guilford loved her.

"Please call for a hackney for me, Pratt," she said as she handed him the paper to read for himself. "I find I must once again go call upon the author of a *Tattle* story."

"Oh, miss, I am sorry," Pratt said, his face weighed down by his unhappiness as he left with the paper in his hands. "I'll have the hackney waiting for you at the door."

"Thank you, Pratt," she said, rising to dress. "I'll be ready directly."

She only prayed that Guilford could say the same.

* * *

Guilford sank a little lower into the bath, letting the water lap over his chest. He'd gone riding for most of the morning, not genteel riding in the park, but hard riding, pushing himself and his horse as he tried to wear the edge from his frustration. Now he was hot and tired and his stable master was vexed at him for keeping his horse out for so long.

The ride hadn't helped. No matter what he did, he still couldn't banish Amariah from his thoughts, or from the rest of him, either. Telling himself—*ordering* himself—to forget her didn't begin to work. He could accept that she'd refuse his gifts and Bly's tidy contract, but what stung the most was how thoroughly she'd rejected *him*. How had she become such a part of him, anyway? She'd been able to put him aside easily enough. Why in blazes couldn't he do the same with her?

He closed his eyes and swore softly to himself. If she didn't wish to see him, then he didn't want to see her, either. He'd leave town. Scotland, or—

What the devil was *that?*

He pushed himself up, listening. Someone was pounding on his front door as if the whole house were on fire. Where were the servants? Why hadn't anyone answered that blasted door?

Through two floors and closed doors, he still could hear Amariah's voice. He clambered from the bath, water sloshing over the sides to the floor, and hastily grabbed his dressing gown. He knew she must be in the hall outside his bedchamber now, because he'd never heard that particular pleading tone from Dunner as he tried to make her wait outside.

What had become of all her blessed propriety now? Storming into his house like this, up the stairs to his bedchamber as if she'd every right—what about the scandal in that? And why now, when he'd already decided the best, the only course was to put her from his mind forever? Why try to revive it, like a drowned corpse pulled from the sea?

He'd barely tied the sash around his dressing gown when the door flew open and she came striding in, leaving Dunner and two other horrified footmen cowering in her wake.

"Good day, Miss Penny," he said. Her face was flushed, her hair tousled and hat askew, and she seemed to have for once forgotten her gloves. He'd never seen her look more lovely, and it was only partly because he'd thought he'd never see her again at all. "How kind of you to call."

She frowned, her gaze running over him from his dripping hair to his bare feet and the small puddle he was leaving on the floor. Her expression was more determined as her bare hands clutched in tight, pugnacious fists at her sides, and he wasn't quite certain whether she would rather kiss him, or punch him.

"Guilford," she said. "You're soaking wet."

He purposefully did not smile, not until he learned exactly why she'd come here to torment him. "Did you force your way into my house to tell me that?"

"No." She shook her head, swallowed and looked him squarely in the eye. "I came to tell you I love you."

Chapter Thirteen

"You love me?" Guilford asked. "You've come here to tell me that?"

"That," Amariah said, trying to ignore the sizable curtained bed that occupied so much of his bedchamber, "and a great many other things besides."

"I'd like to hear them, Miss Penny," he said, his face as unreadable as a handsome brick wall. "If you'll grant me a few moments to dress, then—"

"I won't," she said, raising her chin. "That is, you're fine as you are now, at least for what I have to say."

Which was, of course, an out-and-out lie. He looked so much like a great shaggy dog that had gone swimming in the river that she half expected him to shake himself and scatter water drops onto her. His dark hair bristled out every which way and his scarlet silk dressing gown—oh, she remembered that dressing gown, from when he'd been the pasha of Grosvenor Square!—clung damply to his shoulders and chest and thighs in a very distracting fashion, but she wasn't about to let him escape to dress, not after she'd come this far.

"Pray, sit, Miss Penny," he said, waving toward the pair of armchairs covered in yellow brocade that flanked the fireplace.

"Thank you, no," she said resolutely. "I'd rather stand."

"Would you like tea?" he asked like any other genial host. "Chocolate?"

She shook her head. Heaven help her, this time he wasn't wearing anything beyond bathwater under that paisley silk dressing gown, was he?

He nodded to the servants to leave, waiting until the door closed softly after them. "So tell me."

She blinked, then recovered, squaring her shoulders and lifting her chin.

"Yes." She must concentrate on his face, only his face. She had always found Guilford the easiest gentleman in the world to talk to. Why now, when it was so important, was it a struggle to find the right words? "I have been considering all you said, Guilford, considering it with great care, and—"

"You're accepting?"

"What, that hideous offer?" she exclaimed. "I most certainly am not!"

"Ah." He didn't smile. "That is just as well, since the offer has been withdrawn. Proceed."

"Thank you." She clasped and unclasped her hands. In her haste, she'd forgotten her gloves, and her hands felt disturbingly naked—a foolish qualm, she knew, compared to him in that dressing gown, let alone what they were discussing. "As I was saying, I've been considering what you told me, and what you were offering, and I must admit that despite the sinfulness of what you proposed, your generosity was most remarkable."

"I was generous because I thought the sin would be remarkable, too," he said bluntly. "Though from your outrage, I must have been mistaken."

Her face grew hot, and she turned away from him, toward the fireplace, so he wouldn't notice and she wouldn't have to see him.

"Then perhaps I was mistaken about coming here at all," she said. "But I wanted you to know that as much money as you were willing to give to St. Crispin's, I now know the extent of what you were really offering, and I appreciate that even more."

"What else was there beyond a thousand pounds a month?" he asked, and she didn't miss the bitterness in his words. "Forgive me, but I must have missed that."

"There *was* much more, Guilford," she said softly. "Think of what you gave me just that one night. You brushed my hair. You told me that ice would lessen the swelling in my arm. You held me when I needed to be held, and told me stories of when you were a boy so I wouldn't be afraid."

"I didn't give you anything," he said, clearly mystified. "I only did what any gentleman would have done in the circumstances."

"Most gentlemen wouldn't have done anything of the sort," she said. "You must recall how much I see of gentlemen every night, Guilford. I'd guess that the majority of them in the same circumstances might have called for Pratt, if I'd been fortunate, and then disappeared as fast as they could so they wouldn't be involved or implicated."

"I couldn't abandon you like that," he said, incredulous. "Not you."

"But you see, that's what makes you different from the other lords." She smiled, even though her back was to him. "You may be miles and miles above me in rank and wealth, but you've never treated me as if there were so much as a hair's breadth distance between us. You've given me that, too, Guilford, and how rare a gift it is!"

"Damnation, Amariah, you're the rare one," he said gruffly. "I couldn't treat you like other women because you're not like any of them, not that I've ever known. I've never made a secret of that, either. You can ask anyone."

"I don't have to," she said, "because I've heard it from you. Which is why I'm here, Guilford, so you can hear the same from me."

"What, that I'm not like any other woman you've known?"

She didn't laugh. She couldn't, even though she knew she was supposed to. Instead she stared at the painting that hung over a black ormolu clock on the mantelpiece, a likeness of two spotted hunting dogs with a dead pheasant on the ground between them. As the clock ticked away the seconds, she struggled to concentrate on the dogs and pheasant, and not let her emotions run completely away with her senses. Too much was at stake.

"Well, yes, Guilford, that, of course," she said softly, striving to sound light and failing miserably. "But also to tell you that—that when you told me you loved me, I couldn't believe it. I couldn't, partly because you're His Grace the Duke of Guilford and I'm only Miss Penny, but mostly because…because I love you, too. There now, I've said it aloud, and I'm done, and I can leave you in peace and not trouble you again."

She turned blindly toward the door and escape, keeping her head bowed without the shield of the hunting dogs to help keep back the tears.

She hadn't counted on him blocking her path, a barricade of dark Indian paisley silk and dark curling hair on a very solid chest, still glistening with droplets of bathwater.

"You can't go yet, Amariah," he said. "Not until you've done one more thing for me."

She looked up at him at last, without any real choice to do otherwise. "I should leave, Guilford."

"I won't let you," he said, his voice so low and deep that she felt it like a caress along her spine. "You've said I've done so much for you, and now it's time for you to do one thing for me."

"One thing, then, Guilford," she said, the words coming out like a breathy sigh. She was sure he was going to ask for a farewell kiss, and she was just as sure she'd grant it. "One thing only."

One side of his mouth quirked up. "Call me by my given name."

She flushed, and wrinkled her nose. "Why that?"

"Because it would give me enormous pleasure to hear it on your lips." He touched his forefinger to her mouth, tracing the bow. "Right there."

"Ask me something else," she said. "Please, Guilford."

His smile curved wider. "You don't know it, do you? You've let me lie on your bed with you, and you don't even remember my name."

"I must have known it sometime," she said in an embarrassed rush, "because I make it a habit to learn the names and titles and addresses of all the members of Penny House, and their wives' names, too, if they're wed."

He sighed dramatically. "But I don't have a wife, and apparently I don't have a first name, either."

"Guilford, please!" she wailed in mortification. "I'm sorry I've forgotten your name, but no one ever uses it, and early on you gave me leave to call you Guilford, the way all your friends do, and since then I've no use to—"

"It's Eliot," he murmured, slanting his head as he ducked beneath the brim of her hat to kiss her. "But since you love me, you can call me Guilford, too."

She closed her eyes and parted her lips for him, closing in

her tears, as well. If this were to be the last kiss they shared, then she wanted it marked by joy, not sorrow. She rested her palms on his shoulders, holding herself steady, because oh, she was feeling wonderfully unsteady by now. His skin was warm, the hair on his chest rough and springy framed by the damp silk of the dressing gown, and this kiss between them was slow and lazy and deep and rich and if it lasted forever, she could be happy forever, too.

She felt the slippery tickle of more silk across her throat as he untied the bonnet strings beneath her chin and pushed the hat backward. The straw brim bounced off her shoulders and tumbled to the floor behind her, and she didn't care. Instead when his arm curled around her waist to draw her closer, she slipped her hands over his shoulders and around his back and arched against him. There was no question now that he wore nothing beneath the dressing gown, for she could feel every muscle, every bone beneath the sleek glide of the scarlet silk. His wet hair flicked against her bare wrists, cool against her skin, the scattered drops leaving tiny cool dots on her muslin gown.

Finally he broke the kiss, their faces still close. "Do you remember my name now, sweetheart?"

"Guilford," she said, her breathing quick, her lips so sensitized from his kiss that it felt odd simply to smile. "But I may also call you Eliot, to surprise you."

"I hate Eliot," he said, "so don't surprise me. Tell me, Amariah. You do not really intend to leave now, do you?"

Her smile faded. She knew what he meant: that enormous curtained bed was reminder enough if she didn't. "You tell me the answer to that."

"I won't," he said, brushing his fingers over her cheek. "I can't. It's your decision to make. What you want, and what you'll take."

"Or what we'll both give to each other." She moved her hands restlessly over his arms, unable not to touch him. "No gold this time, or ruby bracelets. I'll never make a mercenary."

"No?" His eyes were full of question, if not out-and-out doubt. "You are certain, sweetheart?"

"Yes," she said firmly. "I know most say it's impossible for men and women to be friends, but we were long before this. I trust you. You give yourself to me, and I shall give myself to you, and that's all the contract we'll need. I love you, Guilford, or Eliot, or whomever you are."

That made him laugh, a deep chuckle.

"And I love you, and could never wish for anything more," he said, running his hand lightly up and down her spine in a way that made her want to purr like a cat. "But I want you to be sure, sweetheart. The talk, the scandal, the effect on Penny House will still be the same."

"Even if the only honest contributor to the *Covent Garden Tattle* is my dearest friend?"

"Especially not," he said. "You can't keep a secret like this in London."

"You can't keep a secret like this anywhere," she said. Now that she was here with him, she felt braver, more courageous, and ready to take on any mere gossips for the sake of their love. "But I won't be ashamed, Guilford, and I won't let them make me feel that way. So long as I hold my head high and live as I want, then I'll be content."

"With me?" he asked softly, his expression surprisingly vulnerable.

"With you," she said, taking his face in her hands to kiss him. "I love you, Guilford. Oh, how much I love you!"

His answer was a wordless growl, lost between their mouths in their kiss. She circled her arms around the back of his neck, deepening the kiss with him. She'd never tire of kissing him, or pressing against him this way. The thin silk of his dressing gown had already revealed more than it hid, and now as they twined more closely together she was acutely aware of the hard, insistent length of his need against her.

"I've an unfair advantage here," he whispered, his hands shifting around behind her. "Let me help even the odds."

"First you brush my hair, then you undress me," she said, laughing as she stood dutifully still. "You really will have to become my maid."

"Any time you wish it, Miss Penny," he said. He was proving most adept at unfastening the tiny covered buttons along the back of her gown, popping each one free in turn, and finally unhooking the inside tapes that held her skirts in place. The front of her bodice began to fall forward and as she automatically began to catch the soft muslin to hold it in place, he caught her hands instead. "I'm undressing you, sweetheart, not the other way around."

Obediently she released her gown, holding her hands out before her.

"Better, much better," he whispered as he slid the gown and her chemise beneath it from her shoulders and over the tops of her arms. "But I can make it better still."

He bent down and kissed the hollow of her collarbone, and she shivered at the sensation: who would have guessed such a place would be so sensitive?

"You're vastly familiar with ladies' clothes, Guilford," she said, not really wanting to dwell on the reasons for that familiarity, but still unable to resist twitting him.

"I have sisters," he said with such improbable blandness that she laughed out loud.

"Is that like the hairdresser all over again?" she asked.

"You were watching your sisters dress before they went out for the evening, and that was enough to teach you all the finer points of buttons and tapes and hooks and loops?"

Now he was kissing her on the side of her throat, and she shivered again with fresh delight. It was one thing to overhear lovemaking described by the gentlemen in the club—and she'd overheard a great deal more than they'd ever realized; but it was far different to actually do and feel those same things, and discover how much pleasure her own body could give and take.

"Oh, my dear Amariah," he said as he eased the gown's short puffed sleeves down along her arms, moving with such exquisite slowness that the muslin seemed to caress her skin. "Don't you trust me?"

"Implicitly," she whispered, holding her breath as he slipped the bodice lower, lower, until he'd bared her breasts, too. She gasped, and once again her hands fluttered up with modesty.

"Then trust me again," he whispered, gently pushing her hands aside. "Implicitly, or however else you please."

He bent to kiss first one breast, then the other, drawing the soft flesh into his mouth and teasing each nipple with his tongue and lips until it stood rosy and taut, and she was moaning with the unexpected pleasure as she cradled his head. Her heart was racing and her body felt on fire, coaxed to this heat by Guilford's touch and *she did not want it to stop*.

"There now," he whispered, kissing her lips again. "I told you to trust me, didn't I?"

Before she could answer, he'd bent to slip his arms behind her knees and sweep her off her feet.

That was how the poets always described it—swept away by love, passion, desire—and for once she discovered the poets hadn't exaggerated. She was tall for a woman, yet Guilford plucked her up as if she were no more than a sprite, rocking her back into the crook of his arm to carry her the short distance to the bed.

She sank deep into the featherbed, with only a moment to stare up at the gathered yellow brocade of the canopy overhead before Guilford was there with her, the full sleeves of his red dressing gown fluttering around his arms like wings, her own dark angel.

"Scarlet and gold, like flames," she said breathlessly, reaching up for him. "Like you."

"Like *you*," he said, easing himself over her. "I should have known with fire for hair that the rest of you would be just as hot."

This time when he kissed her it was different, more demanding, more passionate. Somehow she'd shed her shoes and her gown, her shift now little more than a twisted tangle of linen around her waist. She slipped her hands inside the dressing gown, running her hands along the length of his back to feel the work and play of his muscles, from the breadth of his shoulders and back down where his waist and hips narrowed. His skin seemed on fire, too, the first coolness of the water she'd felt earlier replaced by a glow that burned from inside him, while the silk of the dressing gown glided over the backs of her hands.

He shifted slightly to one side, his hand gliding over the curve of her hip, lower. Gently he coaxed her legs to part, just enough to slip between them and stroke her in her most secret place. She gasped, clutching at his shoulders.

"Trust me, love," he whispered. "Trust me."

She couldn't catch her breath enough to answer, or to tell him what she'd trust him most to do was not stop what he was doing. She arched against his fingers, wanting more of this wonderful tension he was building in her body. He eased over her, settling himself between her spread legs, parting her, replacing his fingers with something hot, blunt, and infinitely larger. Before she realized what was happening, he was thrusting into her, pushing hard, and she cried out with surprise and a sharp shock of discomfort. He kissed her again, soothing her, letting her grow accustomed to him, even as he began rocking slowly inside her.

And slowly she began to move with him as that strange, pleasurable tension he'd first created with his fingers began to return, only better, because now he was touching and stroking her deep inside and she'd never felt anything remotely like it in her life. Instinctively she curled her legs around his waist, taking him deeper, and he groaned, and it was better for her, too, holding him like that. He began moving faster, harder, until her body felt coiled and tight and aching for something elusive, something more, and then it was there, exploding from inside her like fireworks, or earthquakes, or some other inadequate way those poets used to express this, and they never would get it right, not the way it was between her and Guilford.

Afterward they lay together for a long time, their limbs intimately tangled, in a companionable silence that Amariah found wonderful indeed.

"I love you, Amariah," he whispered at last, smoothing her hair back from her face to kiss her. "You, mind?"

"I love you, too." She smiled up to him, blinking. There were tears in her eyes, not from pain, but because she loved him that much. "That was not at all what I'd expected."

"Nor I, either." He propped himself up on his elbow to look at her. "You were a virgin."

"Well, yes," she said, surprised he'd ask such a question. "What made you think otherwise?"

"I don't know," he said, hedging.

"I do," she said, irritated that he'd think she wouldn't understand. "Because I'm twenty-six, and there's no such creature as a twenty-six-year-old virgin in London. Because of all the gentlemen I greet each night at Penny House. Because—"

"Because none of that matters now," he said, lightly covering her mouth with his fingers to silence her. "Because now you're my Amariah, and my lover, and no one else's. I'm sorry only because I would have done things differently if I'd known I was your first."

She smiled, because that made sense. "Then I'm glad you didn't know, since I wouldn't have wanted you to do anything differently. That was...*marvelous*."

"Yes," he said, and now he smiled, too. "It was deuced marvelous for me, too."

"That's as it should be." She sighed happily as she curled closer to him, his arm draped over her hip. She could not imagine feeling any more content, or more cherished, either. "It's quite strange to think that I'm here with you, in this outlandish bed that's as big as a stable yard, with neither of us wearing a stitch to speak of, and yet, because it's you, I'm not in the least ashamed."

"Because it's you," he repeated, "and you're a true wanton."

She gave him a genteel jab in the ribs with her elbow. "And who made me that way, I ask you?"

"True wantons are born that way," he said. "I had nothing whatsoever to do with converting you."

"Liar," she said, making it more an endearment than a fault.

"Not with you. I wouldn't dare." He lifted her hand to his lips and kissed her fingers. "No regrets?"

She knew what he meant by that, too. "I don't wish I'd

waited for a husband, no. I *am* twenty-six, Guilford, and well accustomed to being my own mistress and no one else's. A husband would try to rule my life for me, and we'd both be miserable. But worse, by law Penny House would become his from the day we wed, and I could not abide that."

"That's all true enough," he said, so uncharacteristically thoughtful that she twisted around to see his face.

Had he heard any of her own doubts? Had she unwittingly betrayed her longings for a man who'd be there at her side for life, or the children that she'd most likely never bear? Was he thinking the same thoughts as she, that dukes dutifully married the daughters of other peers, while the daughters of country vicars married far more ordinary men?

Did he perhaps know her as well as she claimed she knew him?

"It is true," she insisted, as much to herself as to him. "And besides, if I were married, I wouldn't be here with you."

His smile was dear enough to break her heart, and more than enough to make her lean forward and kiss him—a sweet kiss, more pledge than passion. Strange to realize she'd now learned the difference.

The onyx and ormolu clock on the mantel chimed, five quick bells. She sighed, and flopped back onto the pillow. "How can it be so late, Guilford?"

"But it's not late," he protested. "It's early."

"For Penny House, it's late," she said ruefully. "I should be back by now. There's always so much to do before opening, and I must be—"

"Stay," he said, cradling her cheek in the palm of his hand. "Don't go. Stay the night with me instead."

She stared at him, the suggestion almost unfathomable. "Every night since we've opened, I've always been at the

ont door. I haven't missed one, not even the other night af-
r I'd hurt my arm."

"Then let this be the first," he said, his voice dropping
wer as he leaned forward and kissed her, a reminder of what
ey'd just done and a promise of what they'd do again. "For
e, love."

She smiled, feeling the pull of responsibility against the
re of remaining here with him. She'd never done such a
icked, selfish act in her life. She looked at Guilford's sleepy
lue eyes, bare chest and half smile, and decided it might be
igh time she did.

"I'll have one of your servants carry a note to Pratt," she
aid, looping her arms around the back of Guilford's neck to
raw him down on the pillows with her. "He can take my
uties for this one night."

"No wonder I love you," he said, easing down over her.
How could I not?"

Westbrook sauntered up the steps of Penny House with
tanton, ready to receive his usual warm welcome from Ama-
iah Penny. He hadn't exactly been bragging about those
varm welcomes to Stanton, but he hadn't been downplaying
hem, either, and he was looking forward to Stanton seeing
ne for himself. Besides, he was feeling powerfully lucky to-
iight; maybe he really would match those winnings he'd cre-
ited for himself on that promissory note.

But instead of the divine Miss Penny, lemon-faced old
'ratt was standing in her place and greeting the members as
hey arrived.

"See here, now, Pratt, where's Miss Penny?" he demanded.
Where've you hidden her?"

Pratt bowed, unperturbed. "I'm sorry, my lord, but Miss

Penny will not be joining us tonight. I'm afraid she's not fee
ing well, and sends her deepest regrets."

"Not well?" Westbrook couldn't believe it, or didn't wa
to. "How can she not be here? Damnation, she's always here

Pratt bowed again. "I am sorry, my lord. Miss Penny doe
enjoy extraordinary good health, but this night, she is indis
posed."

"Indisposed, my ass," Westbrook muttered as he and Stanto
made their way back into the hall. "That woman's never sick.

Stanton shrugged. "Tonight she is," he said. "But you kno
how women are, claiming they're poorly to weasel out o
their responsibilities. Maybe she heard you were coming, ol
fellow, and that was enough to put her off her feed."

Westbrook scowled at the other man. "I say, that's damne
nonsense, Stanton. Miss Penny regards me as one of her spe
cial members here. She's not about to avoid me like that, an
that's the truth."

"Well, you'd know," Stanton said, clearly enjoying West
brook's discomfiture. "You've had enough other ladies giv
you that old excuse before, that I'd think you'd recognize th
signs by now."

"Stow it, Stanton," Westbrook said as they headed u
the stairs to the hazard room. "What you don't know abou
women would fill the whole ocean to India and back."

The hazard room was crowded, with most of the seats
taken around the large oval table. A game was already in
progress, but Westbrook still pushed his way to an empty
chair, ready to jump in as soon as he could.

Tonight was going to be his night, he knew it. If he won,
truly won, then Amariah would smile at him again, and Stanton would have to eat his words. He could almost feel luck hovering over him like a golden cloud, ready to shower good

ortune all over him, and eagerly he watched the caster rattle
he dice in the box before he tossed them across the green cloth.

"My lord," said the liveried footman, bending close to
whisper in his ear. "If you please, Mr. Walthrip would like a
word in private."

Surprised, Westbrook twisted around. The director of the
hazard table hardly ever spoke at all, let alone to anyone in
private. "Walthrip wants to see me?"

"This way, my lord," the footman said, ushering him from
he table. "Mr. Walthrip will address you back here, in his private closet."

Westbrook shoved back his chair from the table and fol-
owed, puffed up with self-importance.

"The director wants to see me in private," he said to Stan-
on as he passed by. "Likely Miss Penny asked him to speak
o me about some special question of the game."

Mr. Walthrip's private closet was hardly the grand space
Westbrook had expected for such an eminence: a tiny space
without windows, scarcely large enough for a straight-backed
chair and a tall, narrow accountant's desk with a stool tucked
n the kneehole. There were nothing decorative or personal to
he space, only a ledger, a pen and an inkwell on the desk, and
a single candlestick.

The hazard director was waiting, his wispy white hair lit
from behind like ethereal floss, his black-coated shoulders
rounded forward as if he were permanently surveying the
hazard table.

"Come in, my lord, if you please," he said in his dry, grav-
elly voice. "I thank you for coming."

"Not at all, Walthrip," Westbrook said heartily, dropping
into the single chair. "Always ready to oblige."

"Yes, my lord. I shall consume as little of your time as pos-

sible." Walthrip glanced at the open ledger, running one fir
ger along the entries, stopping at one. He tapped his finge
twice on the entry, closed the book and looked back to West
brook. "You inquired last evening as to an extension of you
line at the hazard table. I regret that the house has decided tha
such an extension is not possible at this time."

Westbrook stared, stunned. It wasn't just the disgrace o
being rejected here; his uncle had refused him another ad
vance against his income and his inheritance, cutting him of
for the next two months.

"What in blazes do you mean, the 'house' decided agains
me?" he demanded. "The bricks, the mortar, the tiles on th
roof? Give me a real name, Walthrip! Tell me who believe
I'm not gentleman enough!"

Walthrip let his blue-veined hand drift through the air. "It's
not a question of honor, your grace. No one has called tha
into question. All that is required is a payment on your ac
count, and—"

"This is not to be borne!" Westbrook jumped to his feet
slamming his fist on the tall desk beside the closed ledger. "I
am a gentleman, a lord and a member of this club, and I will
not be treated with such little respect!"

At once the door behind him opened, and two of the large-
boned guards silently appeared, their hands folded before
them and their faces grim.

"A simple payment, my lord," Walthrip said, "and we shall
be happy to welcome you back to the table."

"Your table be damned!" Westbrook kicked at the chair before he shoved past the two guards. He turned down the stairs,
looking for Pratt, and acutely aware of the guards following
close behind him.

Pratt was still at the front door, greeting newcomers, as if

othing had happened, as if Westbrook hadn't suffered the
ost humiliating shame he could recall.

"I have to speak to Miss Penny, Pratt," he whispered ur-
ently. "That old bastard Walthrip just cut me off from the
azard table, and I've a right to know why. Miss Penny would
ever treat me like that!"

Pratt's face might have been carved from ivory. "Mr. Wal-
hrip was simply relaying a decision by the house, my lord.
Miss Penny does not hold that responsibility. Now if you
lease, my lord, I suggest that you calm yourself before—"

"Of course Miss Penny can fix things," Westbrook insisted.
"This place's called Penny House, isn't it?"

The other gentlemen around him were watching curiously,
s if he were some sort of penniless vagabond or peddler
bout to be tossed out on his ear by those two guards.

"Miss Penny can do whatever she wants for her friends,"
e continued, his voice rising with his anxiety, "and she's a
ersonal friend of mine."

Stanton appeared from nowhere to take his arm. "Come
long, Westbrook, I'll see you home, there's a good fellow."

"Not before I see Miss Penny," Westbrook insisted, trying
o shake him off. "You call her down here, and ask her yourself. She'll tell you. She's considering me for a place on the
membership committee, you know, and she'd never treat me
like this. I know the way upstairs to her rooms, Pratt, and I—"

The guards' hands were gentle but firm on his shoulders,
guiding him toward the front door as the other gentlemen
seemed to melt away from his path.

"Good evening, my lord," Pratt was saying, but it was already too late to reply. Through the door, down the steps, into the street, and the thing was done.

And so, Westbrook realized too late, was he.

Chapter Fourteen

~~~~~~~~~~

She smiled up at him in the chaise, and Guilford decided he'
never seen a more satisfied woman in his life. Her eyes wer
heavy lidded and languid from too much loving and too lit
tle sleep, her cheeks flushed like a feverish wanton, her mouth
still swollen, almost bruised from his kisses. She lay curle
against him with her stocking feet on the seat beside her, he
hand resting on his thigh and his arm across her shoulder.

His servants had pressed the wrinkles from her gown an
her hair was pinned neatly in a tight knot at the back of he
head, but even a blind man would be able to tell the differ
ence in her between this afternoon and yesterday. She'
wanted to keep their liaison a secret between them as long a
they could, but without a miracle, every gentleman at Penn
House would see at once that Miss Amariah Penny had take
a lover.

"I wish this day would never end," she said softly, gazing
up at him. "I love you that much, Guilford."

He sighed, as unwilling as she was to have this time end
"But if the day never ended, then I wouldn't be able to look
forward to having you with me again tonight."

"It will seem more like morning," she said, her regret genuine. "I won't turn the locks for the night until long after all of you gentlemen leave."

"I'll wait," he said. "I have powerful incentive."

She chuckled, vibrating against him. She was so warm and soft in his arms that he was tempted to suggest they have one last round with her astride him with her skirts flying, here in the chaise.

"Perhaps I'll have Pratt turn ahead the clocks," she said, "and announce closing three hours early."

"You'd do that?" he asked, only half in jest. After last night, he believed she'd do most anything.

She shook her head, and sighed forlornly. "No. As much as I might wish it, my conscience wouldn't let me. I'm already hearing my father's voice scolding me for not being there last night or this morning."

The last thing he wanted in the carriage with them was the righteous voice of the late Reverend Penny, not after all Guilford had done with the man's daughter in the last twenty-four hours. "I'm sure Pratt will have handled everything exactly as you would have yourself."

"Likely better," she said, leaning forward to look from the window as the carriage slowed. "Oh, no. We're here."

She plucked her hat from the opposite bench and retrieved her slippers from the floor of the carriage, hurriedly digging her toes into them and smoothing her skirts before the footman opened the door. He was well aware of how much Penny House meant to her, but that didn't mean he enjoyed competing with it. He'd never had to win a woman away from a rival that was stone, mortar and dice.

"Don't run from me yet," he said softly, pulling her onto his lap. "One last favor."

She sighed with contentment, immediately relaxing against
him, and he knew for this minute, anyway, he'd won.

"Anything you wish," she said, grinning wickedly. "Anything at all, *Eliot.*"

"To hell with Eliot," he said, whispering so close to her ear
that he felt her delighted shiver in response. "I want to be in
your thoughts every minute we're apart."

"You couldn't make me do otherwise," she said, brushing
her lips across his. "Will you do the same for me?"

"Ah, sweetheart," he said, pulling her close to kiss her the
way he'd wanted since they'd left Grosvenor Square. "You already know the answer to that."

The door swung open, the footman laboring to keep his
face a properly blank mask as Amariah scrambled from Guilford's lap and grabbed her hat.

"Tonight, my love," she said breathlessly. "And every minute in between!"

He let her run up the steps alone, the way she'd wished,
but he couldn't help leaning from the door of the chaise to
watch her, her skirts fluttering around her ankles and her coppery hair glinting in the afternoon sun. Just before she reached
the door, she glanced back over her shoulder at him. She
didn't do anything as girlish as to wave, or even smile, but the
look in her eyes alone was more than enough to prove that she
was already thinking of him, and in a most fine and flattering
fashion, too.

Her footman opened the door, and she disappeared inside
Penny House, yet still he lingered.

Every minute, hell. He'd think of her every second.

Ever since Amariah had come to London with her sisters,
Penny House had been the center of her life. So why, then,

when she stepped inside the front hall, did it now feel as if she were a stranger entering a foreign world?

"Good day, Miss Penny!" Pratt exclaimed as he rushed into the hall to greet her. "How glad we are to have you safely returned!"

She smiled, uncomprehending. "I wasn't gone that long, Pratt. You make it sound as if I'd gone to India and back."

"As you say, miss, as you say." Pratt nodded, but no matter what he said, his relief that she'd come back was palpable. Had he really thought she wouldn't come back to Penny House, that she'd let herself be carried off by Guilford forever? "As soon as you are available, miss, I need a word with you. There was a bit of unpleasantness last evening."

"Unpleasantness?" She glanced in the front room to make sure it was empty. "Come in here, Pratt, and tell me all."

She took the nearest armchair, suddenly feeling the effects of little sleep.

Pratt came and stood before her, giving her a quick nod before he began. "Lord Westbrook visited us last night. As we'd suspected, he wished to play at hazard, and Mr. Walthrip asked to see him in private."

"Did Mr. Walthrip explain the terms under which his lordship might play again?"

"Perfectly, miss," Pratt said. "You know that Mr. Walthrip has had much experience with such unhappy discussions."

"Too much experience," Amariah said with a sigh. "I don't know what it is about hazard that makes gentlemen more reckless than at any other game."

"Mr. Walthrip also mentioned that, by his records, Lord Westbrook had not won in several months."

Amariah frowned. "But what of that promissory note from Lord Stanton?"

"Mr. Walthrip says Lord Stanton never plays at hazard," Pratt said, "let alone loses to Lord Westbrook. But since the two gentlemen are friends, perhaps the answer lies between them."

"Curious." She'd have to find that note and look at it again and perhaps ask Mr. Fewler's advice. "I'm guessing that his lordship did not accept Mr. Walthrip's news meekly?"

"No, miss." Pratt seemed to wince at the recollection. "He had to be escorted from the club."

Amariah shook her head. "I'm sorry for that, considering his circumstances, but ill behavior cannot be tolerated. Most likely this morning he'll realize his folly, and make arrangements to restore his privileges at the hazard table. That's what usually happens in these cases."

Pratt hesitated. "This wasn't usual, miss. He demanded to speak to you, claiming that he was a privileged friend of yours, and that you'd make special arrangements on his behalf. He did not accept that you were, ah, indisposed, and tried to force his way up the stairs to your rooms."

Damnation, as Guilford would say. The last thing she or the club needed was having any member claim special privileges from her. "And others noticed?"

"It was difficult not to notice, miss," Pratt said. "His lordship was intemperate."

"You mean he was loud and violent?"

Pratt didn't hesitate now. "Yes, miss. He was."

"At least it sounds as if there were plenty of witnesses." She tapped her fingers on the arm of the chair. She should have been here to calm the baron before he lost his temper, and before he'd made these outrageous claims. Now the damage was done, and she was left with no choice. "All his lordship's privileges are suspended until the situation can be reviewed by a meeting of the membership committee. I'll go write the letter now, and we'll have it delivered to him at once. Tell the guards at the door that Lord Westbrook is not to be admitted under any circumstances."

She rose to go upstairs, already composing the letter in her head. Poor Westbrook had wanted to be considered for the membership committee, and now instead he was to be reviewed by it.

"Excuse me, miss," Pratt said, "but Mr. Fewler would like a word with you, as well."

She sighed, and dropped back into the chair as the head of the private guards came striding in to the room. How many others were waiting in the hall for "words" with her, anyway?

"Miss Penny, good day," he said brusquely. "First I must inquire as to the state of your injuries."

She held out her arm for him to see. "It looks dreadful now, I know, and it's still tender to touch, but much improved."

"No lasting pain?" he asked sternly, inspecting her arm as if he expected to see the injury had deteriorated, not improved. "Nothing that hinders your movements?"

It certainly hadn't hindered her last night with Guilford. "Nothing lasting, no."

"Then it's good that you have so many witnesses who can swear to your suffering in court," he said, almost disappointed. "We'll need that for charges. You see, Miss Penny, I now have fresh information about your attacker."

"You do?" she asked eagerly. "Who was it, Mr. Fewler?"

He frowned. "We do not have a name as yet, but I expect to very shortly. I've spoken to many of the drivers waiting with their carriages, and learned that soon after you were attacked, a gentleman was seen hurrying from the club and down the street."

"A gentleman? A member of the club?"

"By his dress and from how he used the front door, yes, he must be a member," Fewler said. "At the time, everyone assumed he was ill, or merely distraught over a loss, but now I'd wager he was the one in your quarters."

She didn't like suspecting one of the members. Not only would it make a great scandal for the club, but she'd always thought of them as gentlemen, not villains, and many she'd come to regard as friends. "No one saw his face to identify him?"

"I haven't found anyone yet, no," Fewler said. "But we will. I feel sure of that. In the meantime, I'd advise you to take extra care of your person. If this rascal learns we're close to pinching him, then he may try to strike back at you. I'll assign two of my men to stay with you at all times so that—"

"No!" she exclaimed, thinking how complicated seeing Guilford would become with a pair of burly guards trailing after her. "That is, thank you, Mr. Fewler, but I don't believe it's necessary."

"Forgive, miss, but you must do as he says," Pratt said, standing beside Fewler to contribute to the air of disapproval coming toward Amariah. "The danger is too great."

Fewler nodded in grave agreement. "Miss Penny, considering how you have already been attacked, I must insist that—"

"If I leave Penny House alone, either on foot or in a hackney, then I'll take your guards," she promised, knowing full well that those two possibilities were slim indeed. "Otherwise I'll always be in company, and safe among friends."

Fewler shook his glossy head, skeptical. "I'm not sure that's a proper solution, Miss Penny."

"And I say it is, Mr. Fewler." She rose again, determined this time to escape up the stairs to her room. Confronted with all this complicated reality, her time with Guilford almost

emed like a beautiful, insubstantial dream. She might have
omised to think of him, but she hadn't known she'd have
much else crowding those thoughts for her attention.

What would Guilford be doing now? she wondered. *He'd*
d her he'd meant to go back to bed and lie on the same
eets from last night and dream of her. She could imagine him,
ked and sprawled in the middle of that huge bed, with his—

"Forgive me, Miss Penny." The maidservant bobbed a
ick curtsy, her face pink at having interrupted Amariah
re in the hall. "But th' boy jus' brought this down to th'
chen, an' Mrs. Todd said t' fetch it t' you at once."

She held out the tray with the folded newssheet on it, the
est issue of the *Tattle*. With new interest, Amariah took the
per from the tray, and began to glance through the pages,
oking for anything that Guilford might have written.

And stopped cold.

By all our freshest advices, His Grace the Duke of
G***f**d has found a new Plaything of Passion with
which to amuse himself this Season….

"A 'Plaything of Passion'?" Stanton read aloud as his brows
se with surprise. "That's painting it a bit scarlet, isn't it?"

"Well, the *Tattle* already calls her the Red Queen, so I sup-
se they should be calling her scarlet," Westbrook said, peer-
g over Stanton's shoulder to read for himself. "Besides, all
did was give the printer a few suggestions. He's the one
at wrote it."

"The one that Guilford will come after with a horsewhip,
u mean." Stanton lowered his voice and glanced uneasily
ound the tavern where they'd stopped for a pint after rid-
g. There were few customers at this time of day, but it paid

to be careful. "Guilford will, too, when he sees this. 'The V[
tal Virago': now that *was* you, Westbrook!"

"I thought it was a rather good turn of phrase," Westbro[
said with malicious pride. He was still stinging from the h[
miliation of being banned from the hazard table and toss[
from Penny House, as if he were some low dunning trad[
man. If Miss Penny had been the great friend to him she'd p[
tended to be, she would never have let that happen, not to hi[
But she'd proved herself as false as any of Mrs. Poynto[
whores, maybe worse, since she hadn't even had the coura[
that night to tell him to his face. "I could've said far more[

"Be glad you didn't," Stanton warned. "Guilford alrea[
has it in for you. That printer fellow will spill your name f[
enough, and when Guilford learns that you were—"

"He was the one who called her a virago first!" protest[
Westbrook. "He wrote it himself in the book!"

"Yes, and struck it out, too," Stanton said. "That's one [
the ways we knew he was taken with the Penny woman. Wh[
I said we should let the *Tattle* know, too, I meant a line or t[
in sport, to even things a bit with Guilford. I'd no noti[
you'd drag the poor woman's name through the muck w[
that printer as you did."

Westbrook dragged his thumb through the foam that clu[
to the side of his glass. Everyone knew his disgrace, and w[
had happened, and the reason why. Even the chit who'd dra[
this ale had looked down her pert nose at him. He was d[
graced everywhere he went, and it was all the fault of An[
riah Penny.

"She deserved it, Stanton," he said, "after what she did to m[

"You're the idiot who did it to himself!" Stanton lean[
closer. "You pay up what you owe, and they'll let you back i[

"She shouldn't have let it happen," Westbrook said m[

ly, staring at his glass. "If she'd liked me as well as she
imed, then she wouldn't've let them do that to me."

Stanton tossed the newssheet at Westbrook and picked up
crop and gloves to leave. "You'd do better to consider what
iilford's going to do to you when he reads this."

"She deserves it," Westbrook muttered, though Stanton
d already gone. "She deserves it, and more."

Guilford watched his sister sail across her parlor toward him,
e a man-of-war with all guns blazing bearing down on some
pless prize. He'd told himself he'd answer her invitation to
, but stay for only an hour, less if the tedium or the other com-
ny became too overwhelming. Besides, it was a way to fill
time before he could go to Penny House, and Amariah.

"I'm *so* glad you could join us, Guilford!" she cried in her
and Lady trill, a sound that now, as always, put him imme-
ately on guard. "I've guests who are so eager to meet you!"

His guard went up even higher, and he glanced furtively
ound at the others clustered in his sister's parlor. "Eager
ests" generally meant guests eager to marry and their moth-
, eager for them to marry a peer and, more specifically,
rry him. As a matchmaker, Frances was persistent, if untal-
ted, and even before she'd taken him by the arm and steered
n to a window seat, he'd guessed the latest candidate.

"Guilford, this is Lady Cornelia Stanley." Frances made the
roduction with an extra gush of enthusiasm. "My dear Lady
rnelia, may I introduce you to my brother, Lord Guilford?"

The girl was terrified, her round blue eyes watering with
r as she stared up at him without a word to speak in her
sebud mouth. She *was* pretty, in a candy-box way, but she
s also too young, too bland, too uninteresting.

Too unlike Amariah, *his* Amariah, in every conceivable way.

"How vastly, vastly clever you are, your grace!" Lady Co[...]
nelia's mother said, and the three women all laughed togeth[...]
his sister beaming as proudly as if he were the prize bull [...]
the fair.

Lord, what had he just said without realizing it? He w[...]
thinking of Amariah and what an endlessly superior wom[...]
she was, so at least he must have been smiling when he spo[...]

"I like fireworks, too, your grace," Lady Cornelia whi[...]
pered as her nervous fingers mashed a sweet biscuit into t[...]
palm of her glove.

"Then perhaps we'll all have to make a party of it to [...]
watch them on the river." Frances was smiling so broadly, h[...]
eyes were disappearing above her cheeks. She hooked h[...]
hand into the crook of Guilford's arm. "Pray, excuse us f[...]
just a moment."

She pulled Guilford aside, barely out of hearing. "Isn't s[...]
the most delightful girl?" she asked. "I can tell you like h[...]
and of course she instantly fancied you."

"Oh, Fan, don't," he said wearily. "That poor little g[...]
may be the sweetest child imaginable, but I could never [...]
interested in her as a wife."

Frances jabbed him with her fan. "And why ever not? I s[...]
how you smiled at her."

"Because I was thinking of someone else," he said. "I'd [...]
bored to death with a wife like that."

"A wife is not supposed to be entertainment, Guilfor[...]
Frances said, her tone growing more testy. "You marry [...]
preserve your title, for the family, for the future. You do[...]
choose a wife to relieve your *boredom.*"

"Well, maybe I should," he said, shifting his shoulders [...]
if trying to shrug her away. How many conversations had [...]
had exactly like this, first with his mother and now with Fa[...]

Maybe I should try pleasing myself and not you, and marry woman *I* like."

His sister glared, not believing him. "Guilford, don't be so ovoking. You're not getting any younger. You could fall om your horse, or take fatally ill, and where would the succession be then?"

"Somewhere else, I suppose. I'll be past caring." He had a dden, intense thought of Amariah, and how last night, as e'd lain in his arms, they'd tried to outdo each other with ore and more outrageous riddles until he'd wept with laughr. He'd never be bored with Amariah, that was certain; shy tle Lady Cornelia and the well-bred legions like her would ver be able to keep pace with a woman who was as quick the mistress of Penny House.

"You're smiling again," Frances said suspiciously, leang closer to him as if she could somehow see the cause on s teeth. "What are you thinking of, Guilford? Not that dreadl creature who's your new mistress, I hope."

An odd little pummel of foreboding thumped in his chest. Vhat in blazes are you talking about, Fan?"

"Only what everyone will be talking about, Guilford," she id, waving her arms with dramatic resignation. "I don't know hy I bother to try to find you an acceptable lady wife when you sist on wallowing among the lowest women you can find."

"Fan," he said warily, turning his head to one side. "What this?"

"*This* is the kind of disgraceful gossip with which I must ntend as your sister." She marched to a nearby shelf and ew out an obviously read copy of the *Tattle*. "I'm surprised dy Cornelia and her mother would even deign to be in the me room with you after *this*."

"Oh, Fan," he said. "Why do you even have such a piec
of rubbish in your parlor?"

"Because, Guilford, it's the only way I have to learn of a
your most scandalous behavior." She opened the paper, ta
ping her finger on one article in particular. "*Look* at thi
brother. Look at this! 'Plaything of passion,' indeed!"

"You're mad, Fan." He snatched the paper from her, read
ing it for himself.

By all our freshest advices, His Grace the Duke of
G***f**d has found a new Plaything of Passion with
which to amuse himself this Season. While fine Ladies
Fair at Almack's may vie for his attentions with the
same ferocity as the strutting Actresses & other Whim-
sies of Our Own Covent Garden, His Grace has placed
his Affections (among other more heroic Parts) squarely
in the bed of that most celebrated Vestal Virago of St.
James Street. For all her Genteel Airs to the Contrary,
our reports say she capitulated with Ease & Eagerness
into the arms of the gallant G***f**d, & embraced
Rare Lubricious Delight under His Grace's experienced
Tutelage.

Now well broken to the Spur & the Saddle, we ask
will the Red Queen abandon her post at P***y House
& become one more Meek & Obedient Mare in the
Duke's stable?

Damn, he thought, as he read it a second time to be su
he wasn't imagining what he was reading through the haze
his fury.

Damn, damn, *damn.*

Chapter Fifteen

⁓⁓⁓

Amariah stood in the hall as she had scores of times before, in more evenings than she could remember. She smiled and remembered names and congratulated those upon whom luck had smiled, as if nothing had changed, nothing were different, as if her whole world had not come crashing down into an ignominious, humiliating heap around her feet.

Guilford had asked her to trust him, and she had, freely and joyfully. She'd given him her body and her heart, and worst of all, her soul, and what had he done with her gifts? Tattered them, mocked them, then paraded the sorry remnants into the street for the raucous amusement of all the world.

For the sake of Penny House and those who depended upon her and her, she would be strong. Her body would forget his caresses, and the pleasure he'd given her. She would haughtily stare down the curious and the spiteful, and those who might try to follow in Guilford's footsteps, and ignore the speculation and jests that would inevitably be her lot as this Season's scandal. She would even force herself to be civil to him if they met again, for the sake of the club and to give the gossips no fresh fodder. If she could be strong and do all that, and keep

herself clear of further missteps, then her reputation could b
patched back into place.

But her heart—ah, that she feared was forever broken…

She recognized him at once, though he was still no mo
than a dark silhouette in evening dress coming up the step
his coat black, his shirt an impossibly white linen triangle b
low his chin. Her chest grew tight with anger and her hand
moist with nervousness, yet she kept her smile pasted in place
her bright laugh ready. The other men in the hall and on th
steps recognized him, too, and stepped aside to let him pas
eager to see whatever there would be to see when the two o
them met.

Nothing, she told herself fiercely. *Give them nothing*
watch, or relish, or repeat to their friends!

"Good evening, your grace," she said, her curtsy and bo
exactly as they should be. "How kind of you to visit us tonight

"You've seen the *Tattle,* then," he said. His face was pal
his features drawn so taut she marveled that he could spea
"Amariah, you must believe me when I say I had nothing t
do with that."

"We're most fortunate to have stuffed and roasted grous
in the dining room tonight," she continued, focusing slightl
to the left of his ear, on that little unruly tuft of dark hair, s
she wouldn't see the pain in his eyes, pain that couldn't b
gin to equal what she felt. "I believe there's also a most sple
did puree of chestnuts as an accompaniment."

"You know I couldn't have written that." His voice was
hoarse, tormented whisper. "How could I? I love you, Am
riah. How could I have written such vile rubbish about yo
like that?"

Her cheeks were hot, blushing with shame and anger as s
remembered each appalling word of the "vile rubbish." Ho

deed, could he have come here after writing such hateful
ings? How could he claim to love her?

"Your grace may also enjoy the new claret that has just ar-
ved in our cellar," she said, clipping each word. "Other gen-
emen with educated palates have declared it to be of the first
der. I should like your opinion on its merits, as well."

"Amariah, please, don't do this. Not to me, not to yourself,
t to us."

She struggled to forget what it had been like to kiss that
outh, lean against those shoulders, feel the caresses of those
nds, and she sensed how hard it was for him not to reach
t for her.

"I believe a group of gentlemen in the card room have ar-
nged for whist this evening," she continued, holding her fan
ghtly to keep from betraying the tremble in her hands. "I'm
re your grace would be welcome to join them for a hand or
vo, if that is your pleasure for the evening."

"Amariah, look at me, and tell me you would rather believe
at slander than what I've told you myself," he said, his whis-
r urgent. "Look at me, and tell me you don't love me any
nger."

She looked, and if he could read her true feelings, he must
ve seen more than he wished ever to hear. "As pleasing as
is for me to chat with you, your grace, alas, there are other
ntlemen behind you, and I must ask you to excuse me now,
you please."

"Damnation, it doesn't please me, Amariah!"

"Your grace." This time she couldn't keep the little break
om her voice, or hide the angry tears that blurred his face
fore her. "If you please, your grace."

"Very well, then." He stepped back from her, his bow curt.
'll go. But it's not going to end like this, Amariah. It's not."

She watched him leave, his head as high as hers. She'd sai
she would be strong, and she'd succeeded. She'd vowed n
to lose her temper, and she hadn't. And if she'd done all tha
she would not cry now. She would *not*.

Something poked at her finger, and startled, she looke
down. The delicate pierced blades of her ivory fan lay sha
tered and broken in her hand, snapped by the force of her ow
fingers.

She *would* be strong.

She took a deep breath, then another, and forced herself
smile.

"Good evening, Lord Bennington," she said brightly. "Ho
pleased we are to have you here with us tonight!"

Westbrook stuffed his fare into the hackney driver
grubby, waiting hand, and turned toward Penny House. It wa
ridiculous that he'd have to walk this last block, but the crus
of carriages and chaises before the club tonight was makin
St. James Street impassible. The hackney driver had refuse
to wait any longer, the impudent bastard, and Westbrook ha
been forced to climb out.

He muttered to himself, wondering if the driver had recog
nized him, and known his story. That would have been th
limit, wouldn't it, to be put out of a hackney? Oh, Amaria
Penny had no notion of everything she'd put into motio
against him, no notion at all.

He walked quickly, purposefully, not wanting to see th
line of waiting carriages with their beautiful paint and gil
ing, their matched teams and polished brasses and drivers ar
footmen in well-tailored livery, some even in powdered wig
He didn't want them gawking at him, true, but mostly l
didn't want to be reminded of the gross unfairness of his lif

If there were any justice, one of these carriages would be
is, with the Westbrook arms painted on the door. He'd have
plump, pretty, French milliner tucked away in a flat in Chel-
ea, waiting for him to call whenever it suited him. He'd have
new suit of clothes on his back, instead of this one from last
ear, and diamonds on his shoe buckles, with maybe another
tone pinned to his neckcloth. And there'd be so much gold
a his pockets that they'd bulge from the weight, and Ama-
ah Penny would be begging and scraping for him to come
it at her damned hazard table.

He swung his fist at the iron rail fence beside him, swear-
ag to himself at the gross inequity of it all. If only Uncle Jesse
/ould simply die, so he'd have his inheritance now, when he
ould appreciate it!

"Hey, ho, m'lord," a young man's voice brayed from the row
f waiting carriages. "What say you to a game of hazard, eh?"

Hoots and jeering laughter echoed across the street, picked
p by other drivers, footmen and boys. Furiously Westbrook
pun around, his fist raised and ready to challenge whoever
was that called. But if the man had ever shown his face, he'd
anished now, and with another oath Westbrook shook his
houlders, lowered his fists and turned back toward Penny
louse.

Stanton had wanted to wager that he couldn't keep his
mper tonight. He'd twenty guineas, and Westbrook had been
orely tempted. Taking a score of golden guineas from Stan-
n would be a sweet accomplishment. But in the mood he
as in tonight, he wasn't sure he could win, not with so much
rovocation everywhere he went, and besides, he didn't have
le twenty guineas to prove it.

The glow of the lanterns that flanked the club's door
ashed across the pavement, almost as if they were beckon-

ing him to come and join the others. He couldn't recall see
ing so many gentlemen at the door, almost as if it were for
new play at the theatre. He'd hoped to ruin Penny House with
that scandalous story about Guilford and Amariah Penny in
the *Tattle* today, but it certainly hadn't happened yet.

He paused in the shadows, smoothing the revers of his
coat while he waited for a break at the door. He'd come alone
tonight—he'd had enough of Stanton's company for one day
anyway—and he didn't want to be swallowed up in a large
group. He wanted to make his own entrance, because he had
a plan to restore his fortunes.

It was a good plan, with a good chance of success. If Miss
Penny were there in the hall tonight, he meant to tell her how
upset he'd been by his treatment the other night. He'd make
her understand exactly how much mischief she'd caused in
his life, and make her feel sorry enough for him that she'd
have to tell Walthrip to extend his credit at the hazard table
and let him play again.

A party of officers climbed the steps together, and no one
followed. Westbrook saw his chance, and seized it, hurrying
forward to the white stone steps, flanked by two enormo
footmen in Penny House blue livery.

"Lord Westbrook, if you please," one of them said as he
passed. "It is Lord Westbrook, isn't it, my lord?"

"Why, yes, it is." Westbrook shot his cuffs and stood a frac
tion straighter, using the step to even the difference in height
between him and the footman. But it was nice, damned nice
to be recognized, and greeted by name like this. "I am Lor
Westbrook."

Perhaps Miss Penny had changed her mind already. Per
haps she was willing to let bygones be bygones, and welcom
him back to the hazard table where he belonged.

"Did you read the letter you received from Miss Penny to-
?" the footman asked.

"She wrote to me?" Now that was flattering, a personal let-
from Miss Penny herself. He wished he'd seen it. There
l been a large pile of new mail waiting by his door, but he
ln't bothered to look at it, assuming it was only more
lesmen's bills.

"Yes, my lord." Now the second footman had come to
nd beside the first, an immovable block of royal blue and
rer lace. "She explained everything to you in that letter."

"She did?" he asked happily. "Well, then, since I didn't see
t letter, perhaps I should go on inside and ask her about it
self."

"No, my lord." The footmen exchanged glances. "Miss
nny's letter was to tell you your membership is under re-
w, and until the membership committee can convene and
ke a decision, you are no longer welcome as a member of
ny House."

"Not welcome?" repeated Westbrook, stunned. "What the
ril is that supposed to mean, anyway? I'm a charter mem-
of this infernal place, and I have a right to enter whenever
lease!"

"I am sorry, my lord, but we have our orders not to admit
l," the first footman said, his voice ominous. "Not tonight.
w if you please, my lord, I must ask you to move aside so
t others may enter."

"But if I could only see Miss Penny—"

"Miss Penny is not available, my lord," he said again, more
nly. He crossed his arms over his chest. "Now if you please,
lord—"

"To hell with you!" Westbrook said furiously. "To hell
h you all!"

He wheeled around on his heel, shoving his way past other, more fortunate members waiting for him to step asi

The damned red-haired bitch had gone too far this time wasn't bad enough that she'd branded him as a dishonoral pauper, a gentleman incapable of meeting his obligatio Now she'd had him banned from the entire club, from friends and acquaintances and fellow peers. She'd made h an outcast, unworthy of genteel company, and for that sh have to pay. She'd robbed him of what he deserved. Now was her turn to receive her due.

What *she* deserved: oh, yes, he'd see to that. Even if it to the last farthing in his pocket, he'd see to *that,* and as walked through the night, he almost smiled.

Somehow she'd gotten through this night, though it h seemed the longest she could ever recall.

Amariah walked through the now-deserted rooms w Pratt behind her, carrying the keys, the same walk she ma each night before the big house was darkened and locked, a she finally climbed the stairs to bed. There was seldom a thing out of place or amiss—her staff was thorough, their r tine well practiced. Yet even tonight she followed her us routine, room by room, like a mother doing the same sm things to help send her child to sleep.

But as she came through the last room, the front par someone pounded on the front door so loudly that she gas and jumped, then laughed with exhaustion at her own wearin

"See who that is, Pratt," she called, and the manager pee through one of the side windows. "Is it anyone we know?

"Yes, miss," he said slowly. "It's Lord Guilford."

She caught her breath, held it, then let it out in a long p ing sigh. Pratt was waiting for her decision, his white wig e turned an otherworldly blue by the stained glass night

tern hanging overhead.

"Let him in, Pratt," she said quietly.

"Are you sure, Miss Penny?" Pratt asked, his concern for

so genuine that he was willing to overrule propriety and

estion her order.

"I'm sure," she said, touched. "And thank you, Pratt."

"As you wish, miss," he said, and unbolted the door.

Guilford didn't charge in, the way she'd expected, but

pped through the door with his usual nonchalance and con-

ence, as if completely certain of his reception—a confi-

ice that, to her mind, was more than a little misplaced.

"Good evening, Pratt," he said, handing the manager his

. "Or I suppose it must be good morning by now."

"Yes, my lord, it is," Pratt answered, clearly not sure what

lo next. "Can I help you, my lord?"

"Only one person can help me now, Pratt," Guilford said,

id that's Miss Penny."

"You said it wasn't done between us yet, Guilford. I sup-

e you were right," she said, stepping from the shadows.

r earlier shock of seeing him had gone by now, but the an-

and hurt remained simmering inside her. "Come in here,

l we'll say what we must. You may go upstairs, Pratt."

Pratt nodded, unwilling to abandon her. "Thank you, miss,

I believe I'll go to the kitchen for something to eat before

tire. You may call me there if necessary."

"I'd no idea Pratt was such a faithful watchdog," Guilford

d as soon as the manager's footsteps had disappeared down

kitchen stairs.

"Someone has to watch over me, I suppose." She stood to

side and let him pass through the door to join her. She

n't relight the candles, not wanting to encourage him to

stay longer than was absolutely necessary, and they were l
only in the blue glow of the night lantern and what little lig
from the streetlamps filtered in through the windows. "Af
today's *Tattle,* Pratt doesn't trust you."

"I'm not surprised." He didn't sit, but stood, leaning ba
against the large table in the center of the room as he watch
her. The eerie twilight made the planes of his face stand c
in sharp contrast, all cheekbones and jaw, while it hid wh
ever emotion might be in his eyes. "What of you, Amaria
Do you still trust me?"

"I shouldn't." Still standing near the door, she folded I
arms over her chest, tucking her hands close to her sid
"Yet I let you in here."

"I told you we weren't through," he said, soft and low, I
lover's voice, and so dangerous to her. "Between us, swe
heart, we talk so much that I couldn't fathom it ending wi
out a good loud row."

She smiled, wondering if that was another of his dares
not. "Is that what you expect of me? To shout and claw at yc
eyes like a Billingsgate fishwife?"

"Nothing less," he said, his own smile fleeting. "But ther
no witnesses now, Amariah. No one to watch and judge yc
or say you're weak or that I'm bullying. You see, I know h
the mistress of Penny House approaches such things."

"I thought I knew you, too, Guilford," she said, not bo
ering to hide her anger and resentment.

"Your heart still does," he said. "I didn't write those thir
about you, Amariah. I couldn't, not only because they wer
wretchedly foul and unfair to you, but also because of the tir

"Someone wrote them, Guilford," she said. "They di
write themselves."

"But it couldn't have been me," he insisted. "When wo

ve sat down to write, sweetheart? Between the time the last
ue was printed and the new one, I was entirely with you."

"Don't call me sweetheart," she said, but she was already
ighing what he said. In her anger and shock this afternoon,
: hadn't considered how he'd always been with her, any
re than she'd considered all the scores of people who might
sh her or him ill, and who could have written the hateful
ce rather than him.

"Have you ever heard me speak of you, or any other
man, in such a manner?" he continued. "What reason
uld I have for beginning now?"

"You tell me, Guilford." She didn't really want to admit
t what he was saying made perfect sense, or worse, that he
s right.

"Well, then, you surprised me when you came to my
ase," he said. "I was most pleased that you did, of course,
I hadn't expected it, not at all."

"You couldn't have predicted that I'd come," she said
wly, thinking back over the day, "and so you couldn't have
tten it ahead."

"That's true, as well," he said. "However great my powers
, I haven't yet mastered seeing into the future."

"I'm serious, Guilford."

"I am, too," he said, and she could hear it in his voice.
here's nothing more serious to me than the thought of los-
you."

She walked slowly toward him, her footsteps across the mar-
checkerboard floor echoing in the empty room, and came
top an arm's length away. He smiled, and with both hands,
reached out and shoved his chest as hard as she could.

"Blast you, Guilford, I don't want to lose you, either!" she
d, her frustration spilling over. "I thought I already had,

and yet still I thought of you, over and over and over. As m[u]
as I told myself to break that promise to you, I couldn't d[o]
I could *not* do it!"

"Nor could I." His smile was lopsided, surprisingly uns[...]
as he held his hand out to her. "I asked you to trust me [be]
fore, Amariah, and as I recall it worked out well for us b[...]
at the time."

She looked down at his hand, thinking of how much he v[...]
offering her with so simple a gesture, and how much she'd [...]
offering in return if she took it.

"You'd ask me to trust you again?

"I'm begging you to," he said. "I can't see that I have [...]
other choice, not considering how much I love you."

"Just as I love you," she said, finally linking her fingers i[n]
his. "Oh, Guilford. Why must this be so difficult?"

"Nothing worth having is easy."

She sniffed. "That's a powerfully strange sentiment c[om]
ing from you, considering how everything in your life [has]
been easy."

"Not you," he said. "You know that's true."

She sighed. "We really do belong together, don't we?['']

He drew her in against his chest, his arms settling famili[ar]
around her waist. "No one else would have us, sweethear[t]

"Not like this, Guilford," she said softly. "Never like th[...]

She leaned forward, granting forgiveness with her kiss, [and]
he immediately accepted it. She threaded her fingers thro[ugh]
his hair, losing herself in the kiss. His fingers spread wid[e]
cradle her hips, he traded places with her, lifting her onto [the]
edge of the table without breaking his mouth away from h[er]
He kissed her hungrily, furiously, without bounds and w[ith]
out reason, and she loved it like that, feeling the desire bu[rn]
ing between them.

He pushed her skirts over her knees and she answered by
rting her legs to let him slip between. She was already breath-
g hard, her hands shaking from wanting him as she reached
wn to unbutton the fall on his breeches for him. He shoved
r skirts higher, over her hips, and when he touched her be-
een her legs she was already wet with wanting. The next mo-
ent he was in her, in her deep, and when she curled her legs
ound his waist she groaned as he went deeper still. He pushed
r back farther on the table and she began moving with him,
t and delirious with the urgency of paradise very nearly lost.

"You're so wicked, Guilford," she whispered frantically as
e clung to his shoulders. "Oh, Guilford, you're so wicked
d you're so good and I love you so much, and I—"

"Amariah?"

With a horrified gasp, Amariah opened her eyes, and
isted to look past Guilford's shoulder. How could this be
ssible? One quick glimpse in the half-light, but more than
ough: her sisters, Bethany and Cassia, with their husbands,
chard and William, all still dressed from traveling.

With a groan of shame, she wriggled free of Guilford and
oved down her skirts, while he grabbed for his trousers and
ed his coat to try to shield her as best he could. She slipped
m the table, her slippers making an awkward *clump* on the
or, just as Guilford finished with the last button on his trou-
rs. Swiftly she took his hand, and turned to face her family.

*Oh, Heaven help her, what was she supposed to say in such
circumstance?*

But Richard knew. He left Cassia's side, coming straight
ward them.

"What the hell do you think you're doing, Guilford?" he
manded, his fist raised and aimed for Guilford's jaw. "You
oring bastard, let Amariah go now!"

"No!" Amariah cried, planting herself between Guilfor
and Richard. "It's not as it seemed, Richard, please! I lov
him! *I love him!*"

Guilford pushed her aside. "I can take care of this, Am
riah," he said, lunging toward Richard and seizing him b
the shoulders. The two staggered together, locked in a sile
struggle.

"No, Guilford, you will *not!*" She grabbed the back of h
coat, desperate to pull him away. "You will not fight, *not o
my account!*"

"Richard!" shrieked Cassia, moving with surprising spee
for her pregnancy as she grabbed her husband by the arr
"Stop this at once, Richard! At once! Let Amariah explain

"Enough." With startling calm, Bethany's husband, Wi
liam, the largest of the three men and a retired army maj
who'd served in the war, pushed his way between the oth
two and separated them. "This will accomplish nothing, an
you both know it!"

Breathing hard, Richard and Guilford reluctantly sep
rated, glaring at each other. Amariah took Guilford's han
again and, with a deep breath, once more faced her sisters an
their husbands.

"You all know His Grace the Duke of Guilford," she sai
trying to smile. "He and I have become…close since you le
London."

"Close?" Richard repeated incredulously. "Hell, if th
was close, then I—"

"Hush, Richard," Cassia ordered. "Please, let Amaria
explain."

"Yes, please," Bethany said. "I wish to hear what Amaria
has to say."

Amariah wished to hear what she was going to say, to

er two younger sisters had always looked up to her, and had
ome to her with their most difficult questions and dilemmas
 place of their mother. Now what kind of horrid example
ust she be presenting, caught with her lover in the parlor?

But it was Guilford, her own dear, darling Guilford, who
poke for her, slipping his arm protectively around her
houlders.

"I love Amariah with all my heart," he said, the kind of dec-
ration few men ever make before others, "and I dare to hope
at she loves me the same."

Bethany clapped her hands together, her round face
reathed with joy. "Then we are to have another wedding at
enny House!"

"Don't race ahead so fast, Bethany," Amariah said quickly,
ot daring to look at Guilford's face.

"Then it's true," Richard said, his voice crackling with an-
er. "You've made her your mistress, Guilford, without prom-
ing her anything more lasting than what we just saw."

"He did nothing of the sort, Richard!" Amariah said, des-
erate for a way to make them understand. "It's not like that
etween us!"

"Leave the lady out of this, Blackley," Guilford said sharply.
You've no right to speak of her, or of me, in such a way."

Cassia came to place her hand on Amariah's arm. "Come
ith Bethany and me, Amariah," she said gently. "We'll leave
ese gentlemen to sort this out among themselves."

"There's no need for that," Amariah said, raising her chin
 she felt Guilford's fingers tighten around hers, reassuring
r. "He and I are together in this. Whatever Richard and Wil-
am are going to say to Guilford I should hear, too."

"Then I'm sorry for what I must say, Amariah," Richard
id, "and for what you believe you must hear."

Cassia caught her breath. "Please, Richard, don't, not lik this, not when—"

"It was her decision, Cassia," he said, "and perhaps it's be ter she learn now what manner of man she's found for herself

Guilford made a grumbling sound deep in his chest. "Wh the devil is that supposed to mean, Blackley?"

"It means that everyone in London is speaking of a wag you made regarding this lady," Richard said sharply. "It mear that you bet your friends that you'd be able to seduce Am riah in less than a fortnight. I regret that you appear to ha won, you whoring bastard."

Amariah felt as if all the blood had drained from her, a the warmth gone from her heart as she turned toward Guilfor

Be strong, be strong, no matter what happens next. B strong enough to face this, and decide what is right....

"Is this true, Guilford?" she asked, searching his face f her answer. "Did you truly make such a wager?"

He looked down at their clasped hands, and she knew h answer before he'd spoken. "I asked you before to trust m Amariah, and I'm asking again. That wager—"

"You did," she said softly, too numb to raise her voice an louder. She felt her sisters come to stand beside her, a han on each shoulder, ready to catch her if the black, loveless f ture that yawned before her became too much. "You made wager like that over me. Did you really believe I'd never lear of it?"

"God forgive me, Amariah, I did make such a wager," h said. "But that was before I—"

"Go," she said, turning away. "Go, and this time don come back."

Chapter Sixteen

Guilford couldn't imagine his life without Amariah in it, and yet, because of his own idiocy, he'd just lost the only woman he'd ever really loved.

He drove his fist against the side of the chaise, hard enough to make his knuckles hurt, but not nearly enough to make him forget what he'd done. He was an idiot and a fool. The wager seemed like a thousand years ago, before he'd come to love Amariah, and be changed by her, too.

He should have told her about the wager with Stanton himself, made a jest of it as he'd groveled and apologized and called himself an ass for behaving so badly. She would have been outraged, but she would have forgiven him, and if he'd told it right, she probably would even have laughed. But instead she'd had to hear of it in the worst possible way and from the worst possible messenger. Not that Blackley had been wrong: he *was* a whoring bastard for what he'd done to her.

He shifted restlessly on the seat, already missing her more than he'd thought possible. He had one card left to play, one possible last chance to earn her forgiveness, but it was a very

long shot at best. He doubted she would ever forgive him, b
he was certain he'd never forgive himself.

The chaise stopped. The windows of the *Tattle*'s offic
were dark, but Guilford didn't care. This wasn't a social cal

Already his footman was pounding on the door, loud and in
sistent enough to rouse the entire neighborhood. Windows wen
opening in the surrounding houses and sleepy dogs beginnin
to bark by the time that Dalton, his nightcap sliding over h
forehead, finally opened his door to glare at the footman.

"What the devil do you think you're—" he began, but th
footman cut him off.

"His Grace the Duke of Guilford wishes to speak wit
you," he said, pushing the door open the rest of the way f
Guilford to pass.

"Yes, Dalton, I do want to speak with you," Guilford sa
as he shoved his way into the office. "And I can't wait to he
what you have to say in return."

"Your grace, good, er, good morning," Dalton said, fum
bling with the tinderbox as he lit the candlestick on his des
"To what do I owe this honor, your grace?"

"You know damned well why I'm here," Guilford sai
"That offal your printed in your last issue about Miss Penny-
who gave that to you?"

Dalton swallowed hard, his throat convulsing above th
open neck of his nightshirt. "It's against my policies to reve
my sources, your grace."

"To hell with your policies!" Guilford swept his arm acro
the desk, scattering papers and blocks of type to the floo
"You tell me who gave you those lies, and I may let you sta
in business. You do not, and I'll see this rat hole is boarde
and closed by noon."

"For what reason, your grace?" Dalton asked with a touc

of his daytime belligerence. "You can't shut me down without a reason!"

"The constable will find one that suits," Guilford said. "But you and I will know that it's because you decided to take the blame for slandering one of the finest ladies in London."

"It was Baron Westbrook, your grace!"

"Westbrook?" Guilford repeated, incredulous. "Why would Westbrook come to you?"

"Don't know that, your grace, but he did," Dalton said, nearly babbling now that he'd made up his mind to speak. "He came here with another gentleman, Lord Stanton, but it was Lord Westbrook who did all the talking, telling me all about your, ah, connection with Miss Penny."

"Lies," Guilford said sharply. "He knew nothing."

"I understand that now, your grace," Dalton said, his jowls shaking as he nodded eagerly. "Yet he did seem well acquainted with the lady and her, ah, situation, enough that I accepted what he said. He made it sound as if they'd been more than acquaintances, your grace, if you understand me."

"Westbrook?" Westbrook's name had never been linked to any woman as far as he knew, and certainly not Amariah. It wasn't that he didn't believe Westbrook was capable of such a malicious trick—the braggartly little weasel was—but Guilford couldn't fathom a reason for him going to such extremes to damage Amariah's reputation. "Westbrook said that?"

"Yes, yes!" Dalton said, pushing his nightcap further back on his head so his eyebrows bristled out beneath the hem. "How was I to know otherwise, your grace? But there's no love lost between them now, that's clear enough. He said much worse than I used, your grace. I can swear to that. The other gentleman kept trying to stop him, but Lord Westbrook couldn't be stopped."

"And of course, you had to print it," Guilford said.

Dalton bowed his head, trying to look contrite. "The gentlemen struck me as truthful, your grace."

Guilford shook his head with disgust. He couldn't think of a less truthful pair than Stanton and Westbrook. Now he'd do his best to undo their lies, and try to set things right with Amariah.

"Bring me pen and paper," he said to Dalton. "I'm going to write the real truth for you now, and if you wish to remain in trade, you'll print it."

Then all he'd have to do was pray that Amariah read it, and that she'd be willing to trust him this one final time.

Amariah stared down at the tea she did not want, and listened to the advice from her sisters that she did not wish to hear. They were sitting at the long oak table in the kitchen, one of their favorite places to be together; but for Amariah now, it seemed the most awkward and uncomfortable place in the world.

"It's all well and good to speak of love, Amariah," Cassia said, "but you have to consider the future. You told me that yourself. What if you're already carrying his child? You could be, you know."

"Guilford would honor his responsibilities to any child of his," Amariah said. "I do not worry about that."

"But what of yourself, duck?" Bethany asked, resting her hand over Amariah's. "What of his responsibility to you? If he loves you as he claims, why, then I do not see why he can't—"

"Because he is the Duke of Guilford, and I am only Amariah Penny of Penny House," Amariah said, pulling her hand away. "I knew that before I shared his bed, and I know it still. He's a peer, and I'm common, and he'll never marry me. I wouldn't expect him to."

"Why not?" asked Cassia indignantly. "You're as good as ny queen! He'd be fortunate to have you for his wife!"

Bethany leaned forward. "Has he ever said that to you, mariah? Has he told you you're unworthy?"

Amariah shook her head. "He doesn't have to. I'm among ese great lords and gentlemen every night, and I see how otective they are about their titles and bloodlines."

"Not Guilford?"

"No, but that doesn't mean—"

"It does, Amariah," Bethany said. "Each man is different. ook at William. His father's the Earl of Beckham, yet William feared I wouldn't judge him worthy."

"But that's William, not Guilford." Amariah pushed back er chair and stood. "It's of no account, anyway, now that I've nt him away for good."

Bethany rose, too, clearing away the teacups and wiping the ble. "I saw how he looked at you, Amariah. He loves you, and ou love him. He's not gone forever. He'll come back to you."

Amariah sighed, and smiled sadly. "The real question is hether I can trust him enough to wish him back, Betts, no atter how much I love him."

"If you love him, you will trust him," Cassia said, rising ore slowly, her hand pressed to her lower back as she awned. "Oh, my dears, I must go up to bed. I keep country ours now, not Penny House ones."

Bethany draped the towel over the rod. "I'm coming up-airs, too, before William comes hunting for me."

Amariah turned. "What made you all come here tonight?"

Cassia smiled. "Pratt, of course. He wrote to Richard and e, saying that you'd expressly forbidden him to send again r a surgeon or the constable, but that you'd made no men-n of sisters."

"And we'd stopped at Greenwood on our way back to Lon- don," Bethany said. "It was only coincidence we were there when Pratt wrote."

"Or Providence." Amariah smiled wearily, and kissed both her sisters good-night. "I am glad you're here. It's almost like old times."

"It will be when I'm back in this kitchen in the morning," Bethany said. "Don't stay up too late, Amariah."

"I won't," she said, and made herself smile as they went up the back stairs together. Of course they'd be eager to go; they had husbands waiting in their beds for them, while she'd have only herself, her body still raw and aching with unful- fillment from the interrupted lovemaking.

"Oh, Guilford, Guilford," she whispered unhappily as she pushed the chairs beneath the table. "What have I done? What have *we* done?"

She checked the lock on the back door, gazing up at the little strip of night sky over the chimney pots and rooftops. The moon was almost full, hanging there like a bright silver coin, and impulsively she opened the door to see it better. She half remembered some old tale about the full moon favoring lovers; perhaps if she let the moonlight wash over her, even for a moment, she and Guilford would be favored, too. Smil- ing at herself for believing such foolishness, she still stepped outside into the yard, walking until she had an unobstructed view of the moon, without trees or roofs in her way.

Well, old moon, if ever there was a lovesick lady in need of your help, then here I am.

Here I am....

"How much longer you want t' wait, guv'nor?" asked the taller man in the gray coat, sucking on his unlit pipe as he

...ned against the wall. "Must be close t'dawn. If th'lady ...sn't shown by now, odds are she won't come now."

"If you wish to be paid," Westbrook growled, "then you'll ... it until I dismiss you."

The gray-coated man shrugged, and settled himself more ...mfortably against the wall, while his friend with the shock ...yellow hair dozed where he sat, his head cradled on his bent ...ees.

Anxiously Westbrook rubbed his hand over his jaw. The two ...ere sorry excuses for villains, but when he'd concocted this ...an in the tavern, he hadn't had much better to choose from. ...esides, when this was done, they'd fade away into London, ...ver to be seen again, which was exactly what Westbrook had ...anted. He hadn't told them his name, nor had he asked theirs, ...d he certainly hadn't told them Amariah Penny's name. The ...ss they all knew about one another, the better.

He dug his hands into his pockets, creeping around the cor- ...r to peer at Penny House yet again. His original plan had been ...ll of daring: he'd meant to wait until the house was dark for ...e night, climb over the wall and break in through the kitch- ...n, then climb up the back stairs to her private quarters. He'd ...en there before, and he was sure he'd find the way again.

But things had become more complicated. Soon after he ...turned to Penny House with these two men, a chaise had ...iven through the lane to this back door, and two men and ...o women had entered the house. While he'd watched the ...omen had returned to the kitchen with Amariah, and by the ...ndles they'd lit he'd recognized all three of the Penny sis- ...s, sitting at the table for what seemed like an eternity.

How could he take the bitch by surprise with so many ...hers staying there, too? How could he give her what she ...served for treating him so infamously? How could he ruin

her as thoroughly as she'd ruined him? Furiously Westbro
had watched the sisters, cursing more of his infernal ba
luck.

But then, quite marvelously, everything had changed. Th
two other sisters had gone upstairs, leaving Amariah alon
Then, to his openmouthed amazement, she'd unlocked th
door and come outside into the yard, staring up at the sky, a
defenseless as a new lamb.

"Come along, lads," Westbrook whispered, his voice hoars
with excitement. "Our luck's about to turn for the better."

His heart and his spirit even more exhausted than his body
Guilford slowly climbed from the chaise and up the steps t
his house. The footman opened the door as he always did, re
gardless of the hour, and had begun to close it after Guilfor
when suddenly a small figure darted past him from outdoor
into the house.

"Here now, his grace don't want you in here in the fron
hall!" the footman snapped, grabbing the boy's collar to tos
him back outside.

"Y'grace, y'grace, I have t'talk t'you!" Billy Fox criec
twisting to break free of the footman's grasp. "'Tis a matte
o' life and death!"

"Set him free, Parker," Guilford said, staring down at th
boy. "But he's right, Billy. You don't belong in here, especiall
at this hour. Why aren't you in your quarters asleep?"

"I told you, y'grace, 'tis life and death!" the boy saic
breathing hard. The bandanna he now wore tied over hi
scarred face had slipped in the scuffle, and with both hand
he tugged it back into place, his head turned so he coul
watch Guilford with his good eye. "Beggin' pardon, y'grace
but it can't wait, if you please!"

Guilford sighed, too tired for histrionics. "Billy, I am so weary I might very well collapse on this floor before you. Tell me now, or not at all."

Billy nodded, and gulped before he began. "I was holding the horses, Hop and Buck it was, when you were inside Penny House tonight, y'grace, and I heard things, and I wanted t'tell you then, but Robert sent me home when you went on and I couldn't tell you until now."

"Tell me what, Billy?" Guilford demanded. "What in blazes must you tell me?"

The boy gulped again. "That Lord Westbrook means t'hurt Miss Penny!"

At once Guilford forgot his weariness. "What did you say?"

"I was standing with Hop and Buck, and Lord Westbrook came past, stumbling and carrying on to himself, like he was a common drunkard. He was saying he meant t'come back later to punish Miss Penny, an' hurt her, an' give her what she deserved for treating him so bad and unfair."

First the hateful scandal sheet defaming Amariah, then Dalton's account of Westbrook's irrational, threatening behavior toward her in the *Tattle*'s office, and now this. It all made sense, too much sense, leaving Guilford with a growing sense of dread for Amariah's safety.

With new urgency, he crouched down to the boy's level. "You are certain of what you heard? You're sure this man was Lord Westbrook?"

"Oh, aye, to both, y'grace," Billy said, rubbing beneath his nose with his sleeve. "The other drivers an' coachmen were all callin' after him by name and saying things, and laughing out loud about how unlucky he was at gaming. Only I heard him about Miss Penny on 'count o' being on the pavement.

You'll send a warning t'her, y'grace, won't you? You'll send word for her t'watch after herself?"

"I'll do better than that, Billy," Guilford said grimly. "I'll go to her myself."

Amariah looked up at the moon, and thought of Guilford, and smiled. Not that there was anything really similar about the two—the moon was round and silver and hanging directly over her, while Guilford was tall and lean and dark, and somewhere altogether away from her—but still he filled her thoughts, and made her forget everything else around her.

By the time she heard the footsteps, running across the empty yard toward her, it was too late.

She turned at the sound, and saw a tall man in gray running towards her. She gasped, and instinctively put her arms out to stop him. Instead he grabbed her around the waist, jerking her off her feet. She cried out with shock, and he covered her mouth with a foul-smelling hand that made her gag. Desperately she bucked against him, trying to kick and claw her way free, and now there was a second man who grabbed her legs as they carried her from the bright spill of moonlight in the yard to the dark shadows in the lane behind.

"You've got her!" said a third man in a hoarse, excited whisper. His face was hidden beneath the shadow of his hat, and he'd pulled a scarf over the rest like a highwayman. "Good work, lads, good work! Bring her over here!"

Terrified, she fought still, flailing wildly as they dropped her onto the hard paving stones behind the wall.

"She's a wild one, eh?" said the man with the hidden face. "Hold her down!"

Together the men pinned her to the ground, holding her by

er arms and legs. She twisted against them, wrenching her
head free of the man's hand.

"Who—who are you?" she croaked, gasping for air. "What
do you want from me?"

The man's laugh was muffled by the scarf. "Now why
would I tell you who I am, Miss Penny? Let's just say I'm here
to give you what you deserve for what you did to me."

"I've not done anything!" she cried frantically. "I don't
even know who you are! I've not—"

"Enough of that," the man said sharply, shoving a knotted
handkerchief deep into her mouth. "Ruck up her skirts for me."

The two holding her yanked her skirts high to her waist,
shamefully exposing her to their gaze and the cool night air.
She was sobbing with fear, desperation making her fight still
against their hold on her. The man above her was breathing
hard with excitement as he tore at the buttons on the fall of
his trousers. She squeezed her eyes shut, not wanting to see
more as the tears wet her face.

"I'll give you what you deserve, you bitch," the man said,
his words coming out through gritted teeth as he forced his
knees between her legs and lowered himself over her. "You
ruined me, and now by God I'll ruin you."

"The hell you will, Westbrook!"

Guilford. Guilford's voice, here!

With fresh effort she twisted to one side, just as the man
on top of her abruptly toppled to one side. She recognized
Guilford now, on top of the man with the kerchief, the two of
them rolling over and over in the dirt, swinging their fists and
grunting and swearing and kicking.

She could hear other voices now from inside the house,
drawn by the noise and now shouting alarms, and a glimpse
of bobbing lanterns behind the windows.

The gray-coat man heard it, too, and with a nod to the other man, they let her go and ran, disappearing down the lane and into the dark. She rolled clumsily to her knees, every muscle in her body protesting and her hair straggling across her face. She was still crying, too, unable to stop as she tried to stand.

"Amariah!" Suddenly Guilford was there, lifting her up, holding her, not letting her go. "Are you hurt? Tell me, sweetheart, tell me!"

"I—I'm fine," she sobbed as she clung to him. "Oh, Guilford, if you hadn't—"

"But I did," he said, rocking her gently and stroking her hair to calm her. "Hush, now everything's fine. You're fine, and I love you, and that's all."

But as she looked past his shoulder she saw the other man staggering back to his feet. He reached into his coat and pulled out a pistol, the barrel glinting cruelly in the moonlight.

"Guilford, turn, turn!" she cried, trying desperately to pull him around. "Turn, and look!"

Swiftly he jerked around, taking her with him, but the other man had already raised the gun and pointed it at them. The scarf had been torn from his face and his hat knocked off, and in the moonlight to her shock she recognized Westbrook.

"Drop it, Westbrook," Guilford ordered. "You'll gain nothing this way."

"Won't I?" Westbrook called back, the pistol unsteady in his hands. "Your whore ruined my life, Guilford. She treated me like I was dirt beneath her feet, and made the rest of London laugh at me, too."

His arm tightened around her. "That's not true, Westbrook, and you know it!"

"Damnation, Guilford," Westbrook said, his voice shaking as his thumb began to draw back the trigger. "It *is!*"

She saw the brilliant flash of the gunpowder, heard the sharp explosion of the gun, the sound ricocheting off the walls, and as she braced herself for the impact of the shot she felt the sense of loss and love and longing and the gross unfairness of having her life end like this before it had fairly begun.

Oh, Guilford, I could never tell you how much I love you, how much you mean to me!

But the cry of agonized pain came from Westbrook, not her and not Guilford, and with horror she watched him fall forward, clutching at his arm, while the pistol dropped from his fingers.

"Are you and Miss Penny unharmed, your grace?" asked Fewler, suddenly there bowing before them with his own still-smoking pistol in his hand. "I'm sorry we weren't a few moments earlier to spare you that."

"Better that you came when you did than later," Guilford said, and her sisters were now here, too, both weeping and hugging her and making sure she was all right, and the whole yard seemed full of people talking and pointing and shouting back and forth.

But now Guilford was taking her gently by the hands, turning her to face him as the others stepped back in a ring around them here in the moonlight.

"There's only one way to make all of this right, Amariah," he said gruffly, "and I'll ask it before all these witnesses. I'll ask you. Will you marry me, Amariah?"

She smiled through the tears, her heart so full of love for him she wondered how she'd survive. "Yes," she whispered. "Oh, Guilford, yes!"

The next evening, shortly before opening, Amariah was sitting with Guilford in the front parlor when a footman brought them the newest issue of the *Covent Garden Tattle*.

WE of the Press do not often or willingly make Errors in Fact, worshipping as we do the at Temple of HONESTY. But when we are in fact led astray by False Counsel, we make haste to correct our errors, & humbly return our feet again to the Path of Truth.

So is the case regarding our News in the Issue last, a spurious report regarding the Red Queen, Miss P***y of St. James Street & His Grace the Duke of G***f**d. We must offer our deepest & most abject apologies to this Fair Lady and Gentleman, & trust that the Miscreant who offered such Falsehoods against them cloaked as TRUTH will meet his just & due FATE.

Thus we offer far more felicitous news of this Happy Pair today, & will reward our loyal READERS with the freshest information to be had, viz., that His Grace has offered for the hand of Miss P***y in marriage.

May they be joinèd forever in the Blissful Joys of Hymeneal Union!

May they be find only Love & Contentment in each others arms!

May their union be blessed with Prosperity, Health & Fine Children to preserve their JOY & the Noble Lineage of His Grace!

LET LOVE TRIUMPH OVER ALL!

Amariah looked over the top of the newssheet and frowned suspiciously at Guilford. "When did you write this?"

He glanced up at the ceiling, as if the answer were carved in the plaster. "Sometime last evening, I suppose. I disremember exactly when."

"You wrote it when you went to the *Tattle*'s office, before

u came back to Penny House," she said. "And you wrote it
fore you'd even asked me."

"I told you I didn't recall the exact hour, sweetheart," he
id, trying hard not to laugh.

"What if I'd refused you?" She threw the paper at him. "I
uld have, you know. Why, we would have been the laugh-
gstock of the entire town!"

He dodged the flying paper, and reached out and pulled her
to his lap, and kissed her until she'd nearly forgotten what
e'd been reading.

Nearly, but not quite. "And you told me you couldn't pre-
ct the future."

"For you, I can," he said, pulling her into his arms to kiss
ain. "And I see nothing but love and happiness from your
rfect, handsome husband."

She laughed softly, and thought of how lucky she'd be to
ve such a man as her husband.

"Perfection, Guilford," she whispered. "Perfection."

Afterword

They were wed at Penny House on a warm and sunny a[f]
ternoon in late October, on St. Crispin's Day. Because th[e]
was the third and last of the Penny weddings, the three si[s]
ters worked hard to make it the most memorable. Cassia ha[d]
every room decorated with flowers from her own gree[n]
houses in the country, mixed with bunches of flame-colore[d]
autumn leaves that everyone agreed precisely matched the f[a]
mous Penny sister hair. Bethany's wedding supper wou[ld]
have tempted even the most jaded of palates, complete wi[th]
a wedding cake that was a towering masterpiece of sp[un]
sugar and candied violets. And with her customary dipl[o]
macy, Amariah herself prepared the guest list for the most [de]
sired invitation of the season, with guests that ranged fro[m]
the prince himself to several ministers from the most hu[m]
ble parishes in the city.

But Amariah's greatest feat as a bride was to win ove[r]
Guilford's sister Lady Frances Carroll. With the exact mix [of]
deference, wit and charm, Amariah laid siege to Guilford's ex[
acting oldest sister, and by the time of the wedding, La[dy]

ances herself was overheard to announce that Amariah was
ing to make a perfectly splendid duchess.

But the most notable part of the celebration came after the
edding and the supper. Still in her wedding gown, with a
w diamond and pearl coronet in her hair and her bouquet
hand, Amariah rode with Guilford in a flower-draped open
rriage to White's. There, with the audacious confidence
at came from being the mistress of Penny House, she walked
st the stunned footman and through the sainted door as if
e'd every right to do so, and straight to the infamous bet-
g book.

"This is most irregular, miss, ah, that is, your grace," the
traged manager of the club said, bustling up to Amariah's
de. "Surely you are aware of the club rules, stating that no
dies are permitted!"

"Oh, I know them well," Amariah said and smiled. "This
ill only take a moment, and then I promise to leave before
y of your gentlemen are compromised. Have you found it
t, Guilford?"

The distraught manager turned to the duke as other mem-
rs of the club began to gather from curiosity. "Please, your
ace! This will cause a scandal, and put your own member-
ip at risk! I beg you, your grace, please take her grace away
once!"

"I'm sorry, Duncan," Guilford said as he scanned the pages
the betting book, "but I never have had any control over
is lady's actions, and I don't expect to begin now. Ah, sweet-
art, here we are. 'Twenty guineas that Miss Amariah Penny,
e virago of Penny House, will never wed.'"

"Oh, Guilford, how unfortunate for you." Amariah tucked
r hand into the crook of his arm and gave him a consoling
t. "It seems you have lost."

"Not at all, Amariah," he said, writing the outcome to the wager in the book with a slashing flourish. "Because this time by losing, I've won."

She smiled at him, leaning forward to be kissed. "Then pay up, Guilford," she whispered. "Pay up."

* * * * *

On sale 7th December 2007

HAVEN
by *Carolyn Davidson*

**He thought he'd died and gone to heaven…
until he recognised one of the angels!**

The gunshot wound to Sheriff Aaron McBain's chest
was going to keep him out of commission for a while.
So he spent his time wondering where he'd seen beautiful
Susannah Carvel before. By the time he remembered it
was on a Wanted poster, he knew she couldn't possibly
be guilty of any crime – let alone murder!

Aaron had to prove her innocence and to keep her safe from
harm. Because he was beginning to realise that protecting
Susannah was all that really mattered…

Regency

HOUSEMAID HEIRESS
by Elizabeth Beacon

Miss Alethea Hardy is used to an elegant life. But since
escaping from a repulsive proposal, she has been up
at dawn, fetching and carrying – this heiress is now
a maid! Alethea's life seems to be over until she meets
Marcus Ashfield, Viscount Strensham. A handsome
lord can't be interested in a lowly maid…can he?

Regency

MARRYING CAPTAIN JACK
by Anne Herries

Despite being the belle of every ball, Lucy Horne
cannot forget a man she has met only once before –
the enigmatic and dashing Captain Jack Harcourt.
But secrets from Jack's past in the bloody battlefields of
France threaten to confound all his plans – and he
cannot offer an innocent girl a tainted name…

Regency

MY LORD FOOTMAN
by Claire Thornton

Viscount Blackspur is being blackmailed and the Comtesse de Gilocourt knows more than she's telling. But his playing the footman becomes impossible when all he wants to do is take his beautiful mistress to bed!

HER IRISH WARRIOR
by Michelle Willingham

Irish warrior Bevan MacEgan is bound by honour to protect Genevieve de Renalt. Even as she begins to melt his heart, he keeps her at a distance, until a shocking discovery poses a terrible choice…

STAY FOR CHRISTMAS
by Stacy/Bylin/Lane

Life's never easy in the Wild West, but at Christmas time, even the toughest drifter can find a home. Snuggle up with these tales of new love, old ties, tragedy and festive joy.

Medieval
LORDS & LADIES
COLLECTION

VOLUME FIVE
EXOTIC EAST
The seductive heat of
the desert

Captive of the Harem by Anne Herries
The all-powerful Suleiman bought and paid for the
English rose. But Eleanor is adamant that she will not
become his concubine. Glimpsing the passionate man
behind the mighty ruler, Eleanor is drawn to him – but
can she ever hope to become his one true love?

Pearl Beyond Price by Claire Delacroix
The handsome warrior had taken her from all
that she knew – to a place of passion beyond her
wildest dreams! Their worlds were so different,
yet Kira could not fight her powerful attraction
to the mysterious prince.

Available 2nd November 2007

M&B

MILLS & BOON®
MEDICAL™
Proudly presents

Brides of Penhally Bay

Featuring Dr Nick Tremayne

A pulse-raising collection of emotional, tempting romances and heart-warming stories — devoted doctors, single fathers, Mediterranean heroes, a Sheikh and his guarded heart, royal scandals and miracle babies…

Book One

CHRISTMAS EVE BABY

by Caroline Anderson

Starting 7th December 2007

A COLL...
On...

2 BOOKS AND A SURPRISE GIFT

We would like to take this opportunity to thank you for reading this Mills & Boon® book by offering you the chance to take TWO more specially selected titles from the Historical series absolutely FREE! We're also making this offer to introduce you to the benefits of the Mills & Boon® Reader Service™—

> ★ **FREE home delivery**
> ★ **FREE gifts and competitions**
> ★ **FREE monthly Newsletter**
> ★ **Books available before they're in the shops**
> ★ **Exclusive Reader Service offers**

Accepting these FREE books and gift places you under no obligation to buy; you may cancel at any time, even after receiving your free shipment. Simply complete your details below and return the entire page to the address below. You don't even need a stamp!

YES! Please send me 2 free Historical books and a surprise gift. I understand that unless you hear from me, I will receive 4 superb new titles every month for just £3.69 each, postage and packing free. I am under no obligation to purchase any books and may cancel my subscription at any time. The free books and gift will be mine to keep in any case.

H7ZEE

Ms/Mrs/Miss/Mr.............................Initials ....
BLOCK CAPITALS PLEASE

Surname ....

Address ....

....

....Postcode ....

Send this whole page to:
The Reader Service, FREEPOST CN81, Croydon, CR9 3WZ